...professor. Born and raised in Ohio, he obtained a Ph.D. in human anatomy at Tulane, then spent his entire academic career at the University of Tennessee Health Science Center in Memphis.

In addition to being the author of several dozen scientific articles on wound healing, he has written five medical thrillers and seven forensic mysteries.

The latter feature the hugely overweight and equally brilliant New Orleans medical examiner, Andy Broussard, and his gorgeous psychologist sidekick, Kit Franklyn. It has been said that the novels contain 'lots of Louisiana color, pinpoint plotting and two highly likable characters', whilst the *Los Angeles Times* stated 'the autopsies are detailed enough to make Patricia Cornwell fans move farther south for their forensic fixes ..... splendidly eccentric local denizens, authentic New Orleans and bayou backgrounds'.

> "D.J. Donaldson is superb at spinning medical fact into gripping suspense."
> *- Tess Gerritsen*

Assassination at Bayou Sauvage

D.J. Donaldson

Copyright © D.J. Donaldson 2017

All rights reserved. No part of this publication may be reproduced, stored in a retrieval system, or transmitted, in any form, or by any means (electronic, mechanical, photocopying, recording, or otherwise), without the prior permission of the publisher. Any person who does any unauthorised act in relation to this publication may be liable to criminal prosecution and civil claims for damages.

The right of Donald Donaldson to be identified as
the author of this work has been asserted.

Published in 2017 by Astor and Blue LLC,
Suite 23A, 1330 Avenue Of The Americas, New York, NY 10019, U.S.A.
www.houseofstratus.com

Typeset by Astor + Blue

A catalogue record for this book is available from the Library of Congress
and the British Library.

ISBN (Paperback):	978-1-681209-41-8
ISBN (EPDF):	978-1-681209-39-5
ISBN (EPUB):	978-1-681200-05-7
ISBN (Mobi):	978-1-681209-40-1

This book is sold subject to the condition that it shall not be lent, resold, hired out, or otherwise circulated without the publisher's express prior consent in any form of binding, or cover, other than the original as herein published and without a similar condition being imposed on any subsequent purchaser, or bona fide possessor.

This is a fictional work drawn from the authors' imagination and all characters (alive or dead), places, incidents, quotations, and events portrayed herein are either fictitious, or are used fictiously at the Author's discretion and responsibility, including historical facts and descriptions.

For June, My Everything

Acknowledgment

Profound thanks to Dr. Jerry Francisco, retired Shelby County Tennessee medical examiner, for his help with the forensics in this story. Any mistakes I've made are solely my fault.

Chapter 1

Uncle Joe Broussard's eyes suddenly bulged like a sideshow display. Then they exploded, plastering his glasses with pieces of iris, lens fibers, and vitreous jelly. An instant later, the side of his head erupted, throwing shattered bone, blood, and brain matter into the air in a sickening display. Opposite Joe, across the cypress picnic table where they both sat, Joe's nephew, Andy Broussard, now heard the sound of a single gunshot coming from the swamp to his right. Broussard glanced that way and saw a boat with what appeared to be a single figure in it about 200 yards across the water.

At practically the same instant he saw the boat, Broussard rolled his ample bulk off the seat of the picnic table so that he hit the ground with a thump. On hands and knees he scrambled around behind the stacked cypress logs that supported the table's top and seats. Hands cupped to his mouth he yelled to the throng of his relatives scattered around the picnic area. "Everybody down. Get on the ground and lay as flat as possible." He repeated his instructions, knowing that he hadn't provided a perfect answer to the threat, but didn't want everyone running around and giving the shooter any more clear targets.

Believing that Uncle Joe was almost certainly dead, Broussard crawled over to where Joe's body was hanging backward off the split cypress log on which he'd been sitting. He dragged Joe from the seat, pulled him behind the stacked log table support, and checked for a pulse. There was none.

Broussard pulled out his phone and punched in 911. "This is Dr. Broussard, medical examiner for Orleans Parish. A man has been shot at the new picnic area near the ranger station at the Bayou Sauvage wildlife refuge. The victim I mentioned is dead, but others are at risk."

When Joe was shot, two rangers had been eating their lunch at a picnic table in front of the bungalow that held their local office. Unsure of where the shot had come from they too had hit the ground.

"Where is he?" one of them yelled to Broussard.

"Out on the water," Broussard yelled back, pointing into the swamp. "I've got a man down over here with no pulse. Already called 911."

The shooter's boat was located just off a spit of land full of scrubby woods. Its position meant there was no sight line to the ranger's boat dock on the right of two large cypress trees. Still unsure of the killer's exact location, the rangers rose into a crouching run and headed for the dock. When they reached their boat, one of them jumped in, grabbed a pair of binoculars, and dashed to the cypress nearest the picnic grounds. From behind the tree, he put the lenses to his eyes and swept the swamp until he located the shooter, now clearly visible from this vantage point.

The ranger rushed back to his partner and spoke briefly to him while pointing in the shooter's direction. They piled into their boat and a few seconds later, were roaring toward the source of all the trouble.

The two rangers were either among the bravest men Broussard had ever seen or were not very smart, because they headed directly for the killer, making no attempt to pursue an erratic course that would make them elusive targets.

Broussard wanted desperately to see what was about to

happen. Remembering that Renee Lancomb, Uncle Joe's granddaughter, had left her bird-watching binoculars on the picnic table when she'd gone off to play horseshoes, Broussard raised his right hand and groped around the tabletop for them. A moment later, he had them in his possession.

Now what? If the shooter was a marksman using a scope, which seemed like a certainty, and if he was waiting for anyone on the ground to show themselves, the old pathologist's curiosity might do for him what it did to the proverbial cat. But there had been only the one shot, and the shooter's attention must certainly now be centered on the danger posed by the rapidly advancing rangers.

"What's goin' on?" a male voice said from behind Broussard. "Oh shit," the man said as he spotted Uncle Joe.

Looking back at the guy, Broussard saw that it was Joe's bodyguard, with a 9mm automatic in one hand. "Shooter out in the swamp, get down."

The guy hit the dirt and crawled over to check his employer's body.

The bodyguard's arrival had provided the killer with another clear target. The fact he hadn't been shot, reinforced Broussard's belief that it was safe to use the binoculars. Leaning around the picnic table's protective wall of logs, Broussard brought the glasses up, located the shooter, and twirled the focus knob.

As the scene sharpened, Broussard saw why the rangers seemed so unconcerned about the danger they were in. The shooter, dressed in cammies and a cammie cap and wearing sun glasses, was standing in his boat with both hands behind his head in an apparent gesture of surrender. But if Broussard had been in the ranger's boat, he would have warned them not to relax, because the killer's hands weren't visible.

And sure enough, when the rangers were about seventy

yards away, the shooter drew his right hand out in the open. In it was a handgun. With no hesitation, he pointed the muzzle at his own head and pulled the trigger. He then fell sideways out of the boat and into the water.

Chapter 2

Kit Franklyn worked for Broussard as a death investigator, specializing in the psychology of suicidal personalities. Occasionally she helped the NOPD Homicide division with their difficult cases by constructing a personality profile of the killer they were after. Since she'd met Broussard, she'd been nearly killed more times than she could count. Now she always carried a Ladysmith .38 strapped to her right calf, hidden by the pants she would have worn even if she didn't need the gun. Looking at her, no one would know any of this. All they would see is a woman so attractive that other women usually viewed her as unfair competition and men would often walk into things while watching her pass by.

But there was one woman who looked upon Kit with genuine affection. As Kit walked through the doors of Grandma O's restaurant, Grandma Oustellette herself came rushing over to welcome her.

"Hello chil'," Grandma O said, hugging Kit against her considerable chest. Grandma O was dressed as always in a black crushed taffeta dress that made her look even larger than she was. Accustomed to being greeted this way, Kit took a quick deep breath so she could survive the hug without being suffocated.

When Grandma O released her, the old Cajun stepped back and said, "Dere's somethin' different about you today . . ."

Kit made an elaborate gesture of adjusting a lock of her

auburn hair with her left hand.

It was not wasted motion.

"Oh my sakes . . ." Grandma O said, her eyes locking on Kit's ring finger. "He finally did it."

"Last night," Kit said, holding her hand out so Grandma O could see the engagement ring, Kit's boyfriend, alligator farmer, Teddy LaBiche, had given her.

"Wait," Grandma O said, before turning and powering toward the cash register on the bar, her taffeta dress rustling like birch trees in the wind. She opened the cash register, took out something, and headed back to Kit, where she pulled Kit's ring finger up to her face with one hand and popped a jeweler's loop in her right eye with the other.

Tilting Kit's hand so it was optimally illuminated by the lights overhead, Grandma O studied the ring, all the while mumbling to herself: "Center stone old-mine cut with VS2 clarity, caret and a half in size, bezel-mounted, dome-shaped gallery pave-set with other old-mine stones, nice milligrain setting . . ." She lowered Kit's hand and removed the jeweler's loop from her eye. "Dat's a fine ring . . . antique by da look of it."

"It belonged to Teddy's grandmother."

"Dat makes it even better – to be a family heirloom." (She pronounced it *hairloom*.) "Don't he usually drive in from Bayou Coteau on Saturdays in time for lunch?"

"Something came up. A motorboat tore out a piece of the fence around his breeding stock. He'll be here later."

Ignoring Grandma O's look that obviously conveyed her belief that Teddy should not be putting gators ahead of obligations to his fiancée, Kit said, "How do you know so much about diamonds and ring settings?"

"My third husband, Amadee, ran a pawn shop. I used to help out some in dere and I jus' picked it up."

"Seems like a waste to not be using that kind of knowledge anymore."

"Well . . ." Grandma O lowered her voice and looked around to see if anyone else could hear. "Once in a while when someone I been knowin' a long time has a run a bad luck an' needs a loan, I'll see dey get it, but Amadee taught me to never jus' give somebody money. 'Always get collateral,' he said. So I do . . . usually rings. I'm not runnin' a loan business mind you . . . jus' helping friends out from time to time. So when's da weddin' gonna be?"

"We haven't decided yet."

Grandma O's eyes clouded over. "You got him dis far. You gotta haul him in da rest of da way – like a big speckled trout – dey don' want to get in da boat either."

Kit nodded. "Good advice."

Giving out with a loud cackle that made a few of the other patrons in the place flinch in surprise, Grandma O turned and motioned Kit to follow. "C'mon back."

The old Cajun led Kit to the big round table that was permanently reserved for Broussard, but which Kit was also allowed to use.

"What's for lunch?" Grandma O asked as Kit took a seat that faced out onto the rest of the tables.

"A debris po'boy, a house salad, and iced tea."

"You got it . . . or you will in a few minutes."

As Grandma O rustled off to the kitchen, Kit's phone rang. She fished it out of her handbag and glanced at the identity of the caller: Phil Gatlin, Broussard's best friend and oldest detective in Homicide. *What on earth could he want? She wasn't working on anything with him.*

"This is Kit."

"We got a situation," Gatlin said. "I don't want to talk about it over the phone, but it's something Andy thought you should be in on."

"Okay, how do you want to proceed?"

"Where are you?"

"Grandma O's. I just ordered lunch."

"I got a few things to do first. How about I come by and pick you up in thirty."

"See you then."

Chapter 3

To the brilliant sound of Mozart's Violin Concerto #4 issuing from the autopsy room's sound system, Broussard circled the steel table holding the now naked body of the Bayou Sauvage shooter, a lean, moderately muscled male Caucasian between 30 and 40 years old lying face up, his arms aligned along his torso. The old pathologist checked the form on the clipboard in his hand.

"You noted the degree of rigor in his limbs as a three when you prepared him," Broussard said to his assistant, Guy Minoux.

Guy nodded. "Right."

"Did you have to break it, to get him undressed?" He asked the question because once broken, when rigor resumes, it isn't as extensive in the disturbed muscles as in those left alone.

"No, I was careful not to, and the position of his arms made it pretty easy to avoid."

Broussard trusted Guy completely, so that ordinarily, the old pathologist wouldn't have checked the degree of rigor for himself. But it had only been three hours since the gunman had killed himself, and for much of that time the body had been submerged in water that was surely cooler than the ambient spring air. Though the degree of rigor was not a reliable time-of-death indicator, a rating of three seemed high for the circumstances. He explained this to Guy, who nodded and said, "Would you mind checkin' it too. I don't want anybody lookin' at me and rollin' their eyes if this becomes a problem later."

"That part about somebody givin' you a frog eye . . . hope you didn't mean me," Broussard said.

Guy swished his hand at Broussard in a gesture of dismissal. "Nahh, we been through too much of this stuff together for me to think that."

"I'm sure you're right about this, but . . . just to be safe . . ." Broussard headed for the cadaver's right arm. When he was in the proper position, he gently tested the limb's resistance to flexion of the elbow. He tried to raise the arm at the shoulder, then tested the right leg. Nodding, he said, "I agree . . . level three."

He shifted his attention to the head, where he carefully tried to move it from side to side before pulling down on the lower jaw. In keeping with the established principle that rigor begins in the short muscles of the jaw and neck before the long extremity muscles, Broussard judged rigor in the former to be a level four. So there was agreement between these different areas.

Broussard moved to the other side of the head, reached up, and adjusted the light over the table. He then bent down and studied the self-inflicted gunshot wound on the cadaver's temple. What he saw was unexpected. The blast of gasses from the gun had split the man's skin in a star shape and there was no soot around the wound. Of course, immersion in the swamp would likely have washed any gunshot residue from the skin, but that star shape . . .

From the rolling stainless cart nearby he picked up an instant camera and took a shot of the wound. When the latent picture whirred from the camera, he put the camera back on the cart and laid the slowly developing picture beside it.

With a scalpel, Broussard made four incisions that formed a cross in the soft tissue of the scalp, carrying the cuts all the way down to the bone. "Guy, get me four hemostats and come over to the head of the table would you please."

Using a pair of forceps and his scalpel, Broussard began to carefully dissect one quadrant of the soft tissue off the shooter's skull. When Minoux appeared with the hemostats, Broussard lifted the quadrant he'd freed and said, "Use one of those hemostats to hold this tissue back from the wound."

Guy got hold of the pointed end of the quadrant with a hemostat and gently pulled the flap toward him until he felt it begin to resist. Then he let the hemostat dangle so its weight would keep the flap open. In a few more minutes, all four flaps were reflected off the skull. Broussard then blotted away the obscuring blood with a paper towel and issued a satisfied grunt. The soot that had been missing from the skin around the wound was now clearly apparent in a dense deposit on the bone bordering the round hole in the skull, where the swamp water couldn't have reached it. It was all textbook . . . Except . . .

Broussard closed his eyes, his mind turning inward where it was dark and easier to think. Had he been at his desk and not wearing soiled rubber gloves, he would have helped the process along by stroking the bristly hairs on the end of his nose. Unable to do that, it took him a second or two longer to arrive at the question he now asked Minoux.

"Guy, how would you judge the fit of this guy's clothes?"

Confusion at the purpose of the question evident in his furrowed brow, Guy said, "Everything was a little big for him."

Giving a grunt that sounded to Minoux like Broussard had expected him to say something like that, the old pathologist, picked up the camera and took a shot of the soot-marked bone.

While that picture was developing, Broussard again picked up his scalpel, made a deep cut behind the cadaver's left ear, then carried the incision across the top of the head to the same place behind the other ear. As Broussard freed the front half of the scalp from the underlying bone, he couldn't imagine that he would find anything inside the skull that was as interesting as what he'd already seen, but who knows? In any event, since there was no exit wound on the opposite side of the head from the entrance wound, he was sure he would at least find the bullet in there. And most likely, considering its limited penetrating power, it would probably be a .22 caliber round.

He draped the front half of the scalp over the cadaver's forehead and eyes.

Working precisely, with all the dexterity of a pianist Mozart would have envied, Broussard freed the back half of the scalp from the skull and let it dangle so it partially covered the edge of the wooden block supporting the head. He then picked up the electric motor-driven Stryker saw, flicked it on, and plunged its oscillating blade into the skull just above the right ear. With smoke and wet bone meal accompanying movement of the saw blade Broussard made an equatorial cut all around the skull, being careful to keep the blade from penetrating the underlying brain.

It was now time to remove the bony cap he'd freed from the rest of the skull. It came loose with a bit of effort and a sucking sound that always reminded him of walking through swamp muck in rubber boots when he was a kid in Bayou Coteau. Looking at the brain inside, with its lacework of blood vessels covering the rolling hills of white matter, he thought of the old phrase, "He learned it by heart." A mistaken notion by the ancient Greeks that memory and intelligence were centered in the heart. And yet the phrase persists. He shook his head at how much of the past continues into the present. He'd been trying not to think about Uncle Joe, who was being worked on next door by Charlie Franks, the assistant medical examiner. But how could he put aside the sight he'd seen mere hours ago of Joe's brain being blown into a frothy mist? What part of Joe's past had led to his death this morning?

Letting this question percolate for future consideration, Broussard's eyes now went to the large blood clot that covered the right side of the killer's brain, where the bullet had entered the skull and obviously hit a large vessel, most likely a branch of the internal carotid. He then briefly surveyed the lesser clot on the other side, where as the bullet emerged from the brain, it had damaged some smaller vessels. If the slug had pursued a straight course from right to left as it now appeared, it could not have damaged the critical areas that controlled basic body functions such as breathing, heart rate, and blood pressure. Death had almost certainly been caused by overall brain death secondary to blood loss.

"Guy, get a picture of these clots will you please?"

After the requested picture was taken, Broussard stepped in with an aspirator and began to suck out the clots. Removal of the skullcap had also taken with it the adherent dura, the tough fibrous covering of the brain. Peripheral to the cranial saw cut the dura still remained. With the clots removed and the field now clear, Broussard deftly dissected down around the dura and severed the few structures that held the brain in the cranial cavity: the optic nerves, the attachment to the pituitary gland, and the spinal cord.

With the brain now free, Broussard turned it carefully in his hands, checking for any other projectile damage that might have occurred if the bullet had ricocheted after hitting the skull on the side opposite where it had gone in. He found none.

The fresh brain is extremely soft and cannot be sectioned immediately after removal. It must first be hardened in formalin for several days. Broussard therefore, handed the organ to Minoux for further processing.

Returning to the empty cranial cavity, it took only a few seconds for Broussard to find the bullet, which, as he'd expected, looked like a .22 caliber. It was so flattened, it must have been a hollow point, a modification that causes the lead to mushroom when it hits any resistance, thereby greatly increasing the diameter of the bullet. And yes, with closer examination he could see a vague remnant of the pit that made it a hollow point.

Nothing he'd seen since opening the skull had been unexpected. But that didn't change the peculiarities he'd noticed earlier as he examined the entry wound. Because of those circumstances he now wanted to see something that didn't sit on the table in front of him.

A thunderous rumble suddenly drowned out the Mozart piece playing on the stereo. Over by a big jar of formalin that now contained the removed brain hanging by a string, Minoux turned to Broussard, a look of apprehension on his face. "Lordy, Dr. B. I think the buildin' just collapsed."

As Broussard's considerable stomach grumbled again, Broussard said, "Remember that raise we discussed for you last week? I think we may need the money to rebuild."

Laughing at Broussard's comeback, Minoux returned to work.

Broussard stripped off his gloves, washed his hands, and pulled out the drawer where he kept his morgue supply of cellophane-wrapped lemon balls. He unwrapped one and popped it into his mouth, then reached for another.

ASSASSINATION AT BAYOU SAUVAGE

A few seconds later, with one lemon ball in each cheek so that he looked like a contented hamster, he picked up his cell phone and navigated to a familiar number.

Chapter 4

"How are you?" Kit said, getting into Gatlin's ancient Pontiac, which he preferred over a departmental car.

"Can't complain," Gatlin said, the bags under his eyes and overall tired appearance making him look like anything but the skilled detective he was. "Actually I could complain," he added, pulling out of the restaurant parking lot. "And I want to, but I'm trying to be more positive, which ain't exactly easy considering how I make my living."

"So what are we doing?"

"Earlier today, the Broussard clan had a birthday picnic for Andy's Uncle Joe at Bayou Sauvage."

"Where?"

"The wildlife refuge out east. Anyway, Andy and Uncle Joe are having a nice talk and somebody puts a bullet in Uncle Joe's brain. Shooter was in a boat out in the swamp."

"Oh my God . . . and Andy saw it happen?"

"Up close and in living color . . . well, not living . . . but the guy used an M16, so there was a lot of color. There's a ranger station right next to the picnic area and the rangers see it happen. They go after the guy, but weirdly, he doesn't try to run. Instead, he kills himself. That's where you come in."

From where it sat in a holder on the dash, Gatlin's cell phone suddenly blared the voice of Johnny Cash singing "Ring of Fire."

Glancing at the name of the caller as he put the phone to his ear, he said to Kit, "It's Andy." Then, after a couple of seconds, he said to the phone, "Yeah, I found her. She's in the car right now. We're on our way to the guy's address."

Gatlin pulled to a stop behind a queue of cars waiting for the light to change, then put the phone on speaker so Kit could hear.

"I need to see the pistol the shooter used on himself," Kit heard Broussard say.

"It's in the evidence room," Gatlin said.

"I don't care where it is at the moment."

"Why do you want to see it?"

"I'm curious about somethin'."

"Me too. So . . .?"

"No deal," Broussard said. "If I learn anything from it, you'll be the first to know, actually, you'll be second because I'll be the first."

"You're just worried that if you tell me what you're thinking, I'll figure out the rest for myself."

"If we weren't such good friends I'd hit that one over the fence. How soon can I expect it?"

"I'll have to make a call or two."

"I'll be waiting."

"It hasn't been fully processed. Be careful with it."

"You worried I'll shoot myself?"

"Among other things."

"Good to know you care. Tell Kit hello for me." He hung up.

Gatlin closed out the call on his end and put the phone in his lap. Shaking his head, he looked at Kit. "Old codger just won't loosen up until *he* decides it's time."

"So why do you still push him?"

"Keeps me young."

The light changed and they started moving again. At the first place Gatlin could pull over, he did and again picked up the phone. He scrolled through some numbers and tapped the screen with his finger. With the speaker now off he said, "This is Gatlin. Got anybody who can run the pistol from that Bayou Sauvage deal this morning over to Andy Broussard for me? I know you're shorthanded . . . Okay, thanks. I'll buy you a Twinkie some day." He put the phone back in its rack and once again got the car underway.

"I guess you're shorthanded because of the blue flu?" Kit said.

Gatlin nodded. "This time it's even affecting the detectives."

"How come *you're* still working?"

"I noticed that our motto, To Protect And Serve, doesn't say anything about taking time off during compensation squabbles."

"You're a good man."

Not looking at her, Gatlin said, "So if *you* were me, you'd do the same thing?"

Kit smiled. "If I were you, I'd *have* to because you're *doing* it. It's a given."

Gatlin rubbed his face with his hand, fuzzing his ample gray eyebrows. "I think you been hanging around Andy too long. But we'll see."

Kit waited for him to explain what he meant by his last comment, but he didn't continue. Rather than press him about it, she let it go. When Gatlin was talking to Broussard on the phone, the old detective said they were headed for the shooter's home, most likely, she thought, to try and figure out why this had happened. Willing to let Gatlin talk or not as he saw fit, she tried to relax and not get too keyed up about what her role in all this might be.

Gatlin made his way to the Crescent City Connection, the

name given to the Mississippi River Bridge that led from New Orleans to the small city of Gretna on the other side. As they drove, Kit recalled how Gretna had become infamous during hurricane Katrina. Unable to provide any services for the army of refugees fleeing New Orleans after it flooded and afraid of having thousands of desperate people roaming his streets, the Gretna mayor ordered the city police to turn everyone back. This was accomplished by a row of uniformed officers carrying shotguns, one cop firing a round over the heads of the crowd. Kit knew that some in New Orleans still held a grudge.

They followed the west-bank leg of I-90 to Belle Chase Highway, where Gatlin took a left, now heading away from the river. They were only a few miles from the French Quarter, but might as well have been a thousand, for they were on a typical urban street lined by fast food joints and other commercial ventures that either didn't bother with any landscaping or thought, once installed, the plants wouldn't need any more care than the asphalt.

A few minutes later, Gatlin turned onto a residential side street where pickup trucks outnumbered cars, and there were far more vehicles than trees. The older houses on the street were up on cement blocks so there was a visible space under them. On the right was a home with a For Sale sign in the yard. Like the other newer homes on the street this one was built on a slab. Gretna hadn't flooded during Katrina, but it was protected by levees just like the regions of New Orleans that had been inundated. Kit wondered if there was anyone within five hundred miles who would buy that house.

Gatlin drove slowly down the street so he could check addresses. He pulled to a stop in front of a newer one-story brick home with a dense strip of banana trees planted along the property line on each side. In the driveway was a blue pickup.

Gatlin pulled into the drive and shut off the engine. "Okay, this is where the shooter lived. If anyone's home, you take the lead."

"Why me?"

"I want to see how you handle yourself as first chair."

"I don't usually work with an audience."

"Me neither, but sometimes it's necessary."

Kit had no idea what he was talking about, but rather than prolong the discussion she said, "Guess it's too soon for you to have a file on the guy."

"You and I are writing it now."

"Do we at least know his name?"

"Martin Hartley."

"Driver's license?"

"Yeah . . . Oh-oh time to get on with it."

Kit looked through the windshield and saw a woman with a suitcase come out of the house. She carried her bag to the back of the truck and put it down in the driveway, then, with a mixed expression of confusion and irritation, watched Gatlin and Kit walk toward her.

The woman was wearing a black one-piece fishnet dress with a mini skirt hemline and sandals. Her choice of attire showed a lot of skin, all of it unblemished and shockingly white. Her face was only moderately attractive and she was a shade overweight, but had nice legs and was so impeccably groomed, Kit imagined that most men would find her worth a look.

"We're sorry to bother you," Kit said. "This is Lieutenant Gatlin from the New Orleans Homicide division and I'm Dr. Franklyn from the Orleans Parish medical examiner's office. Do you know Martin Hartley?"

Her eyes widened, "I'm Mrs. Hartley. Or am I the widow

Hartley?"

The woman's correct assessment of the situation made Kit's job a bit easier. "I'm afraid it's the latter. Your husband shot someone this afternoon at Bayou Sauvage, then killed himself."

"The woman shook her head. "No, none of that is possible. You've made some kind of mistake."

"We found his driver's license on the body." Kit glanced at Gatlin, hoping he had it with him. He did.

Mrs. Hartley examined it then said, "Yeah, that's his, but he doesn't even own a gun. Fishing is his thing. This is the sixth day of his vacation and he's been fishing every day . . . every damn day. We were supposed to go somewhere . . . he promised, but instead he bought a new boat and now I can't get him out of it. He doesn't give a shit for me. Why should I care about him? A couple more minutes and you wouldn't have even found me. Me and my suitcase would have been gone for good." Then her anger seemed to melt away. Her eyes grew misty. "He's dead? Really? It couldn't have been someone else with Martin's license on him?"

That wasn't a question Kit could answer. She looked at Gatlin. "No ma'am, the deceased and the man pictured on the license were the same."

When Kit had first walked up the driveway, she'd thought the woman's normal color was as pale as a person could be. But with Gatlin's answer to her question, something vital drained from her face so she now looked almost translucent.

"I wasn't really leaving for good," she said. "Just for a few days, to get Marty's attention – show him he has to change – that our marriage isn't just about him." She looked at Kit, her eyes devoid of hope. "What am I gonna do now?"

Kit stepped forward and took the woman in her arms. She hugged Kit tightly with both hands and pressed her cheek against Kit's hair.

After a few seconds, feeling the woman's grip relax, Kit released her.

"You said Marty shot someone?" the woman asked. "I'm sure he didn't, but who are you talking about?"

"His name was Joe Broussard," Kit said. "Is that someone you know?"

Seemingly more composed now, the woman said, "That's not a name I've ever heard before."

"He was the retired CEO of Seabed Petroleum."

The woman shook her head. "Means nothing to me."

"Did you see Martin leave this morning?"

"Yes. I warned him he better not go, tried to give him one last chance. But he just kissed me on the cheek and said, 'next week we'll go to Biloxi for a couple days,' but we wouldn't have gone. That's just how he is, makes promises he never keeps."

"He stores his boat here?"

"Right over there, beside the garage. Had the driveway widened to hold it. Could have gone to Disney World for what that cost."

"Is it possible he hid some guns in the boat when you weren't looking?"

"I suppose, but I told you he's not a gun person. Ever watch *The Simpsons*? They had this one episode where Homer tries to buy a gun. When he finds out he'll have to wait a few days for a background check before he can take possession of it he says, 'But I'm mad now.' Marty pointed at the TV and said, 'That's why all guns should be banned'." She hugged herself with both arms and shuddered. "My God. Marti's . . . and here I am talking about some damn TV show."

Kit put her hand on the woman's shoulder. "I'm so sorry for putting you through this. And I don't even know your first name."

"It's Terry."

"Terry, does Martin have a desk inside the house where he pays the bills or does other work?"

"Yes, a small one."

"Would you mind if we looked at it."

"What for?"

"It might help us all understand what happened today."

"I don't know . . ."

"It's actually the quickest way for you to get rid of us."

"Okay . . ." Forgetting her bag, she turned and led them inside.

Chapter 5

Andy Broussard sat rocked back in his desk chair, his chubby fingers folded over his big belly, thinking about what he'd seen so far on the autopsy of the shooter from the picnic. Something was *very* wrong there. A knock at the door brought him out of his reverie.

"Come in."

A grizzled old cop in uniform opened the door. In one hand was a paper evidence bag that looked heavy.

"Dr. Broussard, Lieutenant Gatlin said you wanted this,"

He came forward and put the bag on the desk.

"Appreciate you bringin' it over, especially under the circumstances."

"Because of harassment from other uniforms supporting the slowdown?"

"Exactly."

"I ain't one to be screwed with."

"No, I can see that," Broussard said, reaching for the bag.

"Thought I knew everyone on the force," Broussard said. "But I don't think we've met."

"Just moved here from Baton Rouge." He motioned to the bag. "I was told not to leave it."

"I'll only be a few minutes. If you like you can sit over there." Broussard gestured to a green vinyl sofa with journal articles and books filling all the cushions. "You can put some of that stuff on the floor. Just don't mix up the piles."

Assassination At Bayou Sauvage

"What are we talkin'..." The cop said. "Five minutes... ten...?"

"Five minutes, tops."

The cop went to the sofa and sat on the armrest. From his perch, he said, "They told me it's still loaded, but there's no live round under the hammer. If I was you, I'd assume they're wrong and I wouldn't point it at yourself or me."

Broussard snapped on a pair of rubber gloves, opened the bag, and looked in. Grasping the revolver by the grip, where it's rough texture would have prevented the shooter from leaving a useful print, he withdrew the gun. It was a snub nose Smith and Wesson Airlite .22LR. Keeping the muzzle pointed at the floor, he popped open the cylinder and noted that the cartridge under the hammer had a firing mark denting the rim. There was also a firing dent on the rim of the cartridge just to the left of the first one. None of the remaining six rounds had firing marks. These observations fit perfectly with his growing suspicions about what had really happened at the picnic. Gatlin said the gun hadn't been completely examined yet, so Broussard didn't want to remove any of the cartridges. Instead, he just turned the gun around and looked at them through the cylinder openings. All the remaining unfired rounds were hollow points, just as he expected.

He snapped the cylinder back in place. Turning to the flexible LED light on the table behind him, he bent the light down so it illuminated the interior of the gun's muzzle, which he examined through a swiveling magnifying glass.

From the arm of the sofa, the cop said, "I know you checked, but seeing someone look down the muzzle of a gun gives me the creeps."

"Some folks think most of what I do is creepy," Broussard replied. "But I see your point." From a nearby drawer, he got a cotton-tipped swab and gently ran it around the inside of the muzzle. Then he studied the swab under the magnifying glass. While sliding his chair along the table, he took off his glasses and let them dangle against his chest by the lanyard attached to the temples. He spent the next thirty seconds examining the swab with a dissecting microscope. Satisfied, he put the swab in a plastic tube and screwed a cap on it.

Glasses once again on his face, he carried the gun back to his desk, where he signed and dated the chain of custody form on the evidence bag. He then scribbled a few notes on a yellow pad describing what he'd done with the weapon. After signing and dating the sheet, he tore it off the pad and taped it under the custody form. The gun then went back in the bag.

"Okay, officer . . . ?"

"Two thirty one," the cop said, standing up.

Broussard briefly thought about asking him if now that they knew each other would he mind if Broussard just called him "Two." Then, thinking the guy might not appreciate it, he handed him the bag and just said, "Thanks for bringin' it over."

Now there was one last thing Broussard wanted to do before telling Gatlin what he'd learned. He picked up his phone, hit the call function, scrolled to his contacts, and tapped a number.

"This is Andy. Can you get free for a couple hours? We'll need a boat."

Kit and Gatlin found nothing in Martin Hartley's desk that tied him to Joe Broussard or the events at the picnic.

"I knew this was all a mistake," Terry Hartley said. "Could you just leave now?"

"Just one more thing, and we'll go," Kit said.

"What?"

"Where did Martin work?"

Her expression obviously showing she had no idea why that was important, Terry said, "Courmier furniture rental in Westwego."

"We may want to speak with you again," Kit replied, taking a small red notebook and a pen from her bag. "Do you have a cell phone?"

Terry gave her the number and said, "Where exactly *is* Marty?"

"He's at the medical examiner's facilities." Kit dug again in her purse and produced her business card. Handing it to Terry, she said, "Here's the address. I'll call and let you when he'll be released. Again, I'm so sorry this happened. We'll see ourselves out. Oh, and don't forget, you left your bag by the truck."

Terry didn't seem to care about her bag. Instead of following them out, she sank into a leather armchair and covered her face with her hands.

Outside in the car, Gatlin said, "Mostly you did okay, but never make contact with a suspect unless you're frisking them and have them at a physical disadvantage. You *hugged* the woman. She could have pulled a knife, then we'd have had a problem."

"She *wasn't* a suspect. And I was just showing her some compassion."

"Yeah, compassion, that's another word for 'mistake.' She and Marty could have been in on this together. You didn't know *what* her role was."

Gatlin had never spoken to her like this before and she didn't like it. "I thought you brought me along to help judge the psychological status of Martin Hartley."

"That's true . . . partly."

"Well, here's what I concluded: Something's very wrong with the scenario you laid out for me. Martin was not a candidate for suicide."

"Why do you say that? He and wife were on thin ice. That alone could drive a man over the edge."

"You heard what she said. He didn't pay any attention to her complaints. He didn't even know he had a problem with her."

"Maybe *she* had nothing to do with it. Could be he knew he couldn't get away after shooting Uncle Joe and didn't want to spend time in prison or go through a trial with a needle in a vein waiting for him."

"I don't think he's the one."

"Well, that's not in question. There were at least two dozen witnesses that saw him do it."

"The comment Martin made about guns during that cartoon show . . . there was no audience for that. He didn't say it for effect. It's what he believed."

"Maybe his wife was his audience. He was setting her up so she'd say he hated guns if anyone came around asking."

"You can't have it both ways. A moment ago, you suggested he killed himself because he knew he couldn't get away after killing Uncle Joe. So why would he care if anyone came around later asking if he owned a gun?"

Gatlin fuzzed his eyebrows with his catcher's mitt of a hand. "We've lost the thread of what we came here for. There's no question he was the shooter. Mostly I wanted to find out *why* he did it. Maybe we can get a handle on that at what was it . . . Courmier furniture rental."

Chapter 6

Broussard owned six 1957 T-Birds, all in mint condition; original upholstery, original paint, no replacement parts on any of them. Most people who saw him driving one assumed he'd bought them when he was thin and had gradually put on weight until each of them encased him like a fitted shirt. But they were wrong, because he'd *never* been thin. And he didn't care. There were too many other things in his life he did care about: good food, either prepared by him, or any other culinary magician that was his equal, old master paintings with sheep in them, Louis L'Amour novels, and his work.

Today, Broussard was driving his white T-Bird, which now came to a stop in front of the NOPD vehicle impoundment station on Poydras street. In seconds, the door in the little building at the front gate opened and the man he'd called right after examining the revolver came quickly to the car.

He opened the door and got in. "How you doin' today?" Bubba Oustellette said, grinning, his teeth impossibly white against his bushy black beard. Bubba clearly believed that once a man decides on the right clothes for himself, no further thought on the topic is needed. He was dressed just like yesterday and the day before and the year before that: a green baseball cap with the old Tulane logo on it (an ocean wave baring its teeth and carrying a football), navy coveralls over a navy T-shirt, and brown work shoes.

"I'm disturbed," Broussard said, responding to Bubba's greeting. "My Uncle Joe was killed this mornin' . . . and on his birthday of all things."

"I heard about dat," Bubba said. "An' you watched it all happen?"

Broussard nodded. "I saw the bullet hit Joe and I saw the shooter kill himself. He was in a boat about 200 yards away out in the swamp."

"Dat would disturb anybody, seein' a family member go down like dat."

"I didn't know Joe very well. He was kind of reclusive, but he *was* family. That made it personal."

"What does reclusive mean?"

"It means he didn't get out much, didn't like to be around other people."

"Good word, but a bad way for somebody to be." Then remembering that Joe was dead, Bubba crossed himself and said, "*repose en paix* (rest in peace). You said we'd need a boat. You wanna go to where it happened and take a closer look?"

"I do."

"Because somethin' ain't right?"

"Precisely. Did you get us a boat?"

"We could go get mine, but I foun' a better answer. I gotta friend name a T Roy Dugas. He gonna let us use his an' his truck an' trailer too. Bes' part a dat is he lives on da Chef Highway out near Bayou Sauvage."

"Is there anyone you *don't* know?"

A few minutes later, as they turned onto Canal Street, Bubba pointed at a pedestrian walking toward the river. "I don' know *him*."

They took Canal to North Claiborne and turned right. Accompanied by US10, which ran above and beside them for many blocks, they drove without talking, both completely comfortable with the companionable silence. Just before they took the ramp onto US10 Bubba said, "Da Bird sounds good."

"It does, but the red one is runnin' rough."

"I could come by Tuesday aroun' five-thirty and tune it up."

"I'd appreciate it."

Bayou Sauvage consists of 2400 acres of fresh and brackish marshes and lakes just 15 minutes from the French Quarter. All of it is within the city limits, making it the largest urban wildlife refuge in the country. But it's not accessible from US10. When the exit for the Chef Menteur Highway came up, Broussard took it.

As they followed an old truck loaded with bales of flattened cardboard down the off ramp, a chipmunk came from the grassy strip bordering the ramp and darted in front of the truck. When the truck passed, there was the chipmunk lying unmoving on the pavement.

Broussard swerved to avoid running over the animal, then pulled off the ramp onto the wide shoulder.

Knowing what was coming, Bubba said, "Dis ain't a good idea."

"There's no one behind us," Broussard said, opening his door. With an agility that defied the laws of physics, the old pathologist slid smoothly from his seat, closed the driver's door, and hurried back to the furry brown patch on the asphalt.

Through the rear window of the T-Bird, Bubba saw Broussard kneel and pick up the animal.

Returning to the car moments later, Broussard leaned in with the chipmunk cradled in one chubby hand. "He doesn't look hurt at all," Broussard said, somehow getting in with only one available hand. "I think he's just in shock."

"So am I," Bubba said. "Don' dose things sometimes have rabies?"

"Extremely rare in a chipmunk."

"So why'd he run in front a dat truck?"

"Bad judgment. But it wasn't because of rabies. If he was sick, he couldn't have run like that."

"What are you gonna do with it?"

"There's a vet about three miles ahead. I'll drop him off there."

Broussard put the animal between them, on the small shelf behind the seats, and got the T-Bird back on the highway. He then groped around in his shirt pocket for the unwrapped lemon balls he carried when he was driving. He popped one in each cheek then went back to his stash for two more, which he offered to Bubba.

"No thanks, I'm good."

"You worried because I picked up the chipmunk with my bare hands and then handled these?" Broussard asked.

"Never gave it a thought," Bubba said, well aware that Broussard knew he was lying.

"Folks these days are way too fastidious," Broussard said, then thinking that Bubba might not know what fastidious meant, he added, "Too clean. We don't challenge our immune systems nearly enough. A few germs are good for you."

"Well, right now I ain't in da mood for chipmunk germs. But thanks for offerin'."

As they drove, Bubba kept looking over his shoulder at the striped little creature lying behind him.

For long stretches, the Chef Highway is flanked by a wide plain of scrubby vegetation with very few buildings of any kind. Then, like something in a dream, the Buddhist Meditation Center rises from the desolate surroundings, its red tiled roofs, magnificent landscaping, and huge white

Assassination At Bayou Sauvage

Buddhist statue making one doubt their senses. Shortly after they passed the Center, the chipmunk opened its eyes.

Seeing where it was, the little creature hopped to its feet, let out a shrill squeak of surprise, and jumped onto Bubba's cap. From there, it went on a rampage, ricocheting around the car so fast it seemed like there were a dozen of them. At one point, it knocked Broussard's glasses sideways, then bounced off the back window and skittered across Bubba's bare neck.

Broussard got the T-Bird onto the shoulder and Bubba opened his door. In seconds, the animal was out of the car and into the vegetation flanking the asphalt.

"He seems to have recovered," Broussard said, straightening his glasses.

Bubba shut his door and they once more got underway.

"Oh, by the way," Broussard said. "That never happened."

"What never happened?"

"Exactly."

They drove for a while longer, then Broussard said, "Where's T Roy live?"

"Jus' a couple miles on da other side of Sauvage."

In a few more minutes, the marshes of the wildlife refuge appeared, stretching endlessly away from both sides of the road. Shortly after they crossed the eastern boundary of the preserve, a bayou that connected to Lake Catherine appeared on their right. When they reached the bayou inlet, and the lake suddenly filled the visible horizon, Bubba pointed to a very modest little house up on pilings fifteen feet high. "Dat's it."

Broussard carefully navigated the oyster shell driveway and pulled to a stop where the T-Bird wouldn't block the red Chevy pickup and boat sitting in the space under the house.

"You must be *very* good friends for T Roy to let you borrow his rig," Broussard said, gesturing at the truck and boat.

"We are. But even good friends, gotta have collateral."

"What kind of . . ." Broussard looked down his nose at Bubba. "So we have to leave him *my* car."

"He said he wouldn't drive it while we were gone, and before we leave, I'll make sure it won't run."

Reluctantly, Broussard popped the hood release, then pulled the keys from the ignition and got out of the car. Bubba too, disembarked, raised the hood, and fiddled with the engine for a couple of seconds. Then he shut the hood and came around to Broussard for the keys.

"How'd you know I'd go for this deal?" Broussard said.

"I been aroun' long enough to know dat when you gotta hunch about a murder, ain't nothin' gonna stop you."

Bubba went up the tall set of steps to the door on the side of the house, knocked, and went inside. He reappeared less than a minute later, waving the truck's keys.

There was no public boat ramp at the picnic area where the assassination of Uncle Joe took place. With Bubba driving, they therefore headed for a ramp as close to the spot as they could get. Another fifteen minutes found them on the water, Bubba working the outboard motor, Broussard sitting amidships, facing forward.

"I'll bet you da only person to ever be out here in a bow tie," Bubba said, over the sound of the purring motor, which pushed them forward at a casual pace.

"You seem different today," Broussard said over his shoulder. "More . . . assertive."

"I been readin' dis book dat says short people get more respect if dey take da lead in conversations instead of jus' hangin' back an bein' a follower."

"You feel like I don't respect you?"

"Course not. I'm jus' practicin'. Hope you don' mind."

"Not at all. I like it." Broussard was about to ask him if he knew how to get to the picnic area, but considering what Bubba had just said, decided to keep quiet.

Even though it was now late afternoon, the temperature on the bayou was quite comfortable. On the left, they passed an expanse of water hyacinths with exotic lavender blooms whose beauty belied the danger the prolific plants posed to the bayou, which could eventually become choked with their presence. Leaving the hyacinths behind, they entered a region where the edges of the water contained patches of pickerelweed, their leaves all pointing upward like the spears of a chlorophyll army. Ahead, the fin of some kind of large fish was visible for a moment before the sound of the motor and the waves from the bow sent it out of sight.

A few minutes later, Broussard saw a great blue heron stab at the water and come up with a silver fish far too large for it to swallow. But magically the fish disappeared down the bird's gullet, distending the heron's neck as it slid down into the bird's stomach.

Bubba guided the boat confidently through a maze of waterways that sometimes connected with each other by small channels that didn't look passable. Eventually, they rounded a spit of land, and a wide, marshy lake opened before them. Looking to the left, Broussard saw, several hundred yards away, the picnic area where Uncle Joe had been shot earlier that day. He held up his hand. "This is it."

Bubba cut the motor.

Broussard stood up and stared at the distant shore. It had always seemed to him that violent acts continue to echo through time, ethereal remnants persisting long after all the participants are gone. As he stood there now, he felt the shadowy ripples of the morning's horrors washing over him.

He looked back at Bubba. "This is just about where the

shooter's boat was positioned." He scanned the shore, then studied the water on all sides of them.

"What you lookin' for?" Bubba asked.

"I'm not sure. The shooter supposedly killed himself and then fell out of his boat, right over there."

"What you mean supposedly? Didn' dey recover da body?"

"I just finished workin' on it before I called you."

"An somethin' you saw brought you out here."

"Yes."

"It don' seem like bein' here is helpin' you any."

Broussard shook his head. "I was hopin' just seein' it all again close up would give me an idea. But it's not. Maybe what I'm lookin' for is *under* the water."

Bubba stood up and dropped an anchor over the side. "Why didn' you say so sooner?" He threw his cap on the seat beside him, then sat down and took off his shoes and socks.

Seeing what Bubba was about to do, Broussard said, "I'm not sure that's a wise move."

"When my mama's birth sac broke everybody said it was filled with bayou water. Dis is my home."

"I was thinkin' of gators."

"No gators aroun' here. Never have been. Somethin' about it dey don' like."

In seconds, Bubba had his coveralls off. After decades of seeing human bodies in various states of decay, there wasn't much in life that made Broussard squeamish. But this did. Averting his eyes and swatting at a dragonfly that was pestering him, he said, "You know, there may be chipmunk germs in there."

"If dere are, dey better stay of my way."

Bubba went overboard with surprising little splash. "Now what am I lookin' for?" he said, only his head showing. "I heard dere was a handgun an' a rifle involved. Are dey down here?"

"No. Only the shooter went overboard. Both weapons remained in the boat. You gonna open your eyes under there?"

"Always do."

"Look for anything unusual."

Bubba silently disappeared. Broussard checked his watch so he'd know when to start worrying if Bubba didn't come up. At about a minute and ten seconds, Broussard became concerned. But five seconds later, the little Cajun bobbed to the surface and wiped the water from his face and beard. "So far it jus' looks like a normal swampy bottom. Lemme try over dere."

He dog paddled to the opposite side of the boat and sank from sight. He came up forty-five seconds later about fifteen feet away from the boat, back in the direction they'd come in.

"Anything?" Broussard asked.

"Dere's a steel rebar driven into da mud right by da boat, and another one where I am now. I also foun' one between dose two."

"Follow the line of those three and see if there are more."

Bubba slipped from view.

Forty seconds later, he emerged, fifteen feet farther away.

"Foun' three more."

"Can you go again?"

For an answer, he did.

When he surfaced this time, he was out of sight around the spit of land jutting toward the boat. "Three more."

"That's enough," Broussard shouted. "Come on back."

Broussard took out his phone and tapped Gatlin's number. "This is Andy. Stop whatever you're doin'. It's a waste of time. Meet me in my office in forty minutes and I'll tell you why."

Chapter 7

This time it was Gatlin perched on the arm of Broussard's sofa. "Okay, what have you got?"

Trying to keep a pile of journal articles from toppling into her lap from the sofa cushion next to her, Kit too, waited for Broussard's answer.

"Martin Hartley is not our shooter."

Gatlin stood up. "Yeah, I figured you were gonna say that. Get to the meat, 'cause I don't see how that's possible."

Broussard rocked back in his chair and laced his fingers over his belly. "Hartley has a contact gunshot wound on his temple... textbook example... skin split in a star-shape from the gunpowder gasses, bone around the entrance hole stained with soot."

Gatlin turned his palms to the ceiling and leaned forward in an 'okay, so what', gesture.

"I was watchin' through binoculars when the shooter apparently killed himself," Broussard said, "and I distinctly saw light between the gun muzzle and his head. His wound shouldn't have shown contact features."

"Jesus," Gatlin said, then crossed himself for blaspheming. "You were what... 200 yards away?"

Broussard nodded, "Probably."

"Those must have been some pretty great binoculars."

"They were. I'm convinced the space between the muzzle and his head was obvious because the gun wasn't in a direct line with his head, but was several inches behind it. That would also explain why, when I examined the weapon I didn't find any tissue blowback in the muzzle."

"That's not all is it?"

"No. The degree of rigor in the body when I started work on it was too advanced for the time that had elapsed since it hit the water."

Gatlin's mind raced with the implications of what Broussard had told them. "So the shooter's suicide was—"

Not wanting Gatlin to say it before he could, Broussard quickly said, "All an act."

But the old pathologist wasn't quick enough, so that he and Gatlin said those three words exactly in unison.

"You're telling us the real shooter killed Hartley earlier and had the body in the water beside the boat when he pretended to shoot himself," Gatlin said.

"When I called and told you to meet me, Bubba and I were at the spot where it all happened. We found a series of rebars pounded into the bayou where they couldn't be seen from a boat. I'm sure that after the shooter went into the water, he used those rebars to guide him as he swam unseen around the point to where he'd hidden another boat. He never intended his charade to fool us for long, only until he'd escaped."

"Which he did while everyone was focused on retrieving Hartley's body," Gatlin said. Then he thought of something. "Hartley's wife said her husband had been fishing every day this week. I'll bet the shooter cased the location for several days before the picnic and decided to use Hartley because there was a good chance the guy would be there on the big day. My question is, where'd he kill him . . . on the water or somewhere before?"

"On the water would be risky because the sound could

attract a ranger's boat," Broussard said, "but—"

"What if he used a subsonic round," Kit said from the sofa.

Both men looked at her in surprise. "How do you know about that?" Gatlin asked.

"I saw someone at the gun range using them."

"That would definitely make the shot quieter," Broussard said, impressed with her contribution.

Over on the sofa, Kit felt less like a useless observer.

Gatlin rubbed his chin. "Wonder if there are surveillance cameras at the public boat ramps."

"There weren't any where Bubba and I put in," Broussard said. He looked at Kit. "Give us a picture of what kind of man we're lookin' for."

Kit got up and stood by Gatlin. "You said the shot that killed your uncle was made from 200 yards away?"

Broussard nodded.

"And he did it on the first try?"

"Yes."

"I don't think an amateur could do that. And the use of a subsonic round to kill Hartley, both those things suggest you're looking for someone with firearms training, maybe with a military background." She looked at Gatlin. "I assume the serial numbers on both guns were obliterated."

"Completely."

"And he's a planner," Kit said. She turned to Broussard. "Philip said it happened at a birthday picnic for your Uncle. How long ago was the event planned?"

"I got my invitation two weeks ago."

"Delivered how?"

"By mail."

"I'd like to see a list of people who were invited and another one containing the names of those who weren't there."

"You realize you're suggesting the shooter might be a relative," Gatlin said.

"Isn't that always the best place to start looking?" Kit said.

Gatlin looked at Broussard. "I'm satisfied. You willing to give her the release time?"

"Already said I would."

Kit had no idea what had happened to the conversation, because they seemed to have suddenly started a new one that didn't include her. "Am I supposed to understand what just occurred?" She said, shaking her head.

"I've got a proposal for you," Gatlin said.

Kit held out the hand with her new ring on it. "Sorry I'm already engaged. But thanks for the offer."

"I saw the ring and was gonna ask you about it later," Broussard said. "When did *that* happen?"

"Last night. Teddy was planning to ask me Sunday, but couldn't wait." She wanted Broussard to stand up, come around the desk, and hug her, but he didn't.

As Broussard looked at her fondly, he wished he was capable of expressing his delight at the news by giving her a hug, but a public demonstration like that was just not in him. Grandma O had once told him, someone must have put so much starch in his shirts, it got into his brain. Whatever the cause, that's simply who he was. There would be no hug this day or any other. An honest spoken sentiment would have to do. "It's reassuring to know that sometimes good things happen to good people."

Having known him long enough to be fully aware of both his astounding intellect and his rudimentary ability to show affection, Kit accepted his verbal offering of congratulations with complete understanding. "Thank you. I appreciate that." She turned to Gatlin. "You were saying . . ."

"You know we're shorthanded on the force because of the

sick out . . . And nobody thought to make a deal with the creeps in this city to slack off until we get our senses back. What I'm saying is we need help. A call came in this morning about a missing young woman named Betty Bergeron. If you'd be willing to look into it, I'm prepared to make you a temporary homicide detective." Gatlin reached in his jacket pocket and took out what looked like a leather wallet. He flipped it open. "Here's your badge and ID."

"So I've been auditioning this morning?"

"Kind of. I already knew you were good. I just wanted to see once again how you handle yourself."

"That's why you let me take the lead with Terry Hartley."

"Obviously."

"Did you clear this with NOPD command?"

"No, I always run around doing this kind of thing. Makes life interesting to get called up on charges by internal affairs every few months."

Kit looked at Broussard. "Did I hear you say you were willing to give me release time to do this?"

"If it's what you want."

"Just to be sure you understand what you might be getting into, let me tell you all the reasons you should say no," Gatlin said. "Mostly you'll be working alone, at least during your initial inquiries. I don't want you intentionally going into dangerous situations without backup, which would be me. But here's the thing, sometimes you don't know you're in trouble until it's too late. Also, and I'm not proud of this, but even though the force is not officially on strike, some of the other detectives might consider you a union scab. This kind of thing sometimes brings out behavior in people you didn't think they had in them. And a lot of what you'll be doing will be mundane and boring. It ain't a lot of fun to talk to a hundred people that didn't see anything and don't even know what day it is."

"You make it sound so attractive."

His expression now darkened "And the case is time-sensitive."

In Kit's work for Broussard as a death investigator, there was always a need to complete her analysis in a timely fashion. But if things got bogged down, it was just an inconvenience. The subject of her inquiries was never worse off for the delay. The assignment Gatlin was offering her was different. Even the general public knows that when a young woman disappears, her life is most likely in danger. In a high percentage of cases, by the time the victim is missed by someone, they are already dead. But sometimes they aren't. This latter possibility was what Gatlin meant when he called the case time-sensitive.

She nodded, letting him know she understood the stakes.

"I should also mention that a junior homicide detective makes less than you do working for Andy," Gatlin said. "But for compensation you'll stay on the ME payroll."

Kit looked at Broussard. "What should I do?"

"Only what your heart tells you."

After that time she had put her life at risk by running directly toward a guy with an automatic shotgun and disarmed him with only her Ladysmith, there wasn't much she was afraid of. So fear didn't factor into her decision. But the missing young woman did. If the department was shorthanded and couldn't work the case, the girl would almost certainly end up dead. She looked at Gatlin and held out her hand. "I'll need that badge."

Chapter 8

After giving Kit her new badge, Gatlin spent a few minutes with her discussing the fine points of probable cause. Then he turned to Broussard and said, "I don't see any point in hiding the fact the real killer escaped. If we try, we could miss some useful information that people calling in might offer. Besides, to do a decent job of grilling any suspects, I'll have to say what actually happened."

"Will you call Terry Hartley and tell her what we've learned?" Kit asked.

"Yeah. I might as well let the press know too."

When Kit left Broussard's office, it was five o'clock. She and Teddy had reservations for dinner Sunday night at Commander's Palace to celebrate their engagement, and she had planned to spend today looking for a new dress to wear. But there was no time for shopping now. She had to find Betty Bergeron.

She moved quickly down the hall to her office and went inside. There, she turned on her computer and entered the password Gatlin had given her to access the NOPD network. A few more keystrokes and she was looking at Bergeron's meager file.

The young woman had been reported missing by her parents, Acadia and Paul. According to them, the girl that Betty shared an apartment with had called them that morning, saying Betty had not come home for two consecutive nights. The report therefore, was actually a second-hand account. Even so, it was important to begin with the parents.

Acadia and Paul Bergeron lived in Metairie, touted as the first suburb of New Orleans. Lying just to the west of the crescent city, Metairie is built on a ridge of land created by silt and sediment deposited by the Mississippi over thousands of years as the river changed course. After confirming by a quick phone call that both parents were home and weren't planning on going out, Kit headed for her car.

Back in Broussard's office, Gatlin returned to his sofa-arm perch and said, "Okay, let's talk about Uncle Joe. Before you complicated things all I had to do was come up with a motive for what happened. Now, I don't even have the shooter."

Gatlin waited expectantly for a comeback, because that's the way the two friends had been talking to each other for decades. But Broussard simply sat there fiddling with a pen and looking at nothing.

Realizing now that his comment had been in poor taste, Gatlin said. "I've never heard you talk about your uncle. Were you close?"

"Used to be. After my parents were killed and I came to live with my grandmother, Joe would take me fishin' whenever he and his boys would go. And if they had a cookout in the backyard, he'd come and get me. He had two daughters and two sons of his own, already a big family. He sure didn't need anybody else around.

"I remember one time Joe and his boys and I were out on Lake Pontchartrain after dark fishin' for speckled trout. And we weren't catchin' anything. Then the moon peeked over the horizon. Joe pointed at the moon and said, 'Boys, when the moon clears the water, those fish are gonna start hittin'' like crazy.' And they did. I've never seen anything like it since. Most likely it was just a lucky guess, but he had us all thinkin' he was a genius.

"Then . . . after I got older, we just seemed to drift apart. I don't know what happened. There was no reason that I know of. This mornin' at the picnic is the first time I've talked to him in years."

"His wife still living?"

"Died a few years back. I sent some flowers and a card, but had to miss the funeral because of that triple murder at the Lagniappe Mart on Airways."

"Why'd he need a bodyguard?"

"He was an important man before he retired. Had to have made a few people mad through the years. Talk to the bodyguard and ask *him*."

"Top of my 'To-Do list,' which I need to start working on. I'm sorry for what happened."

"Yeah, me too."

After Gatlin left, Broussard sat in his chair and tried to figure out why he hadn't stayed in touch with Uncle Joe. He didn't even know anything about Joe's kids. Why was that?

He thought about his own life . . . his work, his cars, his big kitchen, his western novels, his collection of old master paintings with sheep in them, his table at Grandma O's. He loved them all. But they were *things*.

He thought some more, his finger stroking the bristly hairs on the end of his nose. Had he ever loved a *person*? Was he even capable of that kind of love? Did he love Joe? No . . . If he had, he would have spoken to him regularly, invited him to dinner, done something special for him every birthday. Sure, he was seething with anger at the shooter for taking Joe's life. But in truth that was his usual reaction to murder. He hated murderers, but that didn't mean he loved the victims. He was uncomfortable even thinking about love between male relatives. Love didn't seem like the right word, even if they treated you like their own child. Love was a word to be used only in regard to women.

Okay . . . He had loved Susan, the girl from his long ago past. Or did he? Why had that not worked out? Was it *his* fault for not caring enough? What about Kit? If he'd ever had a daughter, he'd want her to be just like Kit. And he'd do anything to protect her from harm. In fact, had done exactly that a number of times over the years. Did he love *her*? He never swore out loud and rarely did even in his head. But now he wondered, what the hell *is* love?

Practically every home on the Bergeron's street had a nice lawn and well-chosen landscaping, which consisted mostly of shrubs and small trees, nothing large enough to provide any shade. Accustomed to living in the French Quarter, where the two-story buildings crowding the narrow streets often permit only a limited view of the sky, whenever Kit left its confines, she always felt as she did now, uncomfortably exposed. Unlike the Hartley's neighborhood, which had been full of pickup trucks, the vehicles here ran to sedans, economy cars, and a few SUVs.

The Bergeron home was one of only a few two-story buildings on the street. And it was the sole residence with a circular driveway, which occupied most of the front yard. She pulled in behind a silver four-door sedan and got out.

The home's front door opened even before she announced her arrival.

Showing her new badge, Kit introduced herself, feeling extremely awkward about saying she was *Detective* Franklyn.

"We've been waiting all day for someone to contact us," a slim woman with long, straight hair of indeterminate color said, sharply.

Kit didn't feel like starting her inquiry with an apology, so she said, "I understand. But I'm here now."

"Please, come in," a wiry man with closely set eyes said, gently moving the woman out of the way. Both were wearing clothes that Kit thought of as office suitable.

Kit stepped into a room containing an eclectic ensemble of furniture that had clearly not been chosen by someone with a sense of color.

"Is my daughter dead?" the woman asked, her eyes wide and staring.

"Acadia," the man said sternly. "Let the detective handle this conversation." Then to Kit; "Please have a seat."

He waved her to a zebra-striped sofa. While Kit accepted his offer, Paul went to a fluorescent pink armchair and sat down. His wife remained standing, leaning against the front door, her lips compressed into thin veal strips of disapproval.

Kit got out a pen, turned to a fresh page in her notebook, and said, "How old is Betty?"

"She was twenty last month," Paul said. Then, not waiting for more questions, he went on automatic. "She's a junior at Tulane, majoring in molecular biology."

"Must be a smart girl," Kit said, noting what he said.

"Wants to be a genetic counselor," Paul continued. "We don't live that far from Tulane. She could have stayed here, but she just *had* to have her own place. If she was here, we could keep an eye on her."

"That was the problem if you remember," Acadia said.

Paul shot her a disapproving look.

Apart from the stress of having a missing daughter, Kit thought the couple's marriage likely had a lot of other issues.

"So you didn't like her going out on her own," Kit said to Paul.

"It didn't make economic sense."
"Did you argue with her about it?"
"A few times."
"How long ago did she move out?"
Paul shrugged. "Six-seven months ago."
"When did you last see her?"
He looked at Acadia. "How long has it been . . . four or five weeks?"
"Probably four," Acadia said. "We were in the neighborhood and went over to her apartment to see how she was doing. We didn't call first, and she got upset, said we weren't showing her the respect an adult deserves."
Then Paul said to Kit, "Do you have kids?"
"No."
"They're beautiful when they first come out, then they're a pain for the first year and the second. After that it gradually gets better until you can't imagine your life without them." He stared straight ahead for a few seconds, not speaking until his eyes teared up. He wiped at them, glanced at Acadia, then turned quickly back to Kit. "*Is* she dead?"
"At this point, there's absolutely no way to know what's going on," Kit said. "But I promise you I *will* find out. Do you have a recent picture of her?"
Paul took out his cell phone and fiddled with it for a few seconds then came over to where Kit was sitting, turned the screen toward her, and gave her the phone.
The picture was the head and shoulders of an attractive girl with long brown hair and what appeared to be naturally full lips. Her phone was in one hand, meaning it was most likely a 'selfie' taken in front of a mirror. Unlike the silly poses most young woman effect these days when taking an informal picture, she didn't have her tongue out or her fingers up in a v or a hook 'em horns. Her expression was

neutral to slightly toward 'stop bothering me.'

"Where'd you get this?" Kit said handing the phone back.

"Pulled it from her Facebook page."

Pleased to hear that the girl was on Facebook, where a lot of information about her could be easily mined, Kit said, "I'll need a copy of the picture. I could get it from her page but it's awkward to do with my phone. Could you just text it to me?"

"Sure," Paul said. "What's your number?"

In less than a minute Kit had the picture on her phone. "What's her Facebook address?" After Paul gave her that, she said, "Did Betty have any boyfriends?"

"When she still lived here, she rarely dated," Acadia said. "Didn't want anything to interfere with her studies. She was very goal-oriented."

"My report said that you first learned Betty was missing from the girl she shared her apartment with."

That's right," Acadia said. "Her name is Dee Evans. I'm sure she knows more about Betty's current relationships and friends than we do."

"Where's their apartment?"

Paul told her the address.

"I guess you also have Dee Evans' phone number."

With that noted, Kit stood up, put her phone and notebook back in her bag, and fished out a business card, which she handed to Paul. "You've already got my number, but here's my card just in case. If you hear anything, give me a call."

"Please, keep us informed," Acadia said as Kit headed for the door.

Kit mentally sorted through what she might say in response. The only time she was likely to call them before she found their daughter was to ask more questions. So she simply said, "Think positive."

Chapter 9

Back in her car, Kit called Dee Evans to see if she was home. Evans picked up the call on the second ring.

"Hi Dee," Kit said. "I'm from the NOPD. I'm working on finding Betty Bergeron. I was coming over to speak with you but wanted to make sure you were there."

"I'm actually at the drug store a few blocks away. I'll be here another five minutes or so, then I'll go home to meet you."

The girls' apartment was a few blocks from Tulane. Estimating the distance, Kit figured Evans would probably get there first. Before starting the car, Kit went to the web browser on her phone to see if she could bring up Betty's Facebook page. It was a slow and cumbersome process, but in a few minutes, she had the site in front of her, only to discover that the page had almost nothing on it. There was the picture Kit had obtained from Paul Bergeron, but no others. Betty had listed her favorite book as *Origin of Species* by Charles Darwin, her most liked movie was *Terminator* with Arnold Schwarzenegger, and that's it. Hugely disappointed at how useless the page turned out to be, Kit quit the browser and put the phone on the seat beside her.

She took Airlines Highway back into New Orleans. Turning onto South Carrolton, she immediately felt more at home. In most places the urban streets have no character. They could be transplanted from one city to the other with no visual disconnect. Not so on Carrolton. Part of that was the presence of what the natives called the neutral ground, a wide median with small trees planted on each side of two sets of trolley tracks. Equally important to its character were the live oaks on each side of the street, whose twisted limbs formed a leafy canopy over the adjacent lanes of traffic. Somehow all this mitigated the lack of any zoning regulation. She passed a church with a long front walk that sat next to a beadwork-decorated Victorian home built practically against the sidewalk. Next came three more homes equally close to the sidewalk, the first, a New Orleans shotgun, the next two, Queen Anne four squares. Then came a little boutique restaurant with tables out front. Who wouldn't want to live in such a city?

Live in such a . . . She imagined Betty Bergeron sitting at one of the tables at the restaurant. Maybe Betty had never done that. The question now was, would she ever be able to?

The address Kit sought was on Willow Street, which was one way coming toward Carrolton. So she turned onto Jeanette, went down to the correct block, and cut over to Willow, a street also lined by live oaks.

She arrived at the girls' apartment, actually a two-story duplex, just as an attractive platinum blonde emerged from a white Ford Focus that had apparently just pulled into the short driveway. The girl was wearing denim cutoffs so brief you could almost see her butt cheeks.

Kit parked behind the Ford and got out. "I guess you're Dee?"

The girl did an awkward curtsy with her keys dangling from one hand and her drug store purchase from the other. She wore her straight hair in an asymmetric cut, one side ending just below her ear, the other sweeping down below her chin. It looked great, but where her hair was long, it obviously partially blocked her vision.

Kit flashed her badge. "I'm . . ." she hesitated, once again feeling strange about how she was about to introduce herself, ". . . Detective Franklyn."

"I'm glad they sent a female detective," Dee said. "Have you ever like, shot anybody?"

"Actually, I have."

"Did it bother you?"

"Not in the least. Can we go inside and talk?"

"Sure."

Dee led the way and opened the front door.

They stepped into a living room furnished with a lot of inexpensive pale wood furniture, woven rugs, and cheap prints on the wall, showing that it was possible to decorate well and not spend a lot of money.

Dee put her purchase on the counter that separated the living area from a small galley kitchen and invited Kit to have a seat.

A moment later, facing Dee across a blonde coffee table shaped like a big kidney, notebook open, pen ready, Kit said, "When did you first notice that Betty was missing?"

"This morning. Well . . . I first thought something was wrong Friday morning. We have separate bedrooms, but I usually hear her come in after her shift at work. She works nights as a bartender at Gator Willie's and usually gets in like, around 1:00 a.m. I wait tables most nights at Nat's grill. We close at eight, so I'm home before she is. The sound of her key in the front door lock always wakes me up. But Thursday night I didn't wake up, and in the morning she wasn't there. I didn't think too much about it and just went on to school . . . I'm majoring in Social Work at Tulane. Then Friday night, I had to get up and pee at 2:00 a.m. and afterward I looked in her room and she wasn't there. This morning, she still wasn't home. I tried to call her on her cell, but it went right to voice mail, which I think means either her phone was off or her battery was dead. And I don't think she ever just turns it off."

Kit took out her own cell phone. "Let's call her again and see what happens. What's her number?"

Kit punched it into her phone as Dee recited it, then listened to the call. "Direct to voice mail," Kit said. "So when did you last see her?"

"Just before I went to work on Thursday. That would be about 4:30 p.m."

"She have any boyfriends?"

"Not that I know of. She isn't like, very social. So a guy would have a hard time getting the time of day from her."

"But she did set up a Facebook page."

"No, I did that for her. Have you seen it?"

"Yes."

"I made her take the selfie you see on there. Even though her expression shows she was like, kind of pissed at me for pushing her to get on Facebook, you can still tell she's beautiful."

"The page doesn't have hardly anything on it."

"What's that old saying, 'You can lead a horse to water but you can't make 'em swim'."

"That's not exactly quoted right, but I get the idea."

"She comes across as a totally serious self-centered nerd, but she isn't, not really. Like me, she doesn't have much free time, but I know for the last two years she helped serve meals to homeless people at the Orleans Parish sheriff's Thanksgiving dinner, and has donated time to Meals on Wheels. That's more than I can say for myself. I hope she's all right. Is she . . . do you think?"

Ignoring the question, Kit said, "Is her bedroom unlocked?"

"Yeah, want to see it?"

"Please."

A casual search of Betty's bedroom produced nothing that would help find her. The girl didn't keep a diary, but Kit did find a small, jeweled notebook containing all her passwords. Using the one she saw in there for the girl's e-mail account, Kit checked all her messages; both received and sent for the last month. She also reviewed the recently deleted file. In no case, did she find any that suggested it might be from a male friend. Nor was there any evidence of trouble she might be having.

Finished with the computer, Kit shut it off, stood up, and looked at Dee, who had been sitting on the bed watching. "I'm going to hold on to this little notebook for a while."

"Sure, okay."

"Can you think of anyone who might have been upset with Betty for anything?"

Dee's eyebrows knitted together as she thought about the question. Then they arched upward as she obviously remembered something. "I was walking across campus with her a couple weeks ago and this blond guy comes up and says, 'Thought I'd give you another chance. How about a dinner date? You pick the night. We'll go someplace really nice.' Then he reached out and took hold of her wrist.

"Betty yanked her arm free and said, 'I told you I'm not interested. Now get lost.' She took off so fast she left me standing there. And I can tell you, the guy was like, not happy.

"When I caught up to her, I asked about him and she told me his name, but I can't recall it right now. I want to say Leon, but I know that's not it. I've seen him in the LBC eating lunch a few times since then. He's always alone and always gawking at the women."

The LBC was the Lavin-Bernick Center, what other

schools call the University Center. "You said he's blond. How else would you describe him?"

"He's like . . . not distinctive in any way. Average height, not skinny, not fat, not athletic looking."

"What about his hair, long, short . . ."

"Neat. That's about all I can say. But he carries a black backpack covered in yellow emogies. You know, those round faces you can put at the end of sentences in your e-mail to show you're kidding or you're sad. Seems kind of effeminate to me. I'd turn him down just for that. But it is a way to identify him. I'd be glad to ask around and see if anyone at school knows his name."

"I'd appreciate that. Can you tell me anything else that would help me better understand who Betty is?"

Dee thought for a moment then said, "Well, she's kind of paranoid about how the government is trying to spy on everybody. Not long ago she told me I should shut off the tracking function on my phone, like she did hers. Was she right? *Are* we all being watched?"

"I'd like to think not. But I don't know any more about that than you do. Having it on gives your phone added functions and my thought is, if you have nothing to hide, why worry about it?" Realizing that Dee might take what she said the wrong way, Kit added. "I'm not saying Betty is trying to hide anything. Some people are just very protective of their privacy. Nothing wrong with that. Anything more you can think of?"

"Not at the moment."

Kit dug in her bag and gave Dee her card. "Call me anytime."

"Now what happens?"

"Any idea when Gator Willie's opens?"

"Seven o'clock I think. You're going over there?"

"Maybe one of the other employees saw her leave with someone after her shift on Thursday."

"I doubt she'd ever allow herself to be picked up like that."

"It's still a visit I need to make."

There was a rattle of metal outside. Dee glanced at the window. "Now *there's* somebody you should talk to."

Kit glanced at the window and saw a ladder being placed against the building.

"Who's that?"

"Leo Silver, the maintenance guy. I've seen him a couple of times taking pictures of Betty with his phone when she wasn't looking."

"I'm going out there. You should probably stay here."

Outside, Silver was heading up the ladder with a caulking gun in his hand.

"Mr. Silver, I'm Detective Franklyn with the NOPD. Could we talk for a minute?"

His face full of questions, Silver came down. He was wearing a camouflage cap, tan work pants, and a tan T-shirt. He was one of those guys whose neck runs straight down to his shoulders from his ears. He had bushy eyebrows and a struggling mustache that rested over thin, smirking lips. "Talk about what?" he said.

"Betty Bergeron. Know who that is?"

"Yeah. She lives in this side of the building." He pointed at the front door on the right. "What about her?"

"She's missing. Didn't come home either Thursday or Friday night."

"And this concerns me how?"

At this point Kit didn't even know if Betty had worked her Thursday night shift, so she asked Silver, "Did you spend any time over here Thursday afternoon?"

"No. The guy who employees me has six properties. I was

painting the one on Autumn all day Thursday until dusk."

"Alone?"

"No, I had a helper."

"Mind giving me his name and phone number?"

"Are you thinking I did something to the girl?"

"Not at all. I'm just trying to get a feel for the situation. That way I'll know what kind of questions to ask and who could help me."

"I see." He then gave her the information she'd requested. Somehow the guy could smirk even when he was talking.

"What did you do after you left here Thursday?"

"Went home, had dinner and a couple of beers, watched TV, and went to bed."

"Where's home?"

He gave her his address.

"Are you married?"

"No. Hard to believe, isn't it?"

"What programs did you watch?"

"It all runs together. Everything is so lousy, it's hard to remember one show from another."

"Mind if I look at the photos on your phone."

"Don't you need a search warrant to do that?"

"If you're not guilty of anything why would you care?"

"Ever hear of a thing called the US constitution . . . freedom from unreasonable searches and seizures? My phone is none of your business."

"Point taken." She closed her notebook. "We'll talk again."

"I can't wait."

Before hooking up her seatbelt a moment later, she noted the make and license number of Silver's truck, then called Gatlin.

"Haven't learned much, but soon as I get home I'm going to run a background check on a man named Leo Silver." She told him why, and added, "Could you have someone check the DMV for the license number and model car Betty Bergeron drove and then send out a BOLO?" The last acronym meant Be On The Lookout. She wasn't trying to sound like a detective, she'd just heard Gatlin use it once in conversation and it had simply popped out.

"Oh, you already did? Of course you would. I should have realized that. What about a subpoena for her phone records? I just learned that she kept the tracking function on her phone turned off, but knowing about her calls might . . . That's in the works too . . .? Good. Talk to you later."

With Gatlin having already initiated two important facets of the investigation, Kit could have felt like he had intruded into her space. Instead, his preemptive actions just made her respect his abilities even more.

She ended the call, navigated to her web browser, and checked the location of Gator Willie's. It was about a quarter mile from where she sat. But it was too early to head over there now. Besides, she hadn't had anything to eat since lunch.

"Twice in one day, chile'," Grandma O said, twenty minutes later, greeting Kit at the restaurant's front door. "I'm flattered. The old Cajun gestured to the back, "City boy is here too."

In the rear, seated at his regular table, his chair facing the front door, Broussard waved her over.

She wasn't surprised to see him because she'd parked beside his T-Bird.

He stood up and pulled out a chair for her as she approached, something he'd never done before. "Detective Franklyn," have any epiphanies about Betty Bergeron today?"

"Not so far. But it's early yet."

"Sounds like your day isn't over."

"Soon as I finish eating, I'm heading over to the bar where

she worked and see if I can get a lead there. Does Gatlin have any ideas about who's responsible for . . ." She hesitated, trying to find an expression that wasn't cold. "What happened at the picnic?"

Before he could answer, Grandma O steamed over to them and said, "Tonight you're gonna want red beans and rice or crawfish etouffee. Trust me on dis." The tower of taffeta looming over them had by now trained all her regulars not to disagree with her about *anything*.

"Etouffee, and iced tea," Kit said.

Broussard opted for the other dish, but trying to exercise *some* independence added, "with extra Andouille."

"You know I put jus' da right amount in dere to start with," Grandma O said. "But because you had a bad day, dis time I'm not gonna make you do what's right. Remember, dat's only for today."

And off she went to the kitchen.

Broussard watched her leave, then said, "You asked about Philip . . . I haven't heard from him since our meetin' earlier in my office."

"He said you were talking to your uncle at the time."

"About four feet away."

"That's horrible."

"Worse part is, before this mornin' I hadn't spoken to him in years. And now, he's gone." He rubbed his short beard in thought, then said, "There must have been sixty or seventy people at that party and I only recognized a handful. And most of 'em there were *related* to me."

Kit responded, "I've got an uncle that came to our house for dinner every Thanksgiving. He had this big booming voice and could always be counted on to make some off-color joke when we were eating. Everyone tried to ignore it, but it always made my mother blush. My point is that you've probably got some relatives you don't *want* to know."

"You may be right, but Joe wasn't one of 'em."

"Changing subjects . . . why'd you pull my chair out for me?" Kit had long wished that Broussard was *her* uncle but was never sure how he felt about her. So she was always on the lookout for some behavior that would bear on the question.

Above his beard, Broussard's cheeks took on a rosy hue, much like the color of a fully cooked crawfish, a sure sign he was going to give an evasive answer.

"Ahh," he said, looking up. "Here's our food."

For the next few minutes they ate in silence, each of them glancing at the other to assess the status of the conversational skirmish she'd initiated. Then Broussard said, "So . . . pretty soon we're gonna have to change your business cards to say Kit LaBiche . . ."

"Well done," Kit replied, smiling.

Chapter 10

The door opened and Blake Irvin, Uncle Joe's bodyguard, was standing on the other side with a Heineken in his hand.

"Mind if I come in?" Gatlin said.

"Got a warrant?"

Before Gatlin could respond, Irvin stepped back. "Just kidding."

Even with the sunglasses he was wearing when Gatlin first talked to him at the picnic grounds after the shooting, Gatlin had thought the man didn't look very tough. Now, with the glasses off, he looked even softer . . . sure, he was beefy and about six feet two . . . shaved head and a strong chin, but he had thin eyebrows and lots of wrinkles at the corners of his eyes. And his skin was *pink*.

"I'd offer you a beer," the guy said, "but if you're here, you're on duty and I know you don't want to drink while you're working."

"Got time for a talk?"

"Considering that my client got his brains blown out right under my nose, I'll probably be having a lot of time on my hands now." He waved Gatlin to a chair that looked like a fabric-covered breath mint on tiny metal legs.

"I sit in that, I may not be able to get up."

"The sofa then."

The sofa was equally as ugly as the chair, but did seem like something that wouldn't hold you captive after you sat in it.

Irvin somehow dropped smoothly onto the breath mint and stretched out his legs.

"How much you figure it'd cost to open a McDonald's?" Irvin said. "Always kind of liked the fast food business."

"People have short memories," Gatlin replied. "You'll probably be okay."

"You don't really believe that do you?"

"You want the happy answer?"

"Never mind." He shook his head. "Who the hell would have expected him to be shot from the swamp?"

"How far in advance did you know about the picnic?"

"He told me the day before."

"And the location?"

"That too."

Then you should have arranged for somebody to be out there in a boat hours before your client got there. If you were any good at your job.

Gatlin didn't say this aloud because he didn't want to pile onto the guy's troubles. "Why were you hired? Was it a general concern by your client or a specific one?"

"He'd been receiving death threats in the mail."

Gatlin was about to ask why Uncle Joe didn't tell the police about this. But then, even when the force was working at full capacity, they didn't have a great record at dealing with things like that. "Did he know who sent them?"

"He was pretty sure it was a guy named Howard Karpis. Until Mr. B fired Karpis three months ago, the guy was head of exploration and development at Seabed Petroleum."

"Why was he fired?"

"Guess he wasn't finding any oil."

"So he was incompetent."

"Or lazy."

"Why'd Joe think it was Karpis?"

"The guy was fired in front of a bunch of company execs after he gave a report on his department's dismal accomplishments for the last fiscal quarter. Mr. B could be sharp tongued if he was unhappy about something, so he probably ripped the guy a new one right there in public. Karpis came around the table and knocked Mr. B's papers onto the floor, then threatened to kill him. When Mr. B and I discussed it, he didn't go into a lot of detail, like what the guy's actual words were."

"Did he show you the written threats?"

"Yeah."

"What'd they say?"

"Can't recite them exactly, but I remember one said something like, 'Pain and death are part of life'."

"That might not even meet the legal threshold for a threat."

"How about: 'The hour of departure has arrived'."

"Pretty lame."

"I might agree if Mr. B wasn't lying in the morgue. I don't get this line of questioning. You've got the killer. Was it Karpis?"

"We don't have him."

"What, he shot himself than swam away?"

"I can't spend time going into all the details except to say that the killer only pretended to shoot himself and yes, he then swam away. Where'd Joe keep those threats?"

"Desk in his study."

"He live alone?"

"Yeah, wife died a few years ago."

"Got a key to the house?"

"I do."

Irvin now had no reason to be in the house, so Gatlin said, "Better let me have it."

Irvin dug in his pocket, took a key off his ring, and handed it over.

"Did Joe have protection 24 hours a day?"

"Only way to do it. I've got two employees. We each took an eight-hour shift."

"They have keys too, I guess."

"Yeah."

"I'll need their contact information."

While Irvin rattled off the pertinent names and cell phone numbers, Gatlin entered it all in his little black book. "What was the servant situation . . . how many?"

"Cook . . . one maid . . . they were there every day. A gardener who came every other day or so."

"The cook and the maid, either of them live on the premises?"

"No."

"How long had each of the three been employed there?"

"The cook . . . three years. The maid . . . two. The gardener, also two years."

Gatlin nodded and said, more to himself than to Irvin. "All of them hired before the Karpis firing."

"And therefore, known and trustworthy," Irvin said.

"You would think so," Gatlin replied. "Got names and addresses for all of them?"

Given how lax Irvin's procedures were, Gatlin doubted the guy even knew the last names of the three. Surprisingly, he said, "I'll get 'em for you."

"What about Karpis? Wouldn't happen to have *his* address, would you?"

"Considering what I just told you about him, how could I *not* have it?"

He deftly got out of his chair and left the room.

When he came back a few minutes later, he handed Gatlin

a piece of yellow notebook paper. It contained not only the complete names of the three servants they'd been discussing, but also phone numbers. Karpis's address was there too, but no contact information.

Gatlin folded the paper and put it between the pages of his black book. "You wouldn't happen to know who handled Joe's personal legal business would you?"

"Not a clue."

"Joe had two sons and two daughters," Gatlin said. "Was he particularly close to them? Did any of the four regularly come to the house, or did he go to see them?"

"His one daughter would come by every week. I think her name was Amelia."

"She married?"

"No idea."

If Howard Karpis proved to be a viable suspect, the provisions of Joe Broussard's will most likely wouldn't have any bearing on who killed him. But Gatlin had long ago learned that at this stage of any investigation to scoop up every bit of information you can.

"Oh yeah," Irvin said. "About two weeks back, a pretty blonde came to see him. Young . . . probably early twenties."

"You get a name?"

"Elizabeth, I think. Seemed to be another relative."

"Anything else I should know about?"

Irvin shrugged.

Gatlin stood and put his black book in his inside jacket pocket. "Thanks for the information."

"Yeah, okay. If you need anything else, please hesitate to ask."

Gatlin cocked his head and squinted at Irvin. "Was that a joke?"

"Apparently not a good one," Irvin said. "In any event,

don't try to contact me for at least 24 hours, because I'll be too drunk to talk."

Chapter 11

Gator Willie's was so busy Kit could barely get in the door. The clientele looked mostly like college kids trying to be "relevant." That meant mostly clean cut guys wearing one earring and hair standing up like a spiky rooster comb; girls with a small nasal diamond or streaks of some odd color in their hair. She saw no guys with facial tattoos or girls with partially shaved heads or lip rings. That didn't mean everyone there was harmless. Some of the most depraved men that ever lived were normal looking or even handsome. There were also plenty of attractive but cold-blooded females now locked up for life. She had the distinct feeling that someone in Gator Willie's knew where Betty Bergeron was.

At the far end of the big room, about two dozen couples were dancing to a Zydeco song called "Dog Hill" by Boozoo Chavis, her knowledge of the piece coming from years of being around her fiancée, Teddy LaBiche.

Next to the dance floor, surrounded by a clapping throng, was a mechanical gator being ridden by a lanky guy in chinos and a yellow T-shirt. Abruptly the gator gave a wild whirl, then stopped suddenly, sending the guy flying into a bunch of hay bales. Shouts of approval erupted from the witnesses, almost drowning out Dog Hill, which is saying a lot.

Kit turned and headed for the bar, trying not to inadvertently rub against anyone. Finally, seeing a route open before her, she picked up the pace, only to have her way suddenly blocked by a good-looking guy with the requisite prowling-male two-day beard.

"Hey beautiful, can I buy you a beer?"

Kit held up her hand and wiggled her ring finger.

Instead of backing off, he took her hand and kissed her engagement ring.

"Now go in peace my son," Kit said pulling her hand back.

His furrowed brow showed that he didn't get her papal reference.

Just wanting to move on, she pointed at the ring with her other hand. "Engaged."

He gave her his best smile, and it was definitely a good one. "Engagements are like predictions of rain," he said. "You should never ignore a chance to have a little fun because of something that might not even happen."

"Funny you should mention things that aren't going to happen. That would include me spending another second talking to you." She turned casually and made sure to give him a little hip action as she walked away.

At the bar, she slid onto the only empty stool; one covered like all the others in what was probably fake alligator skin. Painted on the big mirror behind the bar was a cartoon alligator on its back drinking beer from a bottle balanced on its legs. The three bartenders were female, all dressed the same; denim shorts and a checkered shirt with the tail tied at the waist. A couple of open buttons at the top showed that the management wouldn't hire anyone who didn't own a push-up bra.

One of the girls came her way. "What can I get you sweetie?"

Noting that the round white badge on the girl's shirt said her name was Claudia, Kit flashed her new ID. "NOPD," she said. "I'm trying to find Betty Bergeron. We're you working

Thursday night?"

The girl's flashing black eyes lost their luster. "Yeah, I was here. Did something happen to her? She's missed a couple shifts."

"We don't know anything yet. Did she work Thursday night?"

"Yeah, she was here."

"She go home alone after her shift?"

"We walked out together, just us."

"How did she seem?"

"What do you mean?"

"Normal . . . Happy . . . Excited?"

Claudia shrugged. "Normal, I guess."

"Not upset at anything?"

"Look, we weren't BFFs or anything, more like . . . just workmates."

"Did you see her get in her car?" At the same moment that Kit asked the question a raucous round of cheers erupted from the mechanical gator pit.

Claudia leaned closer and cupped her ear. "Sorry, what?"

Kit repeated the question.

Claudia had to think a moment, then said, "Actually no. The owner came out and called me back in to remind me to punch out at the end of each shift. I been forgetting to do that. He could have done it for me, but made me do it so I'd remember in the future, like I was his kid or something."

"Did she and the manager get along?"

"He's strict. Everybody here gets yelled at occasionally. But I've never heard of Betty and him having any problem beyond that."

Kit lowered her voice. "Does he ever hit on any of the girls?"

Claudia's brow furrowed and she whispered back, "I'm not

sure he even has a dick although sometimes he acts like one."

"Thursday night did you notice anyone talking to her more than usual . . . hanging around her?"

"When we're on duty it's hectic. I wouldn't notice anything like that. In fact, I better get back to work now."

Kit pointed at one of the other bartenders "Could you send that redhead over here so we can talk?"

"I'll get her."

Over the next few minutes, Kit spoke to the other two girls, but didn't learn anything useful, except that the owner's name was Bill Gauthier, and that he was in his office, just to the left of the bar.

Kit went over and knocked on his door. Because of the noise in the place she leaned in and listened hard to hear if he said, "Come in."

Instead, the door suddenly swung open. Caught off balance, Kit stumbled forward into the arms of a guy whose breath smelled like he'd just gargled with mouthwash.

She pulled free and reached for her ID. "Mr. Gauthier, I'm Detective Franklyn, NOPD, can we talk for a few minutes?"

"Am I allowed to say no?" the guy said, his confident grin making Kit think he would have appreciated a snare drum rim shot for his witty response.

"You could," Kit said, "But that sort of thing always makes investigators suspicious."

He stepped back and motioned her in. "Can't have that. So, sure, I got some time . . . not much though. I was about to come out and see why you were botherin' my girls."

"How did you . . ." Then Kit saw two banks of monitors to the right of his desk. She noted that some were showing events taking place in various parts of the bar while others were eyes on the parking lot.

"I'm guessin' you're here to talk about Betty Bergeron,"

Gauthier said.

"If I told you that someone harmed her, what would you say?"

"Did they . . . *is* she hurt?"

"Right now, it's a hypothetical question."

"So you're askin' do I know if anybody has a beef with her?" He shook his head, lips pinched and drooping. "Do I seem like the kind of guy you'd want to discuss your troubles with? Betty served drinks here, I paid her to do it. Employer . . . employee . . . big barrier between us . . . just the way I like it."

Those monitors," Kit said. "Do they automatically record what the cameras see?"

"For a few days, until the data gets written over."

"Think you'd still have the images from Thursday night?"

"Probably."

"Would you be willing to let me look at them?"

"That'll take a long time. You'd be in the way."

"Can they be downloaded onto a flash drive?"

"How big a drive you got?"

Kit dug in her purse and pulled out her secondary key ring. Holding up the flash drive attached to it, she said, "Sixty-four gigs."

Gauthier held out his hand and she gave it to him.

He plugged the drive into the computer wired to the system and made a few mouse clicks.

There ensued an awkward wait while the files were transferred. Looking around the room Kit spotted a rubber alligator with a bloody hand protruding from its open mouth. "Why the alligator theme?" she asked.

"There were alligators around even before the dinosaurs. And they're still here. Whatever killed off the other reptiles didn't affect them. You gotta respect an animal that tough."

"So it's just respect?"

"Okay, you got me detective. I love the damn things."

"I've got a friend who feels the same way." There was no chance she'd tell him she was referring to her fiancée.

"Do you think he's strange?"

"Hardly."

The computer emitted a loud clunk, apparently an indication that the download had been completed, because Gauthier said, "Tell you what. Since we sort of have gators in common. I'm gonna also give you the viewin' software for the files."

He went to the mouse and made a few more selections.

"How long you been a detective?" Gauthier said.

"Why?"

He shrugged. "Seems like an unusual job for a woman . . . I mean one who looks like you."

"Unlike some jobs, appearances aren't very high up the list of qualifications for a detective."

"Guess you're referrin' to the girls I hire. Ones like those out there make more money for the bar and for themselves. Don't blame me. It's on the guys who come in here. They'd rather let somebody with curves and a pretty face take their money." Hearing the computer clunk again, Gauthier reached down, ejected the flash drive, and handed it to her. "Don't know what you're expectin' to find on there."

"A clue maybe," Kit said, "Thanks for the help."

The lot had been so crowded when she'd arrived that Kit had to park partially on the grass at the far end of the asphalt. When she reached the spot, her car looked lower than usual. A quick inspection of the tires with the flashlight app on her cell phone showed that all four were flat.

Chapter 12

Looking closer, Kit could distinctly see that one of her tires had been slashed. Presumably, so had the others. She glanced around her, worried that whoever had done it, might that very moment, be hurtling toward her out of the shadows. But she saw no one.

Feeling that she needed to get into a better lit area, she headed back to the bar's entrance, where, a few steps from the front door, she fished her wallet from her bag and found her triple A card. A moment later, keeping a lookout for anyone suspicious approaching her, she had help on the line.

"Yes . . . Someone has cut all the tires on my car. I can't drive it."

She gave the voice on the other end her name and member number.

She had no idea what they were going to do for her, and as it happened, she didn't find out, because she was informed that her membership had expired two months ago.

"Damn" she muttered. What could she do now?

Calling Gatlin was out of the question. How would that look? On the job for just a couple of hours and now calling him for such a stupid thing. Same for Broussard.

But there *was* one person . . .

Ten seconds later, he answered on the fifth ring. "Bubba, here. Your call is very important to me, so start talkin'."

Not sure if that was a recording, she said, "It's Kit. I've got a problem."

There was a clicking sound and Bubba picked up. "Dr. F. what's da matter?"

She explained what had happened.

"Where are you?" he asked.

She told him the name of the bar. "I don't remember the exact address, but it's on . . ."

"I know exactly where you are. Be dere in about a half hour."

"I'll be inside."

She was soon sitting at the bar, where Claudia came over and said, "More questions?"

"Yeah, would you please get me a Phat Tyre?"

For the next thirty minutes Kit nursed her beer and thought about who could have damaged her car. The most likely culprit was someone involved in the NOPD work slow down . . . cops, detectives, union slugs . . . lot of possibilities. She considered going back to Gauthier's office and checking the surveillance images, but from looking at all the camera coverage earlier she realized the part of the lot where she'd parked was not included.

After what seemed like three hours, her phone rang.

"It's me," Bubba said. "I'm here."

She went outside and saw him standing next to a flatbed truck by the highway.

When she got there, she said, "I'm so sorry to have bothered you."

"You didn't. It was like you knew I was lookin' for some reason to drive dis new truck dat just came in."

By 'came in' he was referring to the police impoundment lot where he worked.

"Will you get in trouble for taking it?"

"Somebody has to make sure it's ready for use. I'm actually

workin' overtime for free. Where you parked?"

Next to Kit's car there was a strip of grass and next to that, the parking area for Oswald's Auto Glass Repair, now closed. This allowed Bubba to get the flatbed close enough so that after he took a quick look at the tires, he was able to jockey her car around and easily drive it up on the truck bed.

"What's the plan?" Kit said, from the front seat of the truck as they pulled onto the street.

"Ain't nothin' can be done about your car tonight. I'll take you home, an' in the mornin' I'll get you fixed up. Paint 'em white and dose tires'd make good planters, but dey ain't gonna carry you anywhere again. Where you wanna get some new ones?"

"Can you find me a good deal?"

"I gotta friend."

"Figured you did."

"Don' mean to poke my nose in, but dat bar don' seem like your kinda place."

"I was there on police business."

"Yeah, Gramma O said you been made a detective."

"How'd she know that?"

"I got friends, but she got ways. Who you think cut your tires? Was it jus' random nasty or somebody dat don't like you in particular?"

"Not sure. Could be I've made some enemies."

"You still got your gun?"

She patted the pant leg that covered her Ladysmith. "Right here."

"Dat's good. Gramma also said you got engaged. Who to?"

"You're kidding, right?"

He glanced at her and grinned, his white teeth flashing even in the poor light. "How's dat gonna work? You gonna move away or is Teddy comin' over here to live?"

Bubba had hit upon a question Kit and Teddy themselves couldn't answer. It was the one thing about their future that worried her. "Negotiations still underway," she said.

For several years, Kit had lived in a French Quarter apartment behind a photo gallery on Toulouse Street. One of the perks of living there was it came with a parking space in an old brick garage, three blocks away on Dauphine. The fact she still lived there after once being attacked in her courtyard and once in her apartment shows how much value parking space has in the Quarter.

Because of its narrow streets and frequent gridlock, driving a huge truck into the Quarter during the day was difficult. On a Saturday night with so many drunks clogging up the place, it was impossible. Bubba therefore, dropped the big truck off at the impoundment lot and they headed for Kit's apartment in Bubba's pickup.

A short while later, heading down North Rampart, Bubba took a right on Toulouse, which fortunately was one-way in the desired direction.

"Just drop me off at Dauphine," Kit said. "No sense you trying to cross Bourbon on a Saturday night. Then you can just take Dauphine to Canal."

"You sure? I don' mind crowds."

"You've done more than enough for one night."

He pulled to a stop at the Dauphine intersection. "Even though tomorrow is Sunday, I can probably get you fixed up with some new tires. I'll call when it's done."

She got out and waited for him to make the turn, then she headed down Toulouse.

Most of the madness during any night in the Quarter was on Bourbon, which was closed to traffic after dark. But some of the mania spilled over onto Toulouse. Several years ago, the living statue acts that populate the Quarter favored covering themselves in gold paint. Of late, silver had become the medium of choice. In the center of the block on her side of the street she saw a silver-skinned guy in a silver tux and top hat holding a silver chain that led to a fake silver alligator. The first time she'd seen him perform she'd watched him for ten minutes waiting for the alligator to do something, but even when the guy would suddenly shift to a new position to prove he was alive the alligator never moved. Even so, she'd given the guy two bucks. Tonight, she edged around the crowd watching him, and kept walking.

At Bourbon Street, the air was filled with earthy smells and the sound of a jazz band. Before crossing the street, she had to wait for a yellow and red Lucky Dog cart to clear the intersection. Whoever had made the carts look like a rolling hot dog had done a great job. Even so, when she'd first moved to New Orleans she'd been afraid to eat anything from a pushcart. But after learning that the great Cajun chef, Paul Prudhomme, would occasionally leave his restaurant and head to Jackson Square for a Lucky Dog, she'd changed her mind. She almost stopped to order one now. But with slashed tires still on her mind, she just wanted to get home. So she simply smiled and nodded at the vendor in his paper hat and red and white striped shirt as he passed.

When she reached the Nolen Boyd art gallery a minute later, she saw Nolen inside talking to a prosperous looking couple that might actually buy something.

On the right side of the gallery, she stepped up to the eight-foot tall, heavy cypress door leading to the rear courtyard, then turned her back to the door, her finger touching the lipstick mace canister on her key ring. She was facing the street because she'd seen a group of loutish looking young men coming her way. To keep from resembling a hooker trying to catch the group's attention, she glanced at her watch then craned her neck to look past them toward the opposite side of the street, as though expecting someone to meet her any minute. When the last of the suspicious men was well out of range, she quickly keyed the lock and slipped inside.

The gallery and the adjacent building formed a long passage leading to the rear courtyard, where her apartment was located. For most of its length the passage had a lattice ceiling covered on top by the branches of an ancient wisteria. During the day, this made the passage a charming, light-dappled avenue. But at night, the Wisteria would have caused it to be a murky twenty-foot stretch were it not for the little lights Boyd had hung along the left wall. He had also placed a coil of razor wire above the big cypress door to keep anyone on the outside from climbing in. As the door shut and locked behind Kit, the tension she felt from being on the Quarter's half lit, humanity-filled streets dissipated.

The lattice-covered walkway opened onto a courtyard equipped with a mercury vapor light on a big pole. Usually the light illuminated a well-kept garden of hostas, autumn ferns, white azaleas, and a small wall fountain. But tonight, like the last two weeks, the courtyard held a hand cement mixer, a big pile of sand, and a mountain of red brick.

Her apartment was to the left, up a flight of wooden stairs. It was located in one wing of a detached building that a hundred years ago, served as homes for the servants that tended the big house now converted to an art gallery. The wing where Kit lived was structurally sound, but the one that formed the back wall of the courtyard was not. In fact, she and someone chasing her had once fallen through its roof.

That was all now being remedied by Leblanc Construction, who had almost completely covered the back wing with metal scaffolding. The deal was that work would not begin until 8:30 a.m. and would cease at 5:00 p.m. So noise was not really a problem. But the mess, especially the dust all over the courtyard and the wooden steps to the second floor, was unsettling. On the positive side of the ledger, she was presently the only tenant.

As she turned the corner of the art gallery and moved fully into the courtyard, she now had a direct sight line to her apartment. That meant the little Westie terrier she'd bought a year ago and who was now alertly standing just outside his doggie door could now also see *her*. Overcome with joy, he came hurtling down the outside steps, his tail wagging so fast it was almost a blur. He slipped and skidded and flopped down the stairs then ran to the gate in a fence the workmen had hastily built to give him just enough of a personal courtyard to do his business.

She opened the gate and snatched the dog into her arms. "Did you miss me sweetie? I missed you." For an answer, the dog began licking her face. The tongue on her first dog, Lucky, was slightly raspy, but Fletcher's was perfectly smooth. This made her skin feel as though it was being rubbed with a piece of wet liver. Despite her love for the little creature, she pulled her face out of licking range and carried him upstairs.

After a quick pit stop in her apartment, she got a pot of coffee started, then went to her computer and plugged in the flash drive containing the surveillance videos from Gator Willie's. With Fletcher lying on the floor beside her chair, she began to remotely relive what might have been the last night of Betty Bergeron's life.

Chapter 13

Disorder in his world always stimulated Broussard's appetite. And it was happening now. He didn't know why, but he suspected the neurons in his brain that had been arguing with each other since he'd begun reflecting on Uncle Joe's death had awakened some of their neighbors. And those other cells likely had connections with his stomach. There was no scientific proof for this; it's just what he believed. So even though he'd already eaten dinner at Grandma O's, he was now home, standing at his gas range. To his right, sat six fully cooked marinated pork chops arranged in a crown on a plate decorated with gold garlands. He poured half a glass of white wine into the pan with the pork chop juices, then added two tablespoons of thickened veal gravy. He turned up the heat and began stirring.

Uncle Joe had been so good to him when he needed a lifeline to survive the empty feeling that had threatened to consume him after his parents were killed. That kind of compassion certainly justified better behavior than years of not even calling the man to see how he was.

Broussard carefully poured the finished sauce over the chops. He carried the meat into the dining room and put the plate on the white tablecloth in front of his place setting.

The least he could now for Uncle Joe was help find the man who'd killed him.

He returned to the kitchen and put the spinach croquettes

into hot olive oil.
But what could he do to further the investigation?
When the croquettes were fully cooked, he spooned them onto a plate and took the dish to the dining room, where after setting it beside the chops, he filled his wine glass with room temperature Gevrey-Chambertin. He then sat down, picked up his glass, and swirled the wine inside. After deeply inhaling the wine's bouquet, he took a small sip. The hot liquid not only warmed his soul, but showed him what he could do to help solve the mystery he'd been so cruelly drawn into. And along the way, he would also learn a lot about all the relatives he had ignored for so long.

Phil Gatlin sighed and looked at the furry object in his hand.
The hobbies of most people are things they're good at. But Phil Gatlin was terrible at the one he chose; fly tying. His hands were too big and he just couldn't get the hang of the whip finish knot, the final step in making a fly. That meant he often had to discard a specimen after wasting fifteen minutes and a lot of material on it. He'd practice just that knot over and over until he was sure he had it, but then when it counted, he'd mess it up. He kept at it because he was by nature an impatient man and figured that fly tying would teach him self-control. Being a perpetual novice at the craft also meant he had to concentrate fully on the process. That in turn enabled him to forget for at least a few minutes the constant clamor in his brain that demanded results in whatever case he was working on. And quieting that voice was important, otherwise he'd try to work 24 hours a day, killing himself and making his wife complain even more about the time he spent on the job.
He picked up a fresh hook and put it in his vice. Then his phone rang.

It was Andy Broussard. "Hey Andy. What's up?"

"Find out anything from Joe's bodyguard?"

The question instantly propelled Gatlin back into the world he loved.

"Joe had been receiving death threats."

"Who from?"

"Not sure, but I've got a possible."

"How good a lead is it?"

"Could turn out to be bupkis."

"I want to help."

"Okay. The bodyguard said Joe's daughter, Amelia, visited him once a week. You know her last name?"

"It's Hebert. She was the one who organized the birthday picnic. At least that's who signed my invitation. For some reason there was no return address on the invitation, so I don't know where she lives, but I've got the RSVP phone number. It's probably hers, but if it isn't, whoever answers could probably put me in touch with her."

"See if she can tell you anything about Joe's will. If not, maybe she could point us toward someone else."

"I'll do that. I'd also like to follow up on Kit's suggestion that we get a list of who was invited to the picnic and who wasn't there. Surely Amelia has the invitation list as well as those who said they were comin'."

"I don't think we should. . ."

"I agree. Just because someone said they were comin' doesn't mean they were present." A pause ensued, then Broussard said, "Shortly before the shootin', Amelia carried a birthday card around the picnic and got everybody to sign it. I wonder if she finished the job and if she still has the card?"

"That's something worth pursuing. But you sure you're alright with snooping around your own relatives."

"Could be that some people who were invited weren't

Broussard blood."

"If you're gonna do this, you have to accept what the evidence tells you, wherever it points."

"I been livin' that way for a long time. Doubt I could change even if I wanted too."

Chapter 14

Kit woke Sunday morning to the sounds of Fletcher barking and a key turning the lock in her front door.

Oh my God. Teddy.

She leapt from the bed and ran to the bathroom, where she tried to repair her hair with her fingers. As she embarked on an economy tour of her teeth with her electric toothbrush, she realized her head felt like she'd been in Gator Willie's all night.

"Hellooo," Teddy called out to her from beside the bathroom door.

They'd awakened next to each other so many times over the last few years seeing her sleep-disheveled wouldn't be anything new for him. But their recent engagement seemed to reset the clock for Kit, which meant this morning, she wanted to look her best. Of course that was no longer possible. But she certainly didn't want him to hear her pee. "Morning," she sang. "I'm running late. Would you make the coffee please?"

When she was sure he'd had time to reach the coffee maker she dropped onto the toilet wanting to be quick and quiet. A moment later, when the flood gates were open, Teddy knocked on the bathroom door and said, "Columbian or Breakfast roast?"

Oh great. "Columbian."

With hopes of a new beginning flushed away, Kit walked

into the kitchen in her nightie. "Are the gators all snug now?" she said, referring to the emergency fence repair he had to make around his breeding stock yesterday.

Teddy looked up from the coffee maker and his dark eyes caught fire. He was across the room in an instant. He took her in his arms and whispered in her ear, "*Tu es la femme de mes reves!*" Knowing that she didn't understand French, he translated in a husky whisper. "You are the woman of my dreams."

He then kissed her gently on the lips. Fletcher barked his approval.

Teddy spoke Cajun French as fluently as English. He came from an aristocratic lineage as evidenced by his fine features and the capital B in his last name, the small b Labiches being less fortunate people.

Kit looked into his eyes and said, "*Amour de ma vie.*" (Love of my life.)

Teddy laughed and spun her around, causing Fletcher to jump out of the way. "Where'd you learn that?"

"From my computer yesterday morning."

"Have any other surprises for me?"

"Actually, I do. Let me get dressed and I'll tell you."

Still holding on to her, he said, "I was hoping the next one might not require clothing."

She gently pulled free. "It's not required . . . more like a temporary condition."

She returned in ten minutes wearing a pink three quarter length collared shirt and white ankle pants that nicely complimented the Silver Millie slings showcasing her shapely feet. She had also taken the time to put on a pair of oversized silver hoop earrings.

"Now <u>that's</u> a nice outfit," Teddy said. "What's the surprise?"

She fished her new badge from her pocket and held it up for Teddy to see. "You're under arrest."

Teddy wouldn't have looked more confused if she'd said she was queen of the alligators.

"I don't understand."

"The NOPD is temporarily understaffed. I'm now an acting homicide detective."

"As of when?"

"Yesterday around five o'clock."

He squinted slyly at her. "Does that mean now I have to do everything you say?"

"The badge means I'm in complete control, but that's nothing new."

He moved in and again took her in his arms. "I never kissed a detective before."

"Sure you did. Just a few minutes ago."

"I mean before today."

"Well, I think you should take full advantage of the opportunity."

They kissed again, long and deep, stopping only when Fletcher began tugging on the leg of Teddy's denim jeans.

"I think he's jealous," Teddy said, stopping to give him his favorite treat; a knuckle-rub on the top of his head.

"Remember how we agreed a moment ago that you had to do everything I asked?"

"Vaguely," Teddy said.

"How about making breakfast for us. I've got everything you need for mushroom omelets, and there are some English muffins in the fridge too."

"And what will you be doing, detective?"

"I'm not sure you want to know." She reached into a nearby drawer for some small pink plastic bags decorated with cartoon paw prints.

"Oh right," Teddy said. "Poop patrol. Seems like a detective shouldn't have to do that."

"Are you saying . . ."

"No ma'am. I wouldn't presume to tell an officer of the law what to do."

Some might think that Kit had gone to a lot of trouble, dressing so well for breakfast at home. But those holding that view would be people who'd been married for many years and had no memory of ever being in the grip of unseasoned love. Kit couldn't imagine that such a time would ever come for her and Teddy.

During breakfast, she told Teddy about the case Gatlin had given her. She described everything she'd done so far to further the investigation, finally saying, "And I stayed up practically all night watching those surveillance videos. But I didn't see a thing that was useful. I'm worried though that I might have missed something. And a girl's life could be at stake."

"Maybe another pair of eyes would help."

"You'd do that . . . watch them again with me?"

"Can I be a deputy?"

"How about I make you deputy superintendent of surveillance video review."

"No man could turn *that* down."

"It's going to be boring, that's actually the problem. It's hard to keep alert."

"Let's do it."

Andy Broussard stood in his huge garage, looking at his fleet of six T-Birds. *Was* he guilty of ranking things before people? Offhand, he couldn't think of any people as beautiful as his cars. Suppose someone stepped out in front of him when he was driving. Would he wreck the car to save the person? No question he would. But in the back of his mind he remembered something Bubba once said, "Anything one man can break another can fix." So that wasn't a real test. Not satisfied that he had answered his own question, he went inside and headed for his study.

At his desk, he picked up the phone and called the RSVP number at the bottom of his invitation to Uncle Joe's birthday picnic. Sunday morning was an impolite time to bother anybody, but it was also a good time to catch people at home. After four rings a woman picked up the phone.

"Amelia? This is Andy Broussard."

"Oh, yes, hello, Andy. My God, wasn't yesterday horrible? I'll never get it out of my mind."

"I know exactly what you mean. I can't tell you how sorry I am about the loss of your father."

"He was getting on in years, and it was natural to start thinking that he wouldn't be around forever, but I didn't expect anything like that."

"Why would you?"

"I remember when we were all kids, you were around a lot. But then . . . what happened?"

"I been askin' myself the same thing."

"I heard on the news that the man who did it escaped. Do the police know who he is and why he did it?"

"No to both questions. But they'll get to the bottom of it. The police would like a list of everyone who was invited to the picnic and also want to know who all was actually there."

"Why ever do they need that?"

"It's just the way these things are done."

"I've got a list on my computer of everyone I invited. I printed it out and when someone called to say they were coming or not, I marked that on the printed list. Right now, I have no idea where the response list is. I may have thrown it away after I made the catering arrangements."

"If I give you my e-mail address, could you send me the invitation list as an attachment?"

"I'll do it as soon as I hang up."

Broussard was determined that no Russian or Chinese computer hacker would ever steal his identity. He was likewise unwilling to have anyone spy on his purchasing habits. In his mind, the best way to avoid both those possibilities was to not have a home computer and do all his shopping either in person or by mail from catalogs. Financial transactions were done in person at his bank. But the ME's operation was fully computerized, because it *had* to be. So that's the e-mail address he gave Amelia.

"Got it," she said.

"At the picnic, you circulated a birthday card for everyone to sign. Were you finished with that before . . . the trouble started?"

"At least ten minutes before."

"Think you got everybody's name who was there?"

"I might have missed some of the children, but I'm sure all the adults signed it."

"What happened to the card?"

She didn't answer.

"Amelia . . . you there?"

"I haven't thought about that card until just now. I have no idea what happened to it. In all the confusion, I may have lost it."

"Was it attached to the clipboard you sent around to give people a smooth signin' surface?"

"No. After everyone signed it, I put it on the picnic table and sat the board on top to keep it from blowing away. I didn't clip it to the board, because I didn't want a pinch crease on the envelope. I certainly don't sound very responsible do I?"

"Under the circumstances, I think you can excuse yourself for losin' track of it."

"Maybe you're right."

"Sorry to keep botherin' you," Broussard said, "But there's one other thing the police wanted to know. Did Joe have any life insurance?"

"No. He cancelled it all when Annie died."

"Did he ever talk to you about his will?"

"As a matter of fact, he did, because I'm named as the executor. That's why I'm so sensitive about losing that card and looking incompetent."

"Do you know the terms of the will . . . who the heirs are?"

"Andy, I don't understand why you're asking these things."

"It's not me. It's the police. They have procedures to follow, reports to be filled out. I'm only askin' to give them a hand."

"Okay, I guess I can tell you. My father's assets are to be liquidated and the proceeds distributed equally among his four children."

"Do they all know that?"

"It's what they assume, but I haven't verified it yet to any of them."

"Now I have to ask somethin' that's probably gonna seem really nosy and I apologize for that. Are any of Joe's kids havin' money problems?"

"I have no idea about Julien's family and Sarah's. But I saw Kay . . . Lewis's wife a few weeks ago, and she was very worried about his business. I think they have a lot of debt, and the last few years his income has dwindled considerably. Scott and I are fine . . . not that I'm comfortable telling you any of this."

"You've been very helpful. I apologize again for the things

I've asked you, but sometimes life gives us difficult tasks."

"Tell me about it. I'm just getting started on the funeral arrangements. I guess the quickest way to let all the relatives know what's going to happen and when, is to put it in his obituary. Exactly where is he?"

"Still at my facility. But he's ready to go. If you've got somethin' to write with I'll give you a number the funeral home can call to make arrangements for pick up."

Broussard gave her the number, then said, "Amelia, I'm so sorry this happened."

"Do the police have any idea who might have done it?"

She had already asked him that earlier, but not wanting to point it out, Broussard simply said, "Right now . . . no."

Broussard's hacking paranoia also extended to his new cell phone, which he had refused to enable for receiving e-mails. Therefore, the only way he could get his hands on the picnic invitation list was to head for the office. But without the signed birthday card, the other list wasn't of much use. So . . . Away he went to his big garage.

Chapter 15

Phil Gatlin was back on the job. And all it cost him to get out of the house on a Sunday was to take his wife to the Golden Corral for breakfast. He was on his way to see Howard Karpis, the guy who'd threatened to kill Uncle Joe. The price for showing up with no warning at a suspect's home was that the guy might not even be there. Such was a detective's life.

Karpis lived about 20 miles south of New Orleans on Bayou Barataria Boulevard, a two lane road that for miles at a time was flanked by scrubby trees and wild vegetation that made the asphalt seem like an avenue to nowhere. As he drove, he idly wondered if Karpis was a relative of the infamous Alvin "Creepy" Karpis, gangster from the 1930's. Alvin was one of only four people the FBI had ever called 'public enemy #1.' If they *were* related would this Karpis even admit it?

Using his home computer, Gatlin had run a background check on Howard Karpis yesterday. He'd found that ten years ago, the guy had done three months in jail followed by a mandatory six weeks in an anger management class after assaulting another driver who'd damaged Karpis's car in a minor traffic accident. Though it had been a decade since that happened, Gatlin felt that even if Howard wasn't related to Alvin Karpis, Howard likely still had those tendencies in him. So, even though he'd already seen the photo on Howard's driver's license, he was eager to get a look at the man in person.

The vegetation abruptly thinned on the right, replaced by a small church clothed in what looked like old time asbestos shingles. Beside the church was a little graveyard enclosed by a low iron fence made to look like cornstalks. Inside the fence the various inhabitants had been placed in a variety of aboveground white marble tombs that would keep the remains from being submerged in ground water.

Then the vegetation returned.

Finally, civilization conquered the landscape. Arriving at Karpis's address a few minutes later, he saw him in the big front yard, trying to wrestle a large section of dying privet hedge out of the ground. As Gatlin pulled into the drive, Karpis stopped working, looked in Gatlin's direction, and took off the gloves he was wearing. Gatlin got out of his car and they met halfway across the lawn.

The first thing that caught Gatlin's eye was the full arm sleeve tattoo of two colorful intertwined Koi on Karpis's right arm. Koi were carp, Gatlin recalled. Carp on a Karpis. How about that.

Karpis had long wavy hair with gray highlights in it. His driver's license said he was fifty-five years old, but he appeared younger. He was lean and muscular, with odd cheekbones that looked like bunions under the corner of each eye, and his nose was slightly askew: A guy that had been around and had enough left to do it all again. If he'd been dressed in cammies, sunglasses, and a cap, would he resemble the body taken from the water at Bayou Sauvage? Gatlin decided that from 200 yards away, he definitely would. And the background check said he was a marksman in the marines.

Gatlin flashed his badge. "Mr. Karpis, I'm Lieutenant Gatlin with the NOPD. I'd like to talk to you about Joe Broussard."

A kaleidoscope of expressions rippled across Karpis's face, reminding Gatlin of a squid he once saw changing color. Gatlin was sure that at the mention of Joe's name, there had been a fleeting look of pleasure on Karpis's face, followed by one of concern, then arrogance. The latter was the one that remained.

"Yeah," Karpis said, "I heard somebody took the old man out. About time." Arrogance now gave way to anger. "That old shit didn't care about anybody but himself. The world is better off with him not in it. In fact, I like what it says in Deuteronomy 5:9 . . ."

Gatlin waited for him to finish his thought, but he let it go. "Never mind. I guess you're here because I threatened him."

"In front of a lot of witnesses, I understand."

"I was upset . . . still am, but you'll be disappointed to know that I didn't do it. Although it was such a slick operation, wish I could say I did."

"Where were you yesterday morning?"

"Fishing."

"Where?"

"Bayou Rigolettes."

He was referring to a body of water about ten miles south.

"You have your own boat?" Gatlin asked.

He gestured to the garage. "Behind the house."

"Where'd you put in?"

"Public boat ramp at Lafitte."

Gatlin was aware of that ramp, had even seen it. "It costs five bucks to put in there. Got your receipt?"

"It blew out of my shirt pocket and into the water while I had my Mercury at full throttle."

"Anybody go with you?"

"I don't like a lot of talking while I'm on the water."

"So that's a 'no'. Stop anywhere to buy bait?"

"Don't need live bait for Speckies. Top water plugs work great if you know which ones to use."

"I wasn't aware of that."

"Doesn't surprise me."

"How many'd you catch?"

"Twenty maybe."

"Where are they?"

"Catch and release, just like bail bonds work in your business."

"Did you kill Joe Broussard?"

Karpis gave Gatlin a sardonic grin. "Small talk is over, I guess. No, I did not kill him."

"Would you be willing to take a lie detector test?"

"No."

"Why not?"

"Suppose you screw it up and say I failed? Then you find some schlub judge to admit it into evidence. Sorry, I don't trust you."

"Did you send him any threatening notes?"

Karpis squinted at Broussard but didn't answer. After another few seconds, he said, "I let him know I was thinking about him a couple times, but I don't believe anything I sent amounts to a real threat, at least not legally."

"Found a new job yet?"

"Not a lot of openings for my skill set."

There were a lot of phrases Gatlin thought should be retired. 'SKILL SET' was one of them. "Mind giving me a phone number where you can be reached?"

"Sure, but you should know I screen my calls."

He recited a number and Gatlin wrote it in his book, then said, "Got any trips scheduled?"

"What are we, best friends now, discussing our future plans?"

"Oh, I think I know your future. That's what you should be preparing for."

Gatlin turned and walked away

Karpis watched until the old detective was in his car and back onto the street. Then Karpis walked over, picked up the shovel near where he'd been working, and threw it across the yard.

Gatlin didn't go back toward the city, but instead headed south, until he could get on the two-lane bridge over Bayou Barataria. Except for a strung-out cluster of small clouds low on the horizon, the sky ahead was clear and blue. Traveling over the treetops and then the bayou stole Gatlin's thoughts and he simply enjoyed the feeling of being above the strife and evil that lay below.

A few minutes later, Gatlin navigated around the curve that brought him onto Jean Lafitte Highway. For the next eight miles, the bayou flirted with the road like an old-time Bourbon Street Burlesque dancer, now showing a bit of itself then hiding the goods behind whatever vegetation was present. As he drove, his mind went back many years to when his son, Andy, was still alive . . . before the meningitis killed the boy and a good part of his mother's good nature. Yes, they still had a grown daughter, but there was no way one remaining child could fill the void left by the death of the other, who would always remain in their memory as a small boy. How many times had he and little Andy hauled their Sea Fox Commander to the Lafitte boat ramp? He didn't know it then, but those were some of the best days he'd ever have in his life. It seemed ironic that he'd spent his life making sure killers were punished, but couldn't do anything to the one that had ravaged his son's brain.

He didn't regularly have thoughts like this. It was just the surroundings that had brought them on. As quickly as they had come, they left, and he continued the trip in a neutral state of mind.

When he finally reached the entrance to the boat ramp's dirt parking lot and drove inside, he found a dozen empty boat trailers and trucks waiting for their owners to return from the water. He parked beside one of them and walked over to the tan kiosk with an outdoor counter. Inside was a kid wearing a pair of big glasses with black frames.

"Yessir. You want a launch ticket?"

"Were you here yesterday morning?"

"All day from 6:00 a.m. 'till 5:00 p.m."

Gatlin took out his cell phone and navigated to the driver's license photo of Howard Karpis. "Was this guy here yesterday?" He held the phone close to the kid's face.

After a few seconds of moving his head around like he was trying to see the picture better, the kid said, "He's got funny cheek bones. I wouldda remembered that. So, no, he wasn't here."

The kid could have been mistaken. But Gatlin didn't believe he was. Heading back to his car, Gatlin imagined the metallic caress of handcuffs against his fingers as he brought them out of his pocket and into position. He even thought he heard the click of the latch teeth engaging over Howard Karpis's wrists. But he had a lot of work to do before that would happen.

The entrance gate to the picnic area at Bayou Sauvage was closed and locked with a big padlock, and there was a strip of crime-scene tape wrapped around the gateposts. Broussard sat in his white T-Bird and assessed the situation. In five minutes of fiddling with his phone, he hadn't been able to contact anyone to let him in. But he was not a man to be thwarted by such a minor problem, especially since the gate was meant only to stop vehicles. There was no fence on either side.

He gracefully slithered out of his car and crunched across the oyster shell pavement to the left end of the gate, where duckweed-covered water almost touched the galvanized anchoring post. Having seen that the right side of the gate would be no better, he took a long look around for gator eyes watching him, then grabbed hold of the gatepost and tried to imitate the time he'd seen one of the flying Wallendas walk across a two-inch steel cable 1500 feet above the ground.

But Wallenda didn't have a ponderous stomach to deal with. That particular encumbrance pushed Broussard away from the post as he passed it, sending both feet into the bayou up to his ankles. Undeterred by this and using the post for leverage, he managed to get back onto the road on the inside. His wet shoes squishing with every step, he walked down the road toward the picnic tables.

Reaching his destination, he saw that no one had cleaned up anything. The picnic tables that people had turned over for protection still lay on their side. On the ground in the middle of the area, beside one of the upended tables, he saw the smashed remains of Uncle Joe's birthday cake. Judging from the small amount that was left, it had surely been sampled by the area wildlife. And there was paper litter everywhere.

As he stood there, he heard the latent echoes of the violence that had been visited upon the place the day before. He thought about walking over and looking at the spot where Joe fell, but then, deciding it would serve no purpose, he began to hunt for that birthday card.

Ten minutes later, he still hadn't found it. He'd even searched through the 55-gallon steel drum with the sign on it that said: *LITTERING MAKES THE GROUNDS AND YOU, LOOK BAD.*

His inability to find the card could mean it wasn't there. In her anxious state, Amelia might have taken it back to her car and it had fallen down between the seats. Not wanting to give up too soon, he took a final survey of the area. He'd been looking at the ground around the tables and had even poked in the nearby weeds. For the first time, he let his gaze sweep upward, out over the water, hoping he might see it floating within reach. And there, about four feet from shore, in a clump of cypress knees, he saw an envelope.

Figuring his shoes were already wet, he took a moment for gator surveillance then waded out, sinking in mud that he should have expected, but didn't. Water edging higher with each step, he kept moving forward, water now to his calves . . . now to just below his knees . . . starting to tickle his lower thighs . . . and . . . he leaned over and snatched the envelope from its resting place. He lifted it to his face and turned it over to see the writing across the front: TO JOE.

Now he was ready to sit down in his office and compare the list of picnic invitees with the names on the card. But that task would not be completed anytime soon, because he had no sooner reached his car than he received a phone call that a man in NOPD custody had unexpectedly died. Considering the potential political consequences of this, and the fact Broussard had agreed with Charlie Franks that this was Broussard's weekend to deal with any time-sensitive issues, he didn't even bother going home to change into dry clothes before heading for the morgue.

Chapter 16

Bubba called Kit a little after 2:00 p.m. on Sunday to say her car was ready. They agreed that Bubba would pick her and Teddy up in front of the photo gallery in thirty minutes and they would then return him to the impoundment lot. In addition to bringing good news about her car, Bubba's call was a welcome break from the hours she and Teddy had spent looking at the surveillance videos from Gator Willie's.

They got back to Kit's apartment around 3:00 p.m., and though it was by now an activity that Kit believed would produce nothing, Teddy wanted to look at the videos again.

Three minutes later, just as Kit returned from a bathroom break, Teddy pointed at the screen and excitedly said, "Look at that!"

He paused the action and hit rewind. "Watch Betty's right hand."

In the video, Kit saw a guy in a blue baseball cap approach the bar from Betty's right side, where her hand rested on the bar while she spoke to a customer. Now that Teddy had focused Kit's attention, she saw the guy in the baseball cap put his hand over Betty's. Without looking at the guy, Betty quickly pulled it away.

"How could I not have seen that?" Kit said. "I've watched it all those times."

"The view is blocked by someone passing," Teddy replied. "It's only apparent for a split second."

Kit wanted to see the guy's face, but he turned to his left and moved out of frame.

"Call up a split screen of all the interior cameras," Kit said.

Teddy complied but they couldn't find the guy in any of them.

"Give me the camera on the outside door."

They sat and watched that view for thirty minutes. Then, "There he is," Kit said, pointing. As he left, his face was clearly visible. "Let me have the mouse."

Teddy moved the mouse and its pad to her side, where she hit rewind and went back to the full-face shot. At that point she stopped the video and did a screen capture.

"Change chairs," she said.

When she was reseated, she cropped the picture of the guy and relayed it to her cell phone. Then she navigated to Dee Evans' phone number and typed a brief text message: *Do you recognize this man?* She attached the photo and sent the message on its way.

"Who'd you send the picture to?" Teddy asked.

"Dee Evans, Betty Bergeron's apartment mate. She told me about a guy whose been harassing Betty, but she didn't remember his name. If that's the guy, we can take his picture around the Tulane campus and the bar and maybe find out who he is."

While they waited for Evans to answer, Teddy said, "You know, I once heard on TV that when the police want to find someone, they ping their cell phone. I'm not exactly sure what that means, but I think the phone provider sends the phone a signal to respond. When it does, the response goes to the nearest cell tower, and from there to some central switchboard at the company. I don't know how close they can get to the exact location of the person that way, but at least it'd get you in the right area."

"I thought about that," Kit said. "But the phone has to be on. And Betty's isn't. I checked that myself. But thanks for the thought."

Kit then remembered that she hadn't yet done a background check on Leo Silver. She told Teddy what she was doing and turned again to her computer. After a short session there, she sat back very disappointed. "He has no criminal record. Not even a parking ticket."

"That doesn't mean he isn't guilty of *something*," Teddy said. "Maybe he just hasn't been caught yet. I wouldn't give up on him."

"I agree. Feel like taking a little ride and talking to some people?"

"That's pretty vague, detective. Could you be more specific?"

"I *was* able to get the picture that's on Silver's driver's license. Let's take that and the one of the guy in the bar over to Betty Bergeron's apartment and show both pictures to the neighbors . . . see if they've noticed anything odd involving either one of them."

A few minutes later, as they crossed the courtyard outside Kit's apartment, they encountered a young guy with fashion model good looks coming in from the lattice panel tunnel. He was carrying three 2 x 6s on one shoulder.

Seeing them, he brushed the dark curls from his forehead and grinned. "Dr. Franklyn, how are you?" Despite the weight he was transporting he stopped walking. "Don't worry, we're not going to make any noise today. Because of the light traffic, it's just easier to bring in supplies on a Sunday."

"Makes sense to me," Kit said. "Teddy, this is Remy LeBlanc. He and his father own the company doing the renovations back here. Remy, this is my fiancée, Teddy

LaBiche."

Because Remy was steadying the lumber with his right hand, Teddy didn't attempt a handshake but simply said, "I admire a man who can carry that much in one trip."

"Got to maximize your effort if you want to make any money in this business. Now, if you'll excuse me, I need to put this stuff down before I drop it. Good meeting you, Teddy."

Out on the street Teddy said, "How do you know his first name?"

Kit gave him a coquettish look. "Jealous?"

"Want me to be?"

"Just a little."

"Okay, maybe this much." He held his thumb and forefinger so close they were almost touching.

"Remy is a distant relative of Andy Broussard. He did some work for Andy a few months ago and when I mentioned to Andy that my landlord was looking for a reliable contractor, he recommended the LeBlancs."

The trip to Betty Bergeron's apartment proved to be a waste of time and they learned nothing useful. They didn't even see Dee Evans. On the way home, Teddy said, "It's nearly five o'clock. Are we going to keep our reservations at Commander's Palace?"

Behind the wheel, Kit inhaled sharply. *Their engagement celebration dinner.* She'd forgotten all about it. "You don't think I'd miss out on seeing you in a jacket and tie, do you? What time are we supposed to be there?"

"Six o'clock."

Considering the garage where she parked was three blocks from her apartment, that wasn't going to leave much time for her to get ready. Teddy could change much faster. So, pushing the speed limit all the way back, she pulled to a stop in front of the photo studio and jumped out. "You park the car and I'll get dressed. With luck, I'll be out of the bathroom by the time you get back."

"You know how that sounded?"

"Very funny."

While Kit ran for the door to the courtyard, Teddy hustled around the front of the car and hopped in without remembering to put the seat back. The true measure of a man's good nature is if he refrains from cursing when he accidently bangs his knee, stubs his toe, or injures himself in some other avoidable way. By this test, Teddy proved himself mortal. But in his defense, he cursed in Cajun French, which at least sounds polite.

For the occasion, Kit wore a silver fringe hem dress that showed off a significant portion of her shapely legs, a major reason why she bought it. Teddy stood about five inches taller than she was, so even with the three-inch stiletto heels on the silver strappy evening shoes she chose, she'd still be looking up at him, exactly how things *should* be. Figuring that it just wouldn't look right if she wore her Ladysmith .38 on her calf as she usually did, she put it in the beaded silver clutch bag she took. Liking the action they provided when she turned her head, and imagining how the restaurant lights would reflect off them, she also wore the sterling silver French wire earrings Teddy had given her for her last birthday.

When she stepped out of the bedroom, now fully dressed, Teddy's mouth dropped open. "Oh my God, you look great."

Teddy was wearing a two button, light gray single-breasted silk suit with one of those lapels that comes off the shoulder and runs down to the first button in a continuous curve, giving the suit a very formal look. The collar on his light blue shirt was a spread design that allowed room for the full Windsor knot on his lilac-colored tie. In Kit's view, he couldn't have chosen better shoes than the tan cap-toe oxfords he'd brought.

"What happened to my alligator farmer?" Kit said.

"Why, do you want him back?"

"Maybe later."

It didn't seem appropriate to arrive at the restaurant in Teddy's red pickup with the Bayou Coteau Alligator Farm logo on each door. Instead, they took Kit's car, Teddy at the wheel.

Sitting down, the part of Kit's dress where the fringe began, rode high on her legs. This made it hard for Teddy to keep his eyes on the road. "Hey LaBiche," Kit said. "We both look too good to be involved in a car wreck tonight."

"I don't know, at least I've got on clean underwear."

Commander's palace on the outside doesn't look like a palace at all, more like a Victorian cottage built for someone with a very large family. In fact, the structure was built by Emile Commander over a hundred years ago for a daughter who never married. It might be supposed that a restaurant often voted best in the city would reside in the French Quarter. But this one sits in the Garden District, where sensibilities are more refined.

The restaurant is surrounded by residential streets and large family homes. What is not present is a parking lot. Since Teddy and Kit were celebrating a major life event, they took advantage of valet parking, not even wondering where the devil they put the cars.

Inside, they were guided to a table that had a great view of the Christmas light-illuminated tropical jungle that comprised the courtyard. Here, looking at the fresh yellow rose and fern centerpiece on a crisp white tablecloth, watching the waiters in black vests bustling about, listening to the murmur of muted conversation . . . it was all so civilized Kit was almost seduced into forgetting about Betty Bergeron. Was this the way Phil Gatlin had spent all those years as a detective, never being able to give himself fully to any other endeavor, his open cases picking at the margins of his attention? When he was telling her all the reasons she should refuse his proposal, he never mentioned that.

"Teddy to Kit . . . come in . . ."

"I'm sorry. My mind wandered."

"To Betty Bergeron?"

"Yes." She reached over and put her hand over his as it rested on the table. "Of all nights, this is one where you deserve my full attention."

"I love that you're concerned about her. Even half your attention is more than any man deserves."

"I'm sure I can do much better than half," she replied, withdrawing her hand as the waiter approached with the huge menus.

Dinner was a culinary experience worthy of the occasion. For an appetizer, Kit had the white shrimp and tasso ham henican while Teddy chose corn fried gulf oysters and crispy braised pork belly both of which arrived looking so artistically arranged, actually eating them seemed like a barbarous act. Before attacking either dish, Teddy held up his wine glass and proposed a toast. "To the most attractive detective there ever was and the alligator cowboy who loves her. May they find contentment and fulfillment in each other that would be impossible by themselves, or with anyone else."

They touched glasses and sealed the toast with a properly decorous sip of what Andy Broussard described as one of man's greatest achievements. (Of course, he once said that of concrete as well.)

For the entrée, they both chose the filet of Black Angus beef, Kit preferring hers with a pink center while Teddy, being more akin to the creatures he lived with daily, wanted his medium rare. Because the filet came with a French potato puree and they had nearly emptied the breadbasket, they ordered no sides with their meat.

In this country, it seems that people often feel they are in violation of some fundamental law if, after a fine dinner, they don't at least *say* they shouldn't have dessert. Neither Kit nor Teddy belonged to that group. With no feelings of guilt, both ordered the praline parfait. Nor did they utter any self-critical comments before or after requesting coffee as well.

A few minutes later, just as Kit took her first bite of parfait and closed her eyes with pleasure, she felt her clutch purse vibrate in her lap. Ordinarily, she wouldn't have looked at her phone while in such a fine place and on such a meaningful occasion. But with a young woman's life possibly in the balance, she couldn't take a chance on ignoring it. She looked at Teddy. "It's my phone. It could be Dee Evans."

She took out her phone and glanced at the screen, a text message. She read it aloud. "That picture you sent is the guy who harassed Betty. And I remember his name. It's Jes DeLeon."

Kit put the phone back in her bag and looked across the table. "I can't wait to see what *his* rap sheet looks like."

"Want to leave now?" He didn't say it petulantly, but more like, 'I'm ready to go, if you are'."

"Just a few more bites. How many engagement dinners am I going to *have* in my life?"

Not even trying for a clever comeback, Teddy grinned and nodded as he returned to his dessert.

Suddenly, Kit said, "Oh my God."

"What?" Teddy said. "Something in your food?"

"I may know how to find Betty Bergeron."

Chapter 17

While they waited for the valet to bring their car around, Kit explained how she was going to find the missing girl. "We couldn't ping her phone, because it was off or the battery was spent. Dee Evans, Betty's apartment mate, said that Betty never shuts her phone down completely, so the battery must be dead. There's a function on the iPhone called send last location. Just before the battery dies, the phone sends Apple the phone's last location. To find it we go on the Apple iCloud site, put in Betty's Apple ID and password, and it'll show us on a map where the phone is."

"Where will you get the ID and password?"

"When I first went to Betty's apartment to talk with Evans about her, I looked around Betty's bedroom. In her desk I found a little book with all her site access information. I've got it at home."

The valet pulled up at the curb with Kit's car. Teddy gave him a five, opened the passenger door for Kit, then went around and got behind the wheel. After a quick check for traffic, Teddy pulled from the curb. "Is that send last location function a default setting on the phone?"

"Okay, that could be a problem. It has to be manually set by the owner. Another potential issue is that Evans said Betty always keeps her tracking setting off. Depending on how she did that, it could also inactivate send last location. So we'll need some luck. And even if we do get lucky, we won't actually be locating *her*, we'll be finding her *phone*, which should probably be in her possession, but possibly isn't."

"Let's not worry about all the things that could go wrong," Teddy said. "It's definitely an idea worth pursuing."

It seemed as though the drive home took twice as long as the trip going *to* the restaurant even though Teddy pushed the speed limit all the way.

When they reached Toulouse Street, Teddy said, "Look, it'll take forever to park the car in your garage. I'll just stop in front of your courtyard and wait on the street while you check this out. Soon as you know one way or the other if this worked, call me. If we're going somewhere, you can change clothes."

"What about you?"

"Just bring me my boots."

Two minutes later, Teddy pulled to a stop and Kit jumped out and headed for the big cypress gate beside the photo gallery.

Reaching her apartment steps, where Fletcher was waiting for her as usual, she gave him a quick rub on the head, then hurried upstairs. Inside, she flew to her computer, navigated to the iCloud site, and reached for Betty's little jeweled notebook. She typed in the girl's ID and password, then, almost holding her breath she chose Find My iPhone. A compass icon appeared and began to rotate back and forth with the word *locating* underneath it.

Did that mean it was working or would the compass finally stop and say something like *no location found?*

Suddenly, there it was! A map with a green dot appeared on the screen. Even with several street names shown, Kit was unsure of the location. She opened a new window, went to Google maps, and entered one of the street names. Now with a map she could manipulate, she zoomed out until she could get her bearings. Then she zoomed in by stages, constructing in her mind a route to the location.

She called Teddy. "Got it. Be down ASAP."

Leaving her restaurant clothes scattered around her room, she threw on a three-quarter sleeve pale blue pullover and a pair of tan pants, then slipped into a pair of running shoes. After strapping her Ladysmith to her calf, she grabbed Teddy's alligator skin boots and headed for the door, where Fletcher sat looking at her quizzically. She gave his ruff a quick scratch. "Gotta go out again, Boy. Be back later."

In the car, by way of greeting, Teddy pointed at one of his ears and said, "you forgot something." Kit reached up and felt the earrings she'd neglected to remove. She took them off now and put them in the glove compartment.

Teddy pulled from the curb. "Where to?"

"Keep going straight to Decatur, then turn left."

"What's our destination?"

"The Holy Cross neighborhood, other side of the industrial canal."

The place she'd named bordered the lower Ninth Ward, where the worst flooding had occurred during hurricane Katrina.

"Nearest bridge across the canal is on St. Claude," Teddy said.

"That's what we want."

Ten minutes later, as they crossed the bridge, Kit said, "We're going to hang a right on Baptist Street . . . there it is. Take it all the way to the end."

They were now heading toward the Mississippi River.

Their route took them past six intersecting streets, each lined with modest well-kept homes. After another block, the road led up to the top of the river levee, where in the dim illumination from a light on a tall pole, they saw a pair of galvanized iron gates.

"Up there?" Teddy asked.

"No, that way," Kit pointed to the left. "Then go slow."

Teddy made the turn and they inched down a street with well-tended grass of the levee on their right and overgrown vegetation and an abandoned house at the end of a long gravel driveway to their left. On each side of the gravel driveway, overgrown scrub, wild vines, and tall grassy weeds created a sprawling morass of green large enough to conceal the ruins of an Aztec temple.

"The cell phone locator dot was right over there, Kit said, pointing to the unkempt side of the road.

Teddy eased onto the right shoulder.

There was a street light about twenty yards down the road on the wilderness side of the asphalt. It produced a cone of light that did nothing to illuminate the house and the jungle around it.

"Now what?" Teddy asked.

"She could be in that house, tied up and near death."

"And the one responsible could be with her and not happy about seeing *us*."

"You never go anywhere without your pistol," Kit said. "You have it now?"

"Yes, but no flashlight."

"I've got a couple."

Teddy knew how fearless Kit could be, sometimes to the point of foolishness. He had a suggestion to make, but held his tongue to see if she needed to hear it.

She got out and looked at the house over the top of the car. She remained there for a while, then came back inside and got out her phone. She punched in Phil Gatlin's number, waited a few seconds, and said, "This is Kit. Hate to bother you, but I tracked Betty Bergeron's phone to an area with an abandoned house near the levee in the Holy Cross area. I really want to go in there and look for her, but I'd feel better with some backup."

She gave Gatlin directions and hung up. Then she looked at Teddy. "Thanks."

"For what?"

"I know that's what you thought I should do. But you let me decide for myself."

Teddy was proud of her for showing such good judgment, but at the same time wondered if she thought he was afraid of going in there.

"And no," she said. "Anyone who makes a living walking around in pits of live alligators isn't likely to be afraid of an abandoned house. I know that if I'd decided to go, you'd have been right there with me."

Teddy nodded. "Are we going to end up like identical twins that complete each other's . . ."

They each said, *sentences* at the same time.

Then, remembering what might be in that house, both of them regretted their moment of self-indulgent word play.

After a short wait, during which Teddy put on his boots, a police car with its blue lights off eased around the corner and drove toward them. It stopped behind Kit's car. Leaving his headlights on, a cop got out and came their way. Teddy rolled down his window.

The cop paused beside Teddy's door. "Sir, please step out of the car."

Teddy did as he asked, making sure he moved slowly to keep the cop from getting nervous.

Kit too, got out and showed him her badge over the top of the car. "It's alright officer, I'm . . ." she hesitated, wondering how she should identify herself, finally just saying it. ". . . I'm Detective Franklyn. I called this in." She pointed at Teddy.

"He's with me."

The cop, a big guy with a heavy, distinctly cleft chin, said, "You mean like a ride-along?"

Figuring there was no point in clarifying Teddy's identity any further she said, "Something like that."

"I'm officer McCoy. Lieutenant Gatlin is on his way. We're supposed to wait for him. What's the deal here?"

"I've traced the phone of a missing young woman to this area. I can't say exactly where it is, but it could be in that house. It's possible the girl and whoever made her disappear are in there too."

He looked at the house. "Don't see any vehicles."

"Hard to see much of anything."

"That's true."

"Anyone else besides Gatlin coming?" Kit said.

"Don't think so."

Conversation then dried up, making the wait for Gatlin an awkward experience. Finally, his old Pontiac rolled around the corner and he pulled in behind the patrol car.

When he approached them, Kit could see he was wearing a black vest, presumably one that could stop a bullet. Without any words of greeting, he looked at Kit and said, "You and Teddy stay here. Officer, let's go."

Weapons drawn, each man holding a flashlight, the two moved toward the house, one on each side of the driveway, where they could dive for cover if necessary. Kit watched them until they approached the house, kicked the door open, and went inside. Through the windows, Kit could see the beams of their lights flicking over the interior.

After about five minutes, during which Kit's heart was racing with apprehension, Gatlin called her cell phone. "I'm here," she said, breathlessly.

"The house is empty," Gatlin said. "We're gonna look

around behind it. I don't think there's any danger in the area. How about you and Teddy work the jungle out front."

"Will do." She looked at Teddy. "That was Gatlin. He wants us to search around out here. But you're not really dressed for it."

"They're just clothes. If they get ruined, I'll buy more. Where are those flashlights you mentioned?"

"There's one in the glove box. You get *it* and I'll get the one in the trunk."

A moment later, flashlight in hand, Kit motioned to the brambles and brush to the left of the house. "You work that side. I'll take the other."

Kit knew when she began this quest for Betty Bergeron's phone that it could lead to the girl's dead body. But she hadn't let that thought possess her, feeling as though if she did, death is what they'd find. Still, as the search now moved to the wilderness around the house, a gratifying result seemed farther away.

Approaching the brush, Kit's senses became more acute, and suddenly she could smell creosote wafting from the coated timbers comprising the dock for the warehouse on the other side of the levee. She heard the rustle of some small animal forcing itself deeper into the green labyrinth ahead. Then she saw something that caused her arms to erupt in gooseflesh. Just ahead of her, the weeds on the edge of the jungle were trampled and there were two parallel tracks that in places had disturbed the growth all the way down to bare dirt, as though . . .

Heart in her mouth, Kit pushed aside the branches of a shrub that prevented her from seeing where the tracks led. In the brambles beyond, she saw a flash of teal fabric and all hope fled.

Chapter 18

The crime scene investigator came out of the brush. Dressed as he was in a white jumpsuit with an attached hoodie and a white mask, the bright lights that had been rigged around the area gave him an unearthly glow. He pulled off his mask. "Okay, Dr. B, You can go in now. You gonna need a hand?"

"If I do, I'll call for help." It was 10:32 p.m. and Broussard was dressed as usual, in slacks, short sleeved white shirt, and a bowtie. He crashed through the bushes to the body of Betty Bergeron and stood for a moment, surveying the scene in the lights the crime scene team had erected. What he saw was a white female dressed in black pants, running shoes, and a teal boat-neck pullover with three-quarter sleeves. She was lying face-up so that he could easily see the small white objects moving between the lids of her closed eyes and her slightly open lips. Her face was swollen and there was a faint roadmap developing in her skin, the result of blood hemolysis in its superficial vessels. In his long career, he'd seen all these things many times. But the vertical slashes in her teal pullover were something new.

As he sat his leather bag on the trampled weeds beside him, he was a collage of emotions. His blood was singing with the chase, but at the same time, he was saddened by the death of someone so young. Compressed between those feelings was rage at the scurrilous perpetrator of this detestable act. From his bag he produced a padded wooden block. Kneeling on the block, he returned to his bag for a pair of rubber gloves that he quickly pulled over his pudgy hands.

Though the crime scene lights were bright, they did not dispel all shadow. This sent him back to his bag for the battery powered headlamp he'd long ago found much more useful than a penlight. He donned the headlamp and switched it on. Aided by the extra light, he examined the discolorations he'd noted a moment earlier on the front and sides of the girl's neck. Satisfied that he'd seen all they had to offer, he lifted the girl's right arm and tested it for rigor, finding as he'd fully expected that it had come and gone. He examined the fingertips of her hand and grunted with recognition. What he hoped to find there did indeed seem to be present.

He then inspected the slashes in the pullover more closely, finding their edges slightly soiled. He rolled up the lower edge of the garment until he could see the skin beneath. Now he understood, not the mind behind this obscene event, but why the fabric around the slashes was not bloodied. Before he'd arrived, the crime scene investigators had done a thorough search of the area and hadn't found a handbag or the girl's cell phone. Though he didn't see a bulge in her pockets that might be her phone, he did a quick pat check anyway. He got up and went back to where everyone waited.

Passing the crime scene investigators, he said, "Okay, you can bag her hands now." Then he looked at his body-removal team. "When they're finished with her hands, you can take her. And be gentle, like she was your own daughter."

Broussard joined Gatlin, Kit, and Teddy, by Kit's car. Without prompting, Broussard told them what he thought. "Death by strangulation."

"How long ago?" Gatlin asked.

"Long enough for the blowfly eggs laid in her eyes and

mouth to hatch. Those flies can smell death from a mile away, so the eggs were probably laid within an hour after she was dumped. I'll have to look at the larvae under a microscope to determine their stage of development but the condition of the body indicates she's been dead for at least two days."

"I've got a surveillance video of her leaving her place of employment last Thursday night . . . actually early Friday morning," Kit said.

"What time exactly did she leave?" Gatlin asked

"The bar closes at 12:30. She came out at 12:45."

"I'd guess she was abducted shortly after she left work," Broussard said.

"That's almost three days ago," Kit said. "Has she been dead all that time?"

"Ask me again tomorrow morning."

"Crime scene guys didn't find her handbag or phone," Gatlin said. "You check her pockets?"

"Not there either."

"Well, it *was* here," Kit said.

"Any way to know *where* she was killed?" Gatlin asked.

Broussard shook his head. "Maybe here, maybe not."

The body removal team approached, pushing a gurney containing the sheet-covered body.

"Was there a cell phone under her?" Broussard asked.

"No sir," Sam Parker, the senior member of the team said.

"I guess her killer took it," Kit said.

"What's with those slashes in her shirt?" Gatlin asked.

"Knife cuts," Broussard said. "She was stabbed fifteen times."

"I don't get it," Gatlin said. "Why no blood on her shirt?"

"He did that after she was dead . . . at least an hour after. No blood pressure, no blood comes out of the wounds."

Kit shuddered. "Fifteen times. That sounds personal."

"Maybe she just reminded him of someone he had a grudge against," Gatlin said. His next question wasn't directed at anyone in particular. "Why the interval between strangling her and stabbing her?"

"Seems to me they had some kind of argument," Kit said. "Whoever was with her became so angry he snapped and choked her to death. Then he panicked and dumped her. Maybe they were already here or he drove here from another place, I don't know. I think he left for a while, not intending to come back, but then remembered her phone. If it was someone she knew, his name might be in her contact list, maybe even some text messages or pictures. So he returned. At some point between the time she was killed and when he came back, the battery on her phone died. That's why I was able to track it to this area. He gets back, finds her bag and her phone, then suddenly, his anger flares up again and he completely loses it, stabbing her until he's spent."

"That's one scenario," Gatlin said.

"What else fits?" Kit asked.

"Somebody she doesn't know abducts and kills her because he hates dark haired attractive girls, or maybe he hit on her where she works or at school and she told him to shove off. He hasn't been taking his medication, he flips out."

Kit now remembered the sandy haired guy at the bar. "There *was* a guy whose been harassing her at school and at work. His name is Jes DeLeon. I just learned his name earlier tonight, so haven't had time to work on him."

"You do a background check on that Leo Silver you told me about?"

Kit was impressed that he remembered the name. "I did, but he has no criminal record. Let's just say it *was* one of those guys. Neither of them is anybody she'd be calling on her phone. Why take it?"

"To sell, maybe. Handbag was gone too. I'm not saying the sequence you laid out for us is wrong. I just don't want you to get wedded to an idea too early. Do that, and it's sometimes hard to accept an alternate explanation even when the evidence is pointing in a new direction."

Teddy thought of an example of how what Gatlin said was true, but since he was merely a bystander in the discussion, he kept it to himself.

"Another piece of advice," Gatlin said. "I'm sure you're aware of the pitfalls in using circumstantial evidence to decide someone is guilty but it's equally risky to *eliminate* a suspect based on it."

Kit nodded. "I'll remember what you said. Not to be a pest about it, but Betty's phone records could be a big help. When exactly will we have them?"

"Soon," Gatlin replied. "Maybe sometime tomorrow."

Kit looked at Broussard. "I assume it'll be awhile yet before you know if she was sexually assaulted."

"That isn't usually determined in the field. But her clothes were all in order. I'm thinkin' she probably wasn't."

"Unless he put everything back in place," Kit said.

Broussard tilted his head and looked at her through the bottom of his glasses. "I've always believed that when the truth is easily obtained, speculation about it is time ill spent . . . But you're right."

"Anything under her nails?" Gatlin asked.

"I think she got him."

"Well, that's it then," Kit said. "We'll get his DNA profile from that."

"Which will take six weeks," Gatlin said. "And if he's never been arrested for a felony, his profile won't be in anybody's database."

"So we keep working," Kit said.

"We keep working," Gatlin agreed.

An hour later, back in Kit's apartment, she went straight to her computer and did a background check on Jes Deleon, Teddy watching over her shoulder.

In a few minutes, she pointed at the screen and said, "A year ago he served 60 days for sexual battery."

"Two months isn't much," Teddy said. "Must have been considered a misdemeanor. Does it say what he did?"

"No."

"Whatever it was, he might be capable of much worse."

"That's what I was thinking."

Kit got up and they both went to the couch, where Kit kicked off her shoes.

"C'mon," Teddy said, "Put 'em up here."

"Just what I've always wanted," Kit said, putting her feet in his lap. "A man who knows his place."

As Teddy began to message Kit's feet, Fletcher stretched out on the floor beside them.

"I'm sorry about tonight," Kit said. "I didn't mean for all that to happen."

"Don't apologize. You did something extremely worthwhile and I was privileged to be a small part of it. One of the things that causes marriages to fall apart is boredom. Looking back on all the things that have happened to me since I've known you, I don't think boring ever gets anywhere near you."

"Are you going home tomorrow?"

"Have to."

They hadn't yet talked about how their marriage was going to work with their respective professions requiring Kit to be in New Orleans, and Teddy, two and a half hours away. Two days ago, in thinking about how this evening would play out, she'd hoped to discuss the distance problem after dinner.

Now, considering what they'd found down by the river, the time just didn't feel right. And that wasn't the only thing the discovery of Betty Bergeron's body had affected.

She looked at Teddy massaging her feet and tried to find the best way to say what was on her mind. Finally, she just came out with it. "Would you mind if tonight in bed we didn't . . . if we just . . ."

"Not at all," Teddy said. "We can't act as though that young woman's death means nothing. We can at least give her tonight."

She'd never had any doubts about Teddy being the man for her, but what he'd just said was so in tune with her feelings she felt closer to him now than ever.

It had been a long day for Broussard. And it wasn't over.

He'd followed the body of Betty Bergeron to the morgue and supervised her transfer from the removal van to autopsy room #1. The complete post mortem could wait until morning, but he needed to do one thing tonight.

Hands gloved, the headlamp he kept in the morgue securely seated on his head, he went to a nearby drawer and withdrew an insulated beaker and a pair of forceps. He carried these items to the sink, turned on the hot water tap, and when the water was as hot as it could get, filled the beaker half full. He then went to the body, where, working carefully, he began picking the largest maggots from around Betty's mouth and dropping them one by one into the beaker. The water would kill them quickly without changing their dimensions. He chose the largest because they were the oldest and would therefore, be the best time of death indicators.

After he had about a dozen specimens, he carried the beaker to the dissecting microscope, withdrew one maggot, and placed it on a small white ruler resting on the microscope stage. With a nearby pen and a note pad, he jotted down the length of the maggot then photographed it with a camera attached to the scope. He dropped that one into a tube of 70% alcohol and repeated the entire procedure with another of the creatures.

When all the chosen maggots were measured and photographed, he averaged the lengths and took the note pad to a battered desk, where he sat down and looked at a graph that plotted maggot length against time for several different temperatures.

He did all this because determining time of death is one of the most difficult tasks he regularly faced. Unless the killer is still stabbing the victim when the cops arrive, figuring out the time of death can be an adventure. The body alone and a lifetime of observer experience rarely provide an entirely satisfactory answer. Other factors are needed. And, depending on later developments, an accurate time can be crucial when a suspect is identified. So, where most people were repulsed by maggots Broussard had such an appreciation for them that when a blowfly got in his house, he'd go to inordinate lengths to let it out rather than hit it with a flyswatter.

Now he was sure, Betty Bergeron had been killed between 1:00 and 2:00 a.m. after she left work Thursday night.

Chapter 19

Broussard had a lot to do today. So he made himself a simple breakfast of eggs en cocotte with cream. Before leaving for the morgue, where he would do the complete autopsy on Betty Bergeron, including scraping the skin cells of her killer from under her fingernails, he went to his study and began comparing the list of birthday picnic invitees with the signatures on Uncle Joe's card. He'd expected to find the invitation list in alphabetical order, but it wasn't. So he worked his way down the invitation list, making a checkmark beside a name, then searching the card for that name. If a name was in both places, it received a plus sign beside the checkmark. If someone was not on the card, they received a minus sign by their checkmark. The job was made more difficult by the haphazard arrangement of signatures on the card.

For the first five names, he found four on the card, interestingly, the person who hadn't signed the card was Lewis Broussard, the only one of Joe's four kids that Amelia said was having financial problems. As Broussard checked off the sixth name on the invitation list, he heard the sound of a horn in the driveway.

He'd stayed home to meet with Remy LeBlanc, his distant cousin contractor, to discuss some work that was needed on the backyard deck. He'd already told Remy what required attention, so when he found him in the backyard a few moments later, Remy was already on his knees examining the deck's joists.

"You're right on time," Broussard said.

"Morning," Remy said, standing up. "You'd be surprised how many jobs we get just by showing up when we're supposed to for an estimate meeting."

"Actually, I wouldn't."

Remy brushed his hand off on his jeans and extended it. They exchanged a warm handshake and Remy said, "I never thanked you for recommending us for that job in the quarter, the one where Dr. Franklyn lives."

"Glad to do it." Having noticed Remy's name on the birthday card as he was searching it, he said, "The picnic Saturday certainly didn't go as anybody planned, did it? How are you handling it?"

Remy shrugged. "I'm okay. But when the shooting started I didn't know *what* was happening. I thought we were all going be targets. And you were sitting right there *by* Joe."

"It wasn't an experience I'll soon forget," Broussard said.

"It sure brought those park rangers out of their bungalow in a hurry."

"We're you and Joe close?"

"He didn't really make himself personally available to people. But when I graduated from high school, he sent me a note saying he had set up a trust for me that would pay for my entire college education or any trade school I wanted to attend. You have to respect a guy who doesn't think the only way to happiness is through college. And to do that for me ...c'mon...sure, I'm a relative, but I'm pretty far downstream. There has to be a special place in hell for the guy who killed Joe. And whenever the guy gets there, I hope it's exquisitely painful."

This recounting of Joe's generosity and wisdom renewed

Broussard's regrets about the distance that had grown between them over time. But all Broussard could do now was learn from the lesson.

"Remy, I'm gonna leave you here alone to look things over. When you've got an estimate for what it'll take to put that deck right, send it to me by e-mail. And let me know when you can start."

Fresh from an early morning jog after seeing Teddy off for his drive home, Kit pressed the door opener on the Dauphine garage where she kept her car. As the opener engaged all its gears and slide upward, she was thinking about Jes Deleon, the guy who'd harassed Betty Bergeron at school and at the bar, touching her on both occasions. Kit had accessed DeLeon's driver's license from the DMV and was planning to head over to the address she'd found on it. His earlier arrest for what appeared to be misdemeanor battery would not have allowed the police to take a DNA sample. That could only be done for a felony. Thus, his DNA profile would not already be in the system.

Presently, what she knew about his relationship with Betty Bergeron did not rise to the level of probable cause for Betty's murder. So at this point, she couldn't force him to give a DNA sample. It would all have to be voluntary. Because of that, she planned to swing by the morgue and pick up some buccal swab kits in the hope she could talk him into cooperating.

When the garage door opened, the overhead lights came on automatically. They would stay on until a few minutes after the door was closed. In the dim light, Kit was shocked at what she saw. Her windshield was shattered by what appeared to be two separate blows from a blunt object like a big wrench. And there was something written on her hood with a Magic Marker.

She walked over and saw what it said: FIRST TIRES, NOW THIS. WHAT'S NEXT? STOP PLAYING DETECTIVE!

Damn it! How did they even get in here?

She walked outside and looked up at the two small windows well above the street. The glass in the one on the right was broken. And it was obvious how the vandal got up there, one foot on that electrical panel down low, then up on the top of the gate next door, and he was there.

She went inside to see how he got down. But there was no apparent answer. Then, looking closer, she saw scrape marks on the brick . . . most likely from his shoes as he lowered himself with a rope held by an accomplice on the street. He'd finished by dropping onto the hood of the other car that parked there.

She went back to her car, and with her phone, took some pictures of the damage and the message on the hood, then called her insurance company.

Lucky her. The policy was current. The agent on the line said that if she sent him photos of the shattered window, including one showing both the car's VIN number and some of the damage, she could proceed immediately with windshield replacement and send the bill to the agency. He also suggested she try to remove the marker with alcohol. If that didn't work, she should take the car to a collision service and have the writing buffed out with rubbing compound, whatever that was.

The mobile windshield guy showed up twenty minutes after she called. He appeared fully able and totally professional in his job and instantly gained Kit's confidence, partly because he didn't even ask her what the message on the hood was all about.

"How long you figure this will take?" she asked.

"Thirty minutes," the guy said.

"I'm going to run an errand. I won't be long."

She left the garage and walked briskly back to Toulouse Street. Half a block down Toulouse, she entered the Nolen Boyd gallery. The owner, a corpulent guy with a face so surrounded by flesh he looked like his features had been painted in the center of a dinner plate, was straightening a picture he'd taken of barges on the Mississippi at sunset. He was her landlord and the owner of the garage on Dauphine. Some time back, she'd worked for him briefly after an experience she didn't really like talking about.

"Nolen, we've got a problem."

Turning, he came toward her, a subtext of mild irritation in his otherwise bland expression. "Whatever happened to 'Hello Nolen. That's a nice shirt. You look handsome today'?"

He knew he wasn't handsome, but had no idea his Hawaiian shirts were all hideous and often food-stained from the Lucky Dogs he loved.

"A self-assured man like you doesn't need flattery," Kit said. "And there are so few of you *in* the world."

"Okay, that's enough BS," he said. "What's the problem?"

"Someone broke into the garage last night and smashed my windshield. They got in through the window on the right, which they broke. We need to get that fixed and have bars put over both of them."

"Okay, I'll see to it."

"When?"

"Next couple days."

"They also damaged the hood of your car climbing down from the broken window."

He now became a full member of the club. "The hell you say. We can't have people just running over us like that. We need those bars ASAP. But I don't know anybody who could do it today."

"I might," Kit said. "C'mon."

She led him outside and through the gate to the back courtyard, where Remy's father, Zachery was setting up some scaffolding.

She waved at him. "Morning. Have a minute to talk?"

As he approached, he took off his hardhat, a gentlemanly act she appreciated.

"Dr. Franklyn, Mr. Boyd, what can I do for you?" He looked like Remy twenty years in the future; skin rougher, some lines at the corners of his eyes and across his forehead, a man who you could point to as evidence that age often improves a man's appearance.

"Someone broke into Nolen's garage last night and damaged both our cars. I know this is an imposition, but is there any chance you could repair the garage window that was knocked out and put some bars over that window and one other? We'd like to have it done today so whoever did the damage can't come back tonight."

LeBlanc looked at Nolen. "It'll slow us down back here."

"I understand."

"Let's go take a look."

As Kit walked down the forensic center's hallway toward Broussard's office forty-five minutes later, she wondered how she was going to end the harassment that had so far been directed at her only through her car. Like the message said on her hood; What *is* next?

She knocked on Broussard's door.

"It's open."

Inside, she found that Gatlin was there too, in his favorite spot; perched on the arm of the green sofa

"Glad you're here," Broussard said from behind his desk.

"We need to have a war council about Betty Bergeron." Each of his cheeks obviously contained a lemon ball. "But I was just about to tell Philip two things. Let me do that then we'll discuss the Bergeron case." He turned to Gatlin. "That death in police custody was unavoidable. The guy died from a ruptured aortic aneurysm. He was a walkin' dead man. No one caused it, it just happened. He couldn't have been saved even if he was in a hospital bed when it tore."

"That's good," Gatlin said. "I mean . . . not for him, but for the arresting officers."

"Death should never be a good thing for anybody," Broussard said. "But we don't live in a world with that kind of purity."

"What was the other thing you wanted to tell me?"

"I found out that Uncle Joe left his money equally to each of his four kids; Julien, Amelia, Sara, and Lewis. All of them are financially secure except for Lewis. His business is in trouble and he's in a lot of debt. Also, I found the birthday card that everyone signed at the picnic. I haven't finished comparin' the invitation list to the names on the card, but I *can* tell you that Lewis didn't sign the card."

"Maybe he was there, but just didn't sign it," Gatlin said.

"Joe's daughter, Amelia, personally took the card around and made sure she got the signatures of every adult present."

"So he could've been the shooter."

There was a time when Kit would have found it shocking that a man could kill his own father for money. But after working with Broussard as long as she had, she was no longer that person.

"Now I've got *two* suspects," Gatlin said. "A guy named Howard Karpis threatened to kill Joe a few months ago. And Karpis's been sending him threatening notes . . . even admitted it to me."

"Why'd he admit it?" Broussard asked.

"Maybe to make me believe him when he said he wasn't the shooter. But the alibi he gave me doesn't check out."

"How well do you like him?"

"Until you told me about Lewis, I *loved* him. Is that it?"

"Wish I had more, but I don't. So let's talk about Betty Bergeron."

Gatlin looked at Kit, "I didn't have a chance to mention it last night, but that was good work finding her body."

"My intent was to find her alive."

"That's always the goal, but in missing persons cases, rarely the result."

"I can say with certainty that she was killed between 1:00 and 2:00 a.m. Thursday night," Broussard said.

"So she was either abducted by someone she didn't know or met with someone she did know right after work," Kit said.

"I forwarded the tissue under her nails to the state crime lab for DNA analysis, which as we've discussed could take six weeks," Broussard said. "But I also sent some over to a lab at Tulane, where they've been workin' on blood typin' of small samples of saliva and tissue. If they're able to do it, we should have those results within 24 hours."

"Isn't that kind of old fashioned stuff?" Kit said. "All those types are shared by a lot of people."

Gatlin finally stood up. "But potentially it could save us a lot of time. If his blood type excludes one of our suspects, we don't have to think about him anymore."

"Speaking of suspects, that guy who harassed Betty at the bar, Jes DeLeon, served 60 days for sexual battery two years ago," Kit said.

"Misdemeanor," Gatlin replied. "Too bad. If he'd been arrested for a felony his DNA profile would already be on record. And what you have won't get us a warrant to swab him."

His comment reminded Kit why she was there. "Let me see what I can do about that." She looked at Broussard. "Do you have a couple of spare buccal sample collectors on hand?"

"Nothin' I like better than a person askin' for somethin' I don't even have to leave my chair to get." He reached down to the desk drawer on his left, removed the items she'd requested, and handed them to her. "Instructions are on the paper sleeves of the swabs."

"You're gonna just talk him into volunteering a sample," Gatlin said with an inflection indicating he didn't think that would work.

"Maybe," Kit said, putting the collectors in her bag. "Depends on how things go."

It appeared to Kit that Gatlin was going to say something more, but he seemed to change his mind. Jumping into the conversational lull, she looked at him and slightly changed the subject, "It could be useful to know where DeLeon went after he left the bar."

"Sorry, no recent phone records or tracking data without a subpoena. In most jurisdictions we could probably get it just with what you've learned. But here, with the judges we have, they require more."

"That's not helpful."

"It's never bothered *me*."

Gatlin was always bantering with Broussard, but rarely with her. She interpreted his sarcastic response as a sign that maybe he was getting used to having her around. "Okay, I'm off to see DeLeon."

She left the office and headed for the elevators.

A moment later, as she stepped forward and pressed the

DOWN button, she heard a loud whistle from the direction of Broussard's office. When she looked that way, she saw Gatlin standing in the hall. "C'mon back," he said. "They've found Betty Bergeron's car."

Chapter 20

Bergeron's vehicle was sitting in the parking lot of a small shopping center. The area around it was already cordoned off with yellow crime scene tape attached to free-standing poles the crime scene van had brought. As Kit and Gatlin parked their respective cars and approached the patrol cruiser next to the van, the lone cop, a young black guy with a thin mustache, stood a little straighter.

"You the one who found it?" Gatlin asked.

"Yes sir," the cop replied.

"Good work."

Gatlin went to the scene tape and held it so Kit could duck under it. Then he followed.

Two white-suited crime scene investigators were working the car like pollinating bees. Gatlin called out to the nearest one, who was looking in the glove box. "Anything of interest yet?"

The guy pulled his head out and turned around. "No blood or weapons, if that's what you mean."

"Either one of those would be start, but we're also looking for a cell phone."

"If it's here, we'll find it."

Gatlin glanced toward the nearest light pole, then surveyed the others. Following his lead, Kit did the same.

"That's not good," Kit said pointing to the pole ten feet away. "No camera."

"But some others have them."

"Look how far away they are."

"Maybe they're extremely long range models."

Kit gestured at the nearest store, which was actually not close. "It's a dollar store. What are the chances?"

"You haven't been a detective long enough to be so pessimistic. Check it out and let me know."

"You're leaving?"

"It's basically your case. I've got to find out who killed Joe Broussard." He began to walk away, then paused and turned around. "What's that writing on your car?"

"Just some harassment for me helping out."

"Sure you can handle it?"

"Oh, I'll handle it. Count on it."

Broussard sat at his desk with Uncle Joe's birthday card and the picnic invitation list, fully expecting that he now had time to complete the cross checking he'd started earlier that morning. He worked for about five minutes in which he didn't find anyone else on the invitation list who hadn't also signed the card. Then on the list he spotted a name that hit him with only slightly less force than the time he'd been struck by lightning while out fishing with Bubba and Gatlin.

He reached for the phone, intending to call Amelia Hebert, Uncle Joe's daughter, and ask why that person was on the list. Then, thinking how this would just be another example of wanting to talk to Amelia only when he needed something, he decided out of respect for their former friendship when they were kids, he should see her in person.

Not wanting to appear rude by dropping by unannounced, he called her.

"This is Amelia."

"Hello Amelia. Andy Broussard calling. Are you available

for a face to face talk?"
"Not at the moment, but what time is it?"
"Ten-thirty."
"How about one o'clock?"
"See you then."
"What'll we be talking about?"
"Let's wait 'til I'm there."

Kit had been staring non-stop at a video surveillance monitor in the dollar store for the last five minutes. One of the distant cameras she and Gatlin had seen outside was positioned so its field of view included the location where Betty Bergeron's car was now parked. The footage she was looking at was from last Thursday night.

Betty had left work at 12:45 a.m. Though the dollar store was ten minutes from Gator Willie's, Kit had asked the store manager to start the review footage at 12:30 a.m. At that time, the entire lot, including the spot Betty's car would eventually occupy was empty.

The lot remained vacant until 12:40, when a broken down pickup truck made an aimless track across the asphalt then drove out of view. At 12:46, a cat in the foreground chased a mouse through the visual field, then both disappeared into the grass and weeds at the edge of the lot. The cat reappeared at 12:50 with the mouse in its mouth. For the next five minutes, Kit had a first-rate view of Darwinian principles in action as the cat dropped to its belly on the blacktop and consumed all of the mouse but its tail.

Then, headlights appeared in the distance; a car turning into the lot from the street. Kit leaned into the monitor, trying to see more than was possible. The car made a wide turn and parked in Betty's spot. It was too far away for Kit to see any detail except that the car was white, the same as Betty drove.

The car sat there alone for three minutes, then another pair of headlights appeared from the street. That car too, made a wide turn.

"Park on my side," Kit muttered, thinking that would give her a better chance to learn something other than the fact the car wasn't light colored. But naturally, it pulled in beside Betty's car on the passenger side, blocking a clear view of it.

Almost immediately, Betty got out of her car and went to the other vehicle. Though she couldn't identify Betty's face, Kit caught a flash of teal, the color of the pullover she was wearing when they'd found her body.

Kit wasn't able to see Betty actually get in the other car, but that's certainly what took place. For the next three minutes, nothing happened. Then, the other car backed up and sped away, heading for the exit. When it reached the street, it hit a curb and fishtailed before it hurtled out of sight, going the opposite direction from which it entered. It was too far away for her to even see the occupants.

Kit felt sick to her stomach because she had probably just witnessed Betty Bergeron's murder.

Chapter 21

Kit left the dollar store and walked across the parking lot toward the crime scene team, who was still working on Bergeron's car. The flash drive in Kit's handbag contained a copy of the surveillance video she'd just watched. Betty Bergeron had voluntarily left her own car and got in the one that had parked beside her, indicating she knew the driver and they were probably friends. And it was almost a certainty the driver of that car was her killer.

The friend angle would seem to eliminate Jes DeLeon. But then she remembered Gatlin's advice about not using circumstantial evidence to *eliminate* a suspect. She had no proof the driver of the other car was a friend. Maybe DeLeon had some hold over Betty and she got in the car because of a threat he'd made.

She ducked under the crime scene tape, walked up to the investigator about to begin vacuuming the trunk of Betty's car, and said, "Anything significant?"

"Sometimes you don't know what's significant until long after you find it. Still no cell phone."

After what she'd seen on the video, it didn't seem likely the car would produce anything of value, but at this point, who could really say? There was nothing she could contribute by just standing there watching, so she returned to her own car.

Her next move seemed obvious. As a first step, she reached into the nearest compartment of the drink holder between seats and picked up the plastic aspirin bottle there. She opened it, shook out the one remaining tablet, and put the bottle in her bag.

Her bag also contained a copy of Jes DeLeon's driver's license and last known address, which was different from the one on his license.

Ten minutes later, Kit drove slowly down Joliet Street, checking the numbers on the houses.

There . . .

She stopped in front of a one-story house painted pale green with turquoise trim. A large yucca plant accessorized with other desert plants in beige-colored pots dominated the front yard. Looking at the house, Kit once again was reminded how hard it was to accept the old saying, 'beauty is in the eye of the beholder.' Surely there must be some universal standards for what's attractive and what isn't. In fact, she knew of one study presenting evidence that people with symmetric faces are preferred as sexual partners, perhaps an evolutionary holdover from when primitive cultures discovered that symmetry of features was correlated with parasite resistance.

She shook her head to clear it of these extraneous thoughts, then looked down the driveway, where she saw an empty car port. So if he wasn't here, where was he?

Kit showed her badge to the clerk behind the counter at the Tulane registrar's office. "I'd like to see the class schedule of a student named Jes DeLeon."

The clerk, a nicely dressed older woman with stiff, dry hair and wrinkled skin she either couldn't hide or had long ago accepted, said, "Do you have a subpoena?"

No, she didn't . . . hadn't even thought about it.

Uncle Joe's daughter, Amelia, lived on one of the residential streets near Commander's Palace, not more than a quarter mile from Broussard's home. Their geographical proximity to each other made him feel even worse about all the years he'd made no effort to keep in touch with her.

He discovered that her home was a tall yellow and white Italianate structure with a two-story porch and ornate corbels under the eaves. The windows on both porches ran from floor to ceiling. Like all other houses in the area, the front yard was nothing more than some foundation shrubbery and a six-foot deep strip of grass behind an attractive wrought iron fence. All in all, a fine domicile.

Today, Broussard had driven his yellow T-Bird. In front of Amelia's house, there was a vacant parking space under a big magnolia. Worried about birds fouling the car's paint, he chose to park two doors down, where no such danger existed.

Moments later, one hand holding the file folder he'd brought, he was on the porch, ringing Amelia's bell, which he could hear only faintly through the home's thick front door. In less than a minute, the door was opened by one of the most elegant looking older women he'd ever seen; tall and slim with a model's long neck, perfect features, silver hair swept up in a cotton candy kind of arrangement, pearl earrings, a multi-strand pearl necklace at her throat, all set off by a black dress with a high neckline.

"Andy," she said with real pleasure in her voice. Before he could respond, she stepped forward and embraced him. Not being a hugger or even a toucher, Broussard didn't know how to react. Not wanting to stand there like an unresponsive sausage, he unenthusiastically lifted his arms and lightly pressed the palm of his free hand against her back.

"Come in, come in," Amelia said, stepping back and gesturing toward the foyer.

And he did, making sure to move far enough inside so she could shut the door.

"Mind if we talk in the kitchen?" Amelia said. "I know that's not considered appropriate in 'polite' circles, but we did it lots of times as kids. Why not now?"

He followed her into a large brightly lit beige kitchen with a huge, granite-topped work island containing a big sink at its far end; a chef's dream. But it looked like Amelia used the island for more than food preparation.

"Please excuse the mess. I handle all my paperwork in here. It's just such a light and pleasant place, it encourages me to do work I'd otherwise put off. You sit there." She gestured to the closest in a line of chairs on one side of the island. "And I'll sit here." She put her hand on the chair tucked under the granite overhang at the near end of the island. "But first, what can I get you to drink? Lemonade, iced tea, something stronger?"

"No thanks, nothing for me." The question Broussard had come to ask her was swelling up inside him and he felt that if he didn't ask it soon, it'd blow the buttons off his shirt, but there was such a thing as timing and manners. "Again, let me say how sorry I was about what happened to your father."

She shook her head. "It doesn't seem real, that I'll never talk to him again. He was there one minute, enjoying the picnic, I think. And then . . . gone . . . forever. How can something so monumental happen that fast? And the way he died was so . . . horrible." Her eyes shifted from sadness to anger. "Do they know yet who did it?"

"Remember how when you're puttin' together a picture puzzle, it's always best to start with the edges? I'd say at this point that's how far the investigation has progressed, just the edges."

In response to her expression of disappointment, he added,

"And now the rest will surely follow."

It was no longer possible to hold in the question he'd come to ask. But before he could speak, the cell phone on the countertop rang.

"This is Amelia."

Broussard couldn't hear what was being said on the other end, but Amelia's eyes grew round, and her jaw dropped open. Even through her makeup, her skin blanched.

"Okay, thanks for calling."

She hung up and her posture slumped. She looked at Broussard. "That was my sister, Sara. What the hell is this world coming to? She said my brother, Julien's, granddaughter has been murdered."

"What's her name?" Broussard asked, already knowing the answer.

"Elizabeth."

"Bergeron?"

"Yes."

Chapter 22

Amelia looked hard at Broussard. "You knew that Elizabeth was dead, didn't you?"

"That's what I came to talk about. I saw her name on the picnic invitation list but I'm sorry to say I didn't know who she was."

"Andy, she was so young."

Broussard nodded. "I don't like thinkin' about that."

Amelia fell into a reverential silence.

Perhaps because she'd just learned about Betty and was still shocked at the news, she didn't try to connect the girl's death with what happened to Uncle Joe. But Broussard's mind was already slogging through the implications. Two killings in one family, just three days apart. Could that merely be a coincidence? He didn't like coincidences. To even consider that as an option in any investigation seemed worthy only of a brain as smooth as an apple.

"Did you know her?" Broussard asked.

"Not very well. But I can imagine how devastated her parents are as well as her grandparents, Julien and Leona. I should tell Scott."

As she punched a number into her phone, Broussard figured Scott was her husband. But he wasn't sure.

After she'd talked with Scott and hung up, Broussard said, "The fact I didn't know I was related to Elizabeth and didn't recognize hardly anyone at the picnic showed me my life has been far too insulated. I want to know the name of every person who was invited and how they're related to each other. Believe me, I know my timin' is awful, considerin' what's happened, but would you be willin' to go over the invitation list with me and tell me who's who?"

Amelia's eyes subtly shifted from reflections on death to once again participating in life. "It'd be my pleasure, Andy."

Broussard opened the file folder he'd brought. "I've got the list and some sheets of paper right here. I'd like to make a pedigree chart to keep it all organized."

"That's sort of the way I made up the list," Amelia said. "I started with my brother Julien and his wife."

Using accepted conventions for constructing a pedigree chart, Broussard had already drawn a square at the top to represent Uncle Joe. He'd then drawn a horizontal line from Joe's square to a circle that indicated Joe's wife, Anne. He now proceeded to add and label symbols for Julien and Leona.

"Then I listed my sister, Sara, and her husband, Noel. Noel's last name is LeBlanc."

"I did know that," Broussard said. "Because of their grandson, Remy."

"You know Remy?"

"Talked to him this mornin' about doin' some more work for me."

"Then you know how good he is."

"I do indeed."

"He was over here two weeks ago, checking on the two men who were replacing some siding on the back of the house. Sat right there where you are and had some lemonade."

Broussard entered Sara and Noel on his chart then looked at the invitation list, where the next names were Amelia's brother, Lewis and his wife Kay. As he put those names on his chart, Amelia said, "Have the police talked to Lewis yet?"

"I don't think so," Broussard said. "Edges first . . ."

"I'm sure he didn't have anything to do with the shooting. You remember how he was like as a kid, wanting to fish with a piece of hot dog rather than put a worm or a minnow on a hook."

"Not sure if that indicates a tender heart or lack of understandin' of where hot dogs come from."

Amelia nodded. "I never thought of that."

"Okay, the next two names on your list are Sherri and David Peltier . . ."

For the next forty-five minutes Amelia spit out names she remembered with such ease Broussard regularly had to slow her down. Finally, he had it all on paper. Looking at the sprawling chart, Broussard shook his head and said, "Uncle Joe and Annie made all that. Makes me feel like an underachiever."

"They only did a small part of it."

"That's true."

When he'd been at the picnic with most of the people now displayed on his pedigree chart, Broussard hadn't given any thought about who they really were, vaguely believing that a lot of them were simply Joe's friends and their kids. But now, as he looked at the names of all his kin displayed in one impressive document, he began to feel uncomfortable, as though he was jammed in an elevator with a lot of strangers.

"Okay," he said, putting the chart in his folder. "Thanks for doin' that." He got out of his chair and headed for the front door.

Behind him, Amelia said, "Again, I'm sure you don't have to worry about Lewis. Will you watch out for him?"

Broussard had no idea exactly what 'watching out for Lewis' meant. And even if he did, he had no reason to influence the investigation in Lewis's favor. But he didn't think he should say that. So he simply said, "It's been great to see you, Amelia. Thanks again for your help."

Kit left the Tulane registrar's office feeling like a dope. Why had she not anticipated that the registrar might balk at simply handing over DeLeon's schedule? It was a rookie mistake. But then of course she *was* a rookie . . . at this kind of stuff anyway. Still, she should have known better.

What to do now? She checked her watch: 12:15.

Dee Evans said that she'd seen DeLeon eating lunch in the LBC. She was now standing on the steps of Gibson Hall, the Gothic architectural centerpiece of the original campus. The LBC was a short distance behind Gibson Hall. To reach it she headed for Engineering Drive, where she fell in behind a co-ed in a short denim skirt and a ruby and blue-striped short sleeved pullover.

As she walked, she passed other students coming her way. Seeing them all she thought about what it was like to be their age – worrying about the next test, the next date, complexion problems – the seniors concerned about that first job. Death was something very few of them ever thought about. Even when they would reach Kit's age, mortality for most of them would still be an abstract concept.

But with the pallid death mask of Betty Bergeron adding yet another layer to the smoldering images of all the other bodies she'd seen in her work, she was far older than her physical age. And in no way did that seem like a good thing.

When she reached the LBC, she went up the steps and wandered around the first floor, her eyes trolling for a black backpack decorated with yellow emogies.

No luck. And if she saw it, that's exactly what it would be, dumb luck.

She went out onto the terrace patio, where she saw some

long-legged girls throwing a Frisbee around the LBC quad. Farther down, two guys were playing catch with a football. The elevated patio was a long rectangle parallel to the quad and it was filled with students sitting on gray metal chairs at yellow-topped tables. Then, at ground level, sitting on a concrete bench ringing a young live oak, she saw a guy drinking from a soda can. Beside him was a black backpack covered in yellow circles.

Chapter 23

Kit found an empty seat on the terrace near the guy she thought was likely Jes DeLeon. Not wanting to just sit there and stare at him, she took out her phone and pretended to be fascinated with its screen, thereby appearing as easily entertained as a lot of the students around her.

DeLeon was watching the Frizbee girls so intently Kit could almost see lascivious thought bubbles over his head. He took his time with his drink, finishing it as the girls departed the quad. He then got up, walked over to a trash receptacle, and tossed the can in.

Kit waited until he was about ten yards away, heading for the front of the LBC. Then she casually went to the trash bin and took off the lid, hoping she'd find his can sitting on top of a lot of paper refuse. She didn't want to talk to him until she'd obtained a sample of his DNA. If she spoke to him and identified herself first, she'd never be able to covertly wait for him to discard some object that might have a few of his cells on it. But the trash container didn't cooperate, because inside, it was *mostly* soda cans. And she hadn't been close enough to see what he was drinking.

She put the top back on the receptacle and looked toward the direction DeLeon had gone, now finding him about thirty yards away.

Trying to appear that she was not following him, she did, making no attempt to close the distance between them.

At Freret Street, he crossed and followed an open-air walkway that had been constructed through Percival Stern Hall so that its second floor arched overhead. Kit knew that on the other side of the walkway, there were many campus buildings he could disappear into. So she picked up the pace to make sure she wouldn't lose him.

When she emerged from under Percival Stern, there he was . . . now about twenty yards in front of her. The walk he was following had buildings on the left and a wide lawn to his right. On other occasions when she'd been to the campus, Kit had enjoyed the gorgeous landscaping, but today she was so intent on keeping contact with DeLeon she didn't even notice it. Just past the three big rusty-metal circle sculptures in front of Stanley Thomas Hall, the walk ran five different ways. He chose the one that would keep him the farthest from any adjacent buildings. Kit now realized they were headed toward the ad building where she'd started this quest.

Five minutes later, with her target still in sight, she left the campus and crossed the near lane of St. Charles Avenue. A streetcar in the neutral ground lumbered past, momentarily blocking her view. When it was out of the way, she saw DeLeon, about fifteen yards down the main walkway into Audubon Park.

Except for DeLeon and Kit, the park entrance was empty, no students or anyone else she could use for cover. But from the moment she'd begun to follow him, she hadn't seen him look her way, so she wasn't worried. Still, she took a branch walkway off to the left that led to a big fountain with a ring of benches around it. By following the right curvature of benches, she could still keep track of DeLeon's movements without risking him looking back toward the entrance and seeing her.

Where the line of benches ended, there was a large live

oak that gave her cover as she stopped and watched DeLeon leave the pavement and step onto the grass bordering the large lagoon that ran the length of the park. He walked to the water's edge and stared into it. Then, as though Kit's wishes could somehow influence the course of events, DeLeon lit a cigarette. Up to that moment, she had no evidence he smoked, but she'd once read an article that said 90% of criminals do. She couldn't vouch for the truth of the article but had followed him, hoping it was right.

He took a few puffs then began strolling to the left, a course that would bring him into a more direct line of sight from where she stood. Realizing how odd it would look if she continued to just stand there, she sat down and put her right leg on the bench. With her body now half turned toward the lagoon, she took out her phone and started moving her finger over the screen as if scrolling through some mesmerizing content.

From the corner of her eye, she saw DeLeon move into sight. He kept walking parallel to the lagoon until he was just to the right of two bronze statues. There, he turned back toward the water.

Kit wanted that cigarette butt when he was finished with it. The article about criminals smoking didn't say anything about what they did with their butts, but Kit suspected they just threw them on the ground. When he did, she'd swoop in, pick it up with a clean tissue, and put it in the empty aspirin bottle she'd brought. Then she had a horrible thought. *Oh no . . . What if he flicked it into the lagoon?*

He took a few more puffs while Kit faked some additional screen gazing. Then . . . Yes . . . he tossed the butt on the grass and stepped on it. Most likely some of the saliva and cells she was after would stick to his shoe, but she knew the PCR replication procedures for multiplying even trace amounts of

DNA could get a profile from a single cell. She also wanted to test the butt for his blood type. Maybe that wouldn't work, but it was worth trying.

DeLeon adjusted his backpack and resumed his stroll along the lagoon. When he was a suitable distance away, Kit got up and hurried toward the water, using the short walkway between benches. In seconds, she was there. But . . . she bent down and . . . found herself looking at a flattened *unsmoked* cigarette.

"Why are you following me and why are you trying to get a sample of my DNA?" a voice said from behind her.

She turned to see Jes DeLeon standing a few feet away. "You've just answered your first question with your second," she said. "Do you know Betty Bergeron?" She knew he did, but wanted to hear what he'd say.

"That's what this is about? You think I'm the one who hurt her?"

The discovery of Betty's body had been on the morning news, the two local papers, and TV. DeLeon wasn't implicating himself by knowing about her death. But why did he say 'hurt' rather than 'killed'? Did he soften the verb because he was involved?

He had a tiny triangular tuft of hair just under the center part of his lower lip, like he thought that was some great magnet for attracting women. His complexion was good and distressingly free of scratches. But he *was* wearing a gray jersey turtleneck, perhaps to hide the marks she was looking for. "I know you spoke to her at Gator Willie's the night she was killed."

"So what?"

"The surveillance tape showed that when you touched her hand at the bar, she wasn't pleased about it. And that night wasn't the first time she rejected your attention. There was at least one other time on the Tulane campus."

"Has someone been gossiping about me?"

"What did you do to get a sexual battery charge on your record?"

"It was a misunderstanding. They said I groped a girl on a crowded bus. I didn't. Someone pushed me against her. By the way, who are you?"

Kit produced her badge and ID. "New Orleans Homicide. Would you mind rolling up your sleeves?"

"Actually, I would."

"Refusing will just make me think you're guilty."

"You already think that."

"Where'd you go after you left Gator Willie's last Thursday night?"

"Home."

"Straight from the bar?"

"Yeah."

"Did you go out again later?"

"No."

"Can anyone verify when you got home?"

"I live alone. So, no."

"Were you angry at being rejected?"

"I think it builds character."

"Would you be willing to take a polygraph test?"

"No."

"Why not?"

"Last time I got involved with cops, I did 60 days for something that happened by accident."

From what he'd just said, Kit already knew the answer to her next question, but she had to try. "How about submitting to a cheek swab. Polygraphs can be a problem if the operator isn't well trained. A DNA profile would absolutely clear you. I can take the sample now."

"You're kidding, right? No way."

Disappointed but not surprised, Kit wasn't ready to leave. "How do you feel about Betty Bergeron being murdered?"

"No one should be able to do that to anyone else, no matter how nasty they are to you."

"Then you think a girl has a right to choose her companions or not as she sees fit."

"Sure, but why act like an ass when someone is just showing that they find you interesting."

"Some guys don't listen when a girl says no."

"And some girls say no before a guy has any chance to show who he is."

"Maybe who you are is obvious."

"Do you dislike me?"

"I don't even know you."

"Exactly, then why am I being jerked around like this?"

"I'm giving you a chance to show *me* who you are."

"I thought it was obvious."

"Not to me, not yet."

"Am I under arrest?"

"No."

"Then as Betty once said to me, 'Get Lost'." He turned and walked away.

Watching him go, Kit mentally summed up what she'd learned. When it came to women, he had a chip on his shoulder and seemed like someone who could lose control if an interaction with a female didn't go his way. But this again brought her hard up against what she'd seen on the dollar store's surveillance video. Betty had voluntarily left her car and gotten into the one that joined her in the parking lot. But Betty didn't like DeLeon. Why would she get in a car with him? Well damn. Maybe that *wasn't* the killer in the other car. If not, DeLeon would still be a possible.

Phil Gatlin stood aside to let two guys leave Marksman Arms, the gun store owned by Lewis Broussard. Inside, the place was full of mostly men, but also a few women, ogling the massive display of firearms hanging on the walls and in glass cases. For a business that was supposed to be in financial trouble it certainly couldn't be from lack of customers.

Before coming over here, Gatlin had obtained a copy of Lewis's driver's license so he'd know what the guy looked like. There seemed to be three clerks in the store, none of them the man he was looking for. Then he saw Lewis come out of a back room. Like the other clerks, he was dressed in green pants and a green T-shirt that had the store's logo on the upper left part of the chest. He came onto the sales floor and walked over to a bank of freestanding shelves, where he put the boxes of ammo he was carrying in the proper place.

Badge and ID in hand, Gatlin stepped up beside him. In a low voice so the whole place wouldn't hear, he said, "Mr. Broussard, I'm Lieutenant Gatlin, NOPD Homicide." At the same time, he flashed his credentials.

"What's this about?" Lewis asked, not in a panicky way, but with simple curiosity.

From the background check he'd run, Gatlin knew that Lewis was a sixty-two-year-old battle-tested former marine, who over a 30-year career, had risen to the rank of captain. And he still looked like it: good posture, short gray hair neatly combed and parted, clean shaven, intelligent eyes, and a countenance that made him look like a man who wouldn't tolerate insubordination.

"Is there a place we could talk in private?" Gatlin said. The man reminded Gatlin so much of his former drill sergeant that he'd almost felt like starting and ending his question with the word, 'sir'.

"Back here," Lewis said, motioning for Gatlin to follow.

They went to a small office with a modest sized glass-topped desk and two dark red-leather visitor's armchairs. Lewis waved Gatlin into one, went behind his desk, and sat in a rolling leather chair with the Marine Corps insignia on the backrest.

The wall behind the desk held a framed picture of Lewis and a four-star general Gatlin thought he recognized. "Isn't that Norman Schwarzkopf?" Gatlin said, pointing at the picture.

"Yeah. He was the CENTCOM commander when I was in Iraq and Afghanistan. Even though he was army, he was a good guy. So when he asked if I'd be willing to stand with him for a snapshot, I said, 'Okay'."

Even if Gatlin hadn't realized on his own that Lewis was joking about which of them wanted the picture, there was a brief twinkle in Lewis's eyes that gave it away. At first it seemed odd that a man who'd just lost his father would be capable of making any kind of joke, but Lewis had probably been saying that about the picture for so long, it was an automatic response.

"So," Lewis said. "You're from Homicide. I guess this about my father."

"That's right."

"I heard the killer got away."

"From the scene, yes. From the consequences, most likely not."

"What brings you here?"

"My understanding is that Joe left his entire estate to be equally divided among his four kids."

"In your mind, does that equal four suspects?"

"At this point I'm not counting, I'm exploring."

"Okay, let's explore."

"I've heard that you're having financial problems. Yet the

business looks successful."

"Who said I'm in trouble?"

"My job is more in the nature of asking questions than answering them."

"It's true. All because I was seduced by my success here into opening a second location in Covington. I paid too much for the building over there and the renovations. The mortgage payments are a sinkhole that's about to suck everything I own into it. I'd walk away, but even that'll be expensive. And yes, my share of the inheritance will save me. But frankly it sickens me to think that I'll benefit by my father's death. I should just give it to charity."

"Will you?"

"I have to think of my family obligations. I took a second mortgage on my house to finance the new shop. And guess who's paying the bills for my wife's mother and father who are both in a nursing home."

"Why didn't you sign the card that was circulated at Joe's birthday party?"

"I wasn't there. I was planning to go, but woke up that morning so sick I couldn't."

"Was your wife ill too?"

"She wasn't even in town. Her sister in Amarillo broke her ankle last week. Kay's been helping *her*."

"Her sister's not married?"

"Divorced."

"When did Kay leave for Amarillo?"

"Last Wednesday."

"When you got sick did you go to an emergency room?"

"I'm a marine. I don't need somebody to wipe my nose."

"Did you call Joe on Saturday and wish him a happy birthday."

"I did . . . About two hours before the event."

"When did you find out about the shooting?"

"Minutes after it happened. My sister, Amelia, called and told me."

"Do you own a boat and trailer?"

"Should have sold it long before now."

"Where do you keep it?"

"At the house, in the garage."

"When's the last time you used it?"

"So long ago I can't remember. How am I doing? Want to cuff me now?"

"Maybe later."

Chapter 24

Broussard was behind his desk as usual. Kit was once again on the green sofa. This time, Gatlin was pacing. Broussard had just told them that Betty Bergeron was Uncle Joe's great granddaughter.

"I think the two murders in the same extended family are probably a coincidence," Gatlin said.

Broussard rocked back in his desk chair. "Doesn't feel like it to me."

"You just don't like coincidences in general. They happen all the time, or there wouldn't be a word in the dictionary for it. We've got separate suspects for each crime – no obvious overlap."

Kit was reluctant to express any view on this matter because she was uncomfortable siding against either of them. But she didn't want to just sit there like a dope. So she stood and walked over to the big rolling whiteboard. Picking up a marker from a tray below, she said, "Let's get what we know up here where we can see it." She started two columns; one headed, BETTY, the other, JOE.

Under BETTY she entered two names: Leo Silver and Jes DeLeon.

"I tracked down Jes DeLeon today. He's *my* prime suspect because as I told you earlier, Betty had rejected has advances on two occasions, one of them in the bar where she works the night she was killed. And he left the bar an hour before her shift ended."

"Any scratches on his face or arms?" Broussard asked.

"Nothing on his face, but he was wearing a turtleneck, so who knows?"

"I guess you're gonna make me ask," Gatlin said. "Cheek swab?"

"He refused."

"Not to be critical, but it would have been a good idea to trail DeLeon awhile before approaching him," Gatlin said. "He might have thrown away something we could use for a sample. I was gonna mention that earlier when you picked up the swabs, but wanted to give you room to function on your own."

Kit was now faced with two options, both of them embarrassing. On the one hand, she could let Gatlin think she was too dumb to have covertly followed DeLeon, or she could admit that he caught her at it. She chose the latter. "I was sure he had no idea I was shadowing him through the campus, but when I tried to pick up what I thought was a cigarette butt he'd discarded but was actually an intact cigarette he used to bait me, he came up behind me and wanted to know what I was doing."

Gatlin nodded. "Okay. Good thought . . . poor execution. If I had to choose I'd pick ideas over technique every time. It's impossible to teach a detective how to think. Technique comes with time. So don't worry about it. What about Leo Silver?"

"Haven't really worked on him."

Gatlin took out some folded papers from his jacket pocket. "I got Betty Bergeron's phone records for the two weeks before she was killed. She didn't use her phone much . . . two calls to her parents, three to her apartment mate, two to a classmate in molecular genetics, three to Gator Willie's . . . and six to a number I've traced to a burner phone."

"You mean one of those prepaid phones you can buy without giving your name?" Kit asked.

"Yes. She also *received* six calls from that phone."

Knowing that drug dealers commonly used burner phones, Kit looked at Broussard. "Any evidence she was using?"

Broussard shook his head. "Tox screen for commonly abused substances was negative."

"It's not just crooks who use burner phones," Gatlin said. "Some people would rather not have the hassle of the paperwork associated with a cell phone plan. They use up the minutes on the phone, then buy more for cash."

"Doesn't pass the smell test to me," Kit said. "I think she and the owner of the burner didn't want any record that they were talking to each other."

"Why would that be if it wasn't drugs?" Gatlin asked.

"Maybe she wasn't using, she was dealing. And that somehow got her killed," Kit suggested.

"Workin' as a bartender she probably barely made enough money to cover her livin' expenses," Broussard said. "Who's been payin' her tuition?"

"I don't know," Kit said. "But I'm going to find out." She looked at Gatlin. "We may not know who owns the burner, but can we get tracking data for it?"

"We'll see," Gatlin said. "It's already in the works. Okay, moving on to Uncle Joe."

Kit walked over to the sofa and sat down, now realizing that the only things she'd written on the board in Betty's column were the names of her two suspects.

Gatlin picked up the whiteboard marker and put Howard Karpis's name under the heading for Uncle Joe. "Haven't done much more on this guy," Gatlin said. "But to summarize what we know: He's admitted sending threatening notes to Joe, and the alibi he gave me for Saturday morning was a lie. I've requested a subpoena for his phone records and tracking data, but so far don't have it.

"Now for Joe's son, Lewis." He put that name on the board under Karpis's. "As Andy said, he's in line for a quarter of Joe's estate as an inheritance. And he needs it because he overextended himself in opening a second location for his gun shop."

"Gun shop . . ." Kit said.

"That got my attention too," Gatlin said. "Plus he was a marine captain. I didn't ask but I'm betting he could make an accurate 200-yard rifle shot with no problem. He was supposed to be at the picnic but said he was so sick that morning he stayed home. But did he really? His wife has been in Amarillo since last Wednesday. She hasn't been around to monitor his movements. Instead of home in bed on Saturday, he could have been in that boat at the picnic."

"Does he own a boat?" Broussard asked.

"He does. Earlier, either you or Kit mentioned that the killer might have cased the swamp around the picnic area looking for a fisherman who's there every day. He could have done that early on Thursday and Friday and still shown up for work at a reasonable time. Again, with no wife at home to see that he's taking the boat out every day, there'd be no one to question him about it."

"Sounds like he's another guy whose tracking records we need," Kit said.

"And if I can catch him in a lie, I'll be able to go after 'em."

"What about fingerprints on the two guns Joe's killer left in Hartley's boat?" Broussard asked.

Gatlin's expression soured and he shook his head. "Got nothing from either one. Both too oily."

"Cartridges then," Broussard countered.

"Clean . . . maybe wore gloves while he was handling them." Gatlin looked at the whiteboard and made a sweeping gesture toward it as though it contained everything they'd just said. "Okay, Andy, connect the dots we just laid out for the two murders."

"We need more dots."

"Glad to hear it," Gatlin said. "I was afraid you come from the same school of dot connectors that drew the constellations. You ever really look at those things? Five dots to make a woman holding a mirror . . . six for a crab . . . nutty."

"Sometimes you have to be willin' to believe before you can see."

"Jesus, you sound like a priest." He crossed himself for saying 'Jesus.' "You been spending too much time with Grandma O."

"Ring of Fire" sent Gatlin's hand to his pocket for his phone. "Gatlin." He listened for a few beats then nodded and said. "On my way." He looked at Broussard. "We'll need you, too."

"For what?"

"Double homicide."

"Where?"

He recited the address and Kit shot to her feet. "It's Betty Bergeron's parents."

Chapter 25

Broussard crossed the Bergeron's living room and slowly made his way toward the hall on the other side, where just around the corner to the right, Gatlin said he'd find the first body. They'd waited for the crime scene team to do its work, then, because the space was so narrow, Gatlin had gone in first, alone, and done his walkthrough. Now it was Broussard's turn.

Nearing the hallway, Broussard saw a trail of bloody footprints that came out of the hall, then turned and continued toward what he believed was the kitchen.

Avoiding the footprints, he moved forward into the hall and immediately saw to his right, a body, face-up, sprawled on the carpet. The victim was dressed in blue-striped pajamas soaked in blood from a crushing head wound so horrendous it took a moment for him to realize he was looking at a male. Next to the victim's right hand was a large carving knife. About eye level on the wall directly up from the body's feet, there was a dent in the sheetrock. Taking into account the fact the head wound was on the victim's right side, it didn't take a genius to figure out that the dent in the wall came from the victim's head bouncing off it after being struck by something that gave the killer a great deal of leverage. For want of a better possibility, Broussard believed it could have been a baseball bat.

Kit had said Betty's parents were Acadia and Paul. He'd also seen that on the pedigree he'd constructed while talking to Amelia. Most likely, hearing some noise in the living room, Paul had grabbed his knife and crept down the hall to see what was going on. The killer meanwhile, had positioned himself to the right of the doorway. Then, perhaps a board squeak gave Paul's position away. Whatever the reason, his killer had stepped around the wall and started a vicious swing of the bat at the same time. The result now lay on the carpet.

Broussard bent over and tried to manipulate the victim's right arm and leg. From this he learned that the body was in full rigor. The need to bend over a corpse whenever he went into the field was one reason he wore a bow tie rather than the long kind.

He stood up and looked down the hall. About six feet ahead, there was a door opening on each side of the hall. The bloody footprints had come out of the one on the left.

Careful not to step on any of the footprints, he moved forward. There was only a faint coppery aroma of blood in the hallway, but as he entered the master bedroom, the scent filled his nostrils.

Across the room, lying by the bed on one side and a tipped over nightstand and lamp on the other was another body, most likely Paul's wife, Acadia. Blood soaked the carpet around the body and great gouts of it had spattered the adjacent wall and headboard of the bed. There was even some on the ceiling. Broussard moved closer, to where he could see the victim better. The blood alone created a hellish scene, but the condition of the victim's head made it far worse. She'd been beaten so badly that at the killer's trial the defense would surely object to showing the jury any photographs of it. Most of the blood on the wall behind her had come from the weapon striking her, spurting outwards from the compression of the blow. All of it on the ceiling was cast-off;

blood that had been flung from the weapon during both its upward and downward motion.

The victim was wearing a sleeveless nightie that left her arms bare. On the upper part of her right arm near the shoulder, there was a bruise whose size and shape reinforced Broussard's belief that the murder weapon had been a baseball bat. The killer had likely not intentionally meant to hit her there, but had done so during his initial attack, before she'd been rendered immobile.

He checked the flexibility of the victim's appendages and found that, like the body in the hall, she was in full rigor. Broussard surveyed the room, first looking at everything he could see from where he stood. Then, he turned around.

On the floor to the right of a chest of drawers, surrounded by broken glass, a battered picture frame lay face-down on the carpet. The wall above the frame had a dent in it, apparently made when the killer had driven the object off the chest with the bat. Broussard walked over, picked up the frame, and turned it over knowing even as he did what he was about to see.

"Okay, your turn," Broussard said to Kit, who was waiting outside on the front porch.

"Is it bad?"

"On a scale of 1 to 10, I'd give it an 11."

"Maybe I'll just let you describe it to me."

"I've seen you handle other scenes as bad as this with no problem."

"I'm not sure that's a reputation I want."

"Well, I need you to go in and at least look at the male in the hallway and tell me if it's Paul Bergeron. The female is in the bedroom. She doesn't have a face to recognize."

Kit let out a sigh and headed for the front door.

She returned a minute later and said, "It's Paul. The female's hair is the same color as his wife's, she's wearing the same engagement and wedding rings, and she has the same strawberry-shaped birthmark I saw on her hand earlier. It has to be her."

Gatlin joined them from doing something in his car, which was parked by the curb out front. "So what did you think?" he said to Broussard.

"They're both in full rigor. So they were likely killed around 12 hours ago."

Gatlin checked his watch. "That would make it 4:00 a.m. this morning."

"Plus or minus a couple hours," Broussard said. "Weapon was likely a baseball bat. Judgin' from the extent of their injuries, the target was the female. The male was just in the way."

Gatlin looked at Kit. "Been inside?"

"Yeah."

"Can you ID the male?"

"It's Betty's father, Paul. The female is wearing the same rings his wife, Acadia, was wearing when I spoke to them earlier. She also has the same hair color and the same birthmark on her hand."

"Okay, we'll double check it with her dental records, but it's her." He looked at Broussard. "Guess you saw the picture frame the killer destroyed."

"Why was the picture face down?" Broussard asked. "You looked at it didn't you?"

"Thought you'd like to see it as I did."

"Picture of whom?" Kit asked.

"Their daughter, Betty," Broussard said.

"That's who killed them," Kit said. "The same person who murdered Betty." She looked at Gatlin to see if he was ready to connect the dots.

"Seems likely," he said. "He could have gotten in using a key from Betty's missing handbag. Question is, what'd she do to make him so angry at her he'd want to destroy her mother like that?"

"I was hopin' he left the murder weapon somewhere in the house," Broussard said. "But I didn't see it. At least we've got his footprints."

"Which may or may not be useful," Gatlin said. "By now he's likely already ditched his shoes. But he probably was still wearing them when he got back in whatever he used to get here. Kit, I'd like for you to canvas the neighborhood and see if anyone saw a third vehicle in the driveway early this morning."

Kit looked at her watch. "It's nearly five o'clock. People should be coming home from work soon. If it's okay with you, I'll wait until a bit later to start. Meanwhile . . ." She pointed at the morning paper, which was still lying in the front yard. Its continued presence there so late in the day along with both cars still in the drive is what prompted the elderly next-door neighbor to check on the victims. "The delivery car for the paper was probably in the neighborhood around the time of the murder. I'll talk to the carrier too."

"Good idea," Gatlin said.

"That burner on Betty's phone records . . . I'm even more interested in it now," Kit said. "I'm betting the owner is who killed her. When we get the tracking records for it, they should also show he was here."

"Unless he was as cagey as Betty about blocking the tracking function," Gatlin said. "In any event, I'll check and make sure the time period covered includes this morning."

"After we know he's the one, can we ping his burner to locate him?"

"I'd probably be on board with that." He looked at Broussard. "I don't want Paul and Acadia's relatives hearing about this on the news. Any idea who I should contact?"

"She was the daughter of Julien Broussard, one of Uncle Joe's boys. Let me see if I can get you his phone number."

Broussard reached for his cell, navigated to a number in his contacts, and pressed the call button. "Amelia . . . this is Andy . . . Listen, I've got some more bad news. We've just found Betty's parents murdered." Her wail of surprise was so loud Broussard had to move the phone away from his ear. "Yes . . . both of 'em. We're not sure yet exactly what happened, but we want to tell Leona and Julien. No. It shouldn't be you. I'm sure they'll have questions and that'd be best handled by . . ." Broussard suddenly saw who should tell them. "Actually, I'll do it. Do you have their number?"

After a short delay, Broussard said, "Hold on, let me put that in my phone." He added the number to his contacts. Amelia gave him another number and he added that as well. "Thanks Amelia, I'll talk to you soon."

"Don't you have to get back to the morgue?" Gatlin said.

"It'll be awhile before our transport gets here. And in any event, Charlie Franks and Guy Minoux can start without me. I won't be long." Instead of leaving, Broussard rubbed his beard and said, "Remember how back in my office I said we needed more dots? If we use Uncle Joe as one dot and Betty Bergeron as another, a straight line drawn between them would go right through Betty's parents."

Gatlin looked at Broussard for a moment and shook his head. "Being a good detective should mean you never have to say to your friends, 'I realize that.' You might suggest to . . . Leona was it?"

Broussard nodded.

". . . and Julien that the line would also go through them."

Chapter 26

Leona and Julien lived in Lakeview, an area of the city that borders the 1300 acre city park. Broussard had not been there since Katrina put it all under water. Now, years later, after all the rebuilding, the houses and yards looked crisp and clean with lots of young trees and a surprising number so large they must have been flood survivors. Judging by the rough condition of the street asphalt, the city though was not doing its part.

Most of the houses were of traditional southern architecture featuring covered porches and columns and siding that was either wood or something that looked like it. But Leona and Julien had gone another way. With its granite steps and limestone block façade, it resembled a museum. There were no driveways on the street so Broussard parked in front of the house, got out of his T-Bird, and went up the short walk to the front door. In a nearby magnolia, a mockingbird ran through its impressive catalogue of songs, showing why, if a house has a resident mockingbird, the place doesn't need anything else with wings.

Broussard had called ahead and without telling the couple why he wanted to see them, arranged for both to be home when he got there.

It was Julien who answered the bell.

"Hello, Andy. Please . . . come in."

As expected, confusion about the purpose of Broussard's

visit was evident on his old friend's face. Julien taught philosophy at Tulane. Anyone who knew him would never again judge a person's intelligence by appearance alone. Julien had large ears, small eyes, and a cranium that almost looked too small to house a normal brain. Even when he was a kid, Julien always wanted to know the deeper meaning of things. It used to drive Uncle Joe crazy. Julien would catch a fish and ask Joe if the fish thought the people in the boat were all monsters or gods. Once when it began to rain while the sun was shining, Julien asked Joe why things sometimes happen that don't make sense. Or he would wonder why he was born a human and not a worm.

When Julien asked one of these questions, Broussard made sure he listened carefully to the answer because most of them were things he too, wondered about. He just didn't know it until Julien brought it up. Broussard had always believed it was Julien that had taught him to think beyond the obvious.

The large room where Broussard now found himself had obviously been professionally decorated. Even though he was there for a distressing purpose, the beauty of the colors on the upholstered furniture; pale orange, beige, stripes of pale green and burnt umber, could not be ignored.

Leona was standing well away from the door, by a large beige chair bearing a diagonal trio of colored stripes. She had a pleasant, open face that Broussard was sure had far fewer lines on it when he'd spoken briefly to her at the picnic before Uncle Joe was shot. And her eyes now had dark bags under them that had not been present then. She was only related to Joe through marriage to Julien, so Broussard figured most of her haggard appearance had probably come about after learning that her granddaughter, Betty, had been killed. Now he was about to make her life even worse.

Without offering a handshake or a chair, Julien said,

"What's going on?"

Julien was on Broussard's right and Leona on his left, positions that made it impossible to see both at the same time. Eyes traveling from one to the other, Broussard said, "I'm sorry to have to tell you that your daughter is dead."

Leona dropped into the chair behind her and put her face in her hands. His vision focusing on some distant place, Julien muttered, "Dear Acadia . . ."

Then Julien's manners kicked in. "Please, Andy . . . have a seat."

Broussard went over and sat in a chair that was the twin of Leona's. Thankfully, Julien sagged onto the end of the sofa near Leona. Broussard could at least now face them at the same time.

"How?" Julien asked.

Broussard didn't mean to take a deep breath before telling them, but it happened anyway. "She and her husband were murdered, we think, by the same person who killed your granddaughter . . . and possibly . . ." he centered his attention on Julien, ". . . your father too."

"Exactly what happened?" Julien asked with a calm voice.

"It might be better if we didn't—"

"I didn't request, 'better'," Julien said. "Please answer my question."

Glancing first at Leona, Broussard said, "They were beaten to death with some kind of blunt object."

Leona began to sob. Her reaction was distressing to witness but at least it was a normal response. Julien, on the other hand seemed untouched.

"The nature of death is something a philosopher often contemplates," Julien said, so placidly Broussard wanted to smack him. "And it boils down to two possibilities. Death is either a wall or a door. If it's a door, the question becomes what's on the other side of that door. I recently read a book written by a famous neurosurgeon who was essentially brain dead for a week with almost no chance he would survive. During his week of no longer being here, he discovered that death is a door, an opening to a plane of existence he summed up in the phrase 'you are loved.' In that place we become one with the universe and all questions are answered. I once believed death was a wall, but after reading his book, I'm now convinced it's a door. If Acadia and Paul, along with my granddaughter and father, have all gone through that door, there's no reason to be sad about it."

Broussard had from time to time considered those two possible results of death. The biggest problem he had at the moment with Julien's discourse on it being a door was that Julien had made no distinction between those who'd led good lives and those who hadn't. If killers and their victims went through the same door to a wondrous new existence, where was justice in that? Julien's view on death needed work.

He looked at Leona to see her reaction to what Julien had said.

"Julien's IQ is 156," she said. "That's considered by some to mean he's a genius. If that's what he thinks, I do too."

All this was not good news for what Broussard was about to tell them. Of course, if Julien was a genius he'd already figured out what was coming. "Whoever's responsible for these deaths seems to be intent on eliminating everyone in the direct lineage leading from your father to your granddaughter."

"Which means I'm now in danger," Julien said.

"That's right. And so is Leona, only because she may become collateral damage when the killer tries to get at you."

"Like what happened to Paul when the creature went

after Acadia," Julien said. "Do the police have any suspects?"

"Several, but right now no arrests are imminent."

"What's the motive?"

"We have no idea."

"I get the feeling you're about to give us some advice."

"Go away somewhere until the killer is caught."

"Where?"

"I don't know, somewhere you're not known. The police here can't protect you. The best thing you can do is disappear for a while."

"We have a funeral . . . actually now three funerals to arrange."

"Betty and her parents can wait. There are ways to keep them . . . until the time is right."

"It seems to be a universal belief that self-preservation is a person's primary function," Julien said. "But in the big picture, once someone passes reproductive age, they are of no value to the species. That's why so many diseases appear in women after menopause. And even though men can still make sperm into later life, a high percentage of those spermatozoa are faulty. It's no great loss to the species for disease to take older men as well."

"You don't care if you live or die?"

"Maybe the door leads to a better existence."

Broussard looked at Leona. "Does he speak for you on this too?"

"I don't want to die, but if Julien believes we shouldn't hide, I'll stay with him."

"I think you're both nuts."

"Read the neurosurgeon's book," Julien said.

"Okay, you won't hide, but let me ask, do you know of anyone who hates the family enough to be doin' this?"

"My father was a powerful man and not altogether a

likeable one, at least not to people who worked for him. I'd look there."

"Any other ideas?"

Julien shook his head.

Broussard looked at Leona, who did the same thing.

"The police need to contact Paul's next of kin," Broussard said. "Do you know who they should call?"

"I believe we *can* help you with that." Julien said.

As Broussard headed back to the morgue after talking with Leona and Julien, he thought about *The Tall Stranger*, the Louis L'Amour western he was reading at home for at least the sixth time. He loved L'Amour's stories for their moral clarity. In the land of L'Amour, there was no ambiguity, dead was dead, no talk of walls and doors. And evil got what it deserved.

In that story Morton Harper tries to trick a wagon train into heading west along a route that will bring them into danger. Rock Bannon warns them about the route and about Harper's motives. But like Julien, no one listens. And people die.

Julien wanted him to read the neurosurgeon's book. Maybe he should have struck a deal, got Julien to read about Morton Harper. Surely being a genius he'd have seen the point.

Chapter 27

Kit had high hopes the paper carrier would have seen the killer's vehicle in the Bergeron's driveway, but her optimism had been crushed by the carrier not even remembering how many cars had *been* in the drive. His lack of awareness most likely had something to do with the smell of pot that enveloped him like a cocoon even though he wasn't smoking it when they'd talked.

Nor had any of the Bergeron's neighbors noticed a strange vehicle in the drive. So as she headed for home via the garage on Dauphine Street, she felt useless and spent. At the garage she paused for a moment to admire the new burglar bars on the windows, a respite that gave her a brief moment of satisfaction in an otherwise frustrating day. And of course, she'd also found a hand car wash that was able to clean the magic marker writing off her hood. Whoopee.

She opened the garage door, drove inside, and parked. As the door closed, her phone rang. It was Teddy.

"Hey, how's your investigation going?"

"Terrible. Not only do we have no idea who killed Betty, this afternoon we found both her parents dead."

Teddy made a sound that reflected at least three different emotions. "They certainly didn't start you off on an easy one."

"We do have one lead. Betty's phone records show she recently made a lot of calls to a number tied to a prepaid disposable phone. I think the owner of that phone killed all of them."

"Why?"

"We believe he was angry over something."

"How you holding up to all that responsibility?"

"I'd be doing better if you were still here."

"Maybe I'd be in the way."

Kit was of two minds on this. Sure, it'd be great to see him, have him hold her in his arms, but could she clear her thoughts and give him her full attention for the evening? Could she partition herself into one compartment for investigator and another for fiancée? Damn it. Where they would live after marriage was not their only problem.

"Have I lost you?" Teddy said, responding to the gap in the conversation.

"I'm here. I can't imagine you ever being in the way. How was *your* day?"

"Didn't get bitten or have to shoot any of the gators to save my life. I'd say it was successful."

"Don't lose any parts. I'd like to keep all of you."

"I like that. It'd make a good bumper sticker. 'Don't lose any parts.' Who could argue with that?"

"I'm sitting in my car in the garage, and the lights are about to go out. So I better go. Love you."

"Me too. We'll talk later."

Keeping her key ring and lipstick mace canister in hand, she got out of the car, walked to the pedestrian door, and stepped outside.

It was nearly seven o'clock and she hadn't yet eaten dinner. Tonight seemed like a good one for a burger at Bunny's Bar and Grill near the corner of Toulouse and Bourbon. But first she needed to go home and check on Fletcher.

When he heard the street gate open, Fletcher shot out of

his doggy door and dashed down the outside steps. She found him jumping up and down with his front paws on the fence, his mouth open, and his tongue hanging out.

Physically, there are two kinds of Westies. One has a longer snout than the other. Though both are cute, the short-snouted ones are impossibly appealing. Fletcher was the latter. Though there was a chance he'd get her dirty if she picked him up, she did it anyway, receiving in turn, his smooth little tongue all over her face.

She scratched his neck briefly, then put him down and went upstairs to make sure his water and food dispenser were working properly. Satisfied that all was well, she looked at him and said, "All right varmint. I'm going to get something to eat. Be a good boy while I'm gone."

Fletcher's ears flipped up to full alert and he cocked his head, trying *sooo* hard to understand. For that brief instant, the dark burden of what happened to the Bergerons left her. But as she went down the steps a moment later, Fletcher at her heels, the dingy specter of their deaths returned.

Rounding the corner at Toulouse and Bourbon, she was hit in the face by one claw of a huge rubber crawfish hat worn by a short guy with a beer in his hand. As she disengaged herself from the encounter and went on her way, she shook her head at the things that could happen to a person in the Quarter.

Bunny's was about half full; five guys at the bar and four occupied tables. Seeing her come in, Bunny waved from behind the bar. Over the sound of Garth Brooks singing, "Friends in Low Places," Bunny called out to her, "Be right with you sweetie."

Kit took a table under a poster showing Bunny in full costume, the way the old gal looked when she'd been one of the hottest exotic dancers on Bourbon Street. Back then she was billed as Bunny LeClair, a name she still used even though the years had stolen her beauty so she now looked nothing like she did when she was young. Kit was one of only a small number of Bunny's friends who knew her real name was Lefkowitz.

As Bunny came her way, Kit once again admired how Bunny had accepted her changed appearance with good natured resignation, refusing to have even the smallest nip or tuck.

"Hey girl, haven't seen you in a while," Bunny said. "Wait, what's that on your ring finger?"

Kit put her hand out to let Bunny take a look.

"Teddy LaBiche right?" Bunny said.

"Who else?"

"I dunno. Women who look like you do get a lot of opportunities."

"It's been Teddy for years and still is."

"I like a woman who knows her mind. So what are you havin'?"

"A double Bunny burger all the way, parmesan fries, and a Fat Tyre."

"You must have had a rough day."

"I'm trying to forget it for a while."

"Then I'll clam up and get your food."

Bunny had the jukebox rigged for free play, allowing each patron to pick up to three songs at a time. Tonight, Kit didn't want to hear any lyrics about death, so she went over and made choices that were all upbeat.

As she returned to her table, Garth Brooks ended and her first selection; George Jones's "I Don't Need No Rockin' Chair," filled the room.

While waiting for her food, Kit looked around at all the pictures of Bunny when she was young. What must it be like to be defined by your looks and then lose them? Most likely no different than retiring from a career as a death investigator. In both cases, that earlier person no longer exists and you just have to live with it. Not thoughts she needed right now.

She let her mind shift into cruise control and simply listened to the music.

The beer that Bunny brought her was ice cold and wonderfully tangy, a perfect complement to the rest of the food she'd ordered. Just as she finished eating, the jukebox began to play, "He Stopped Loving Her Today." Great, the world's saddest love song . . . featuring . . . DEATH.

Suddenly needing the freedom of the streets, she left a generous tip and carried her check to the register, where Bunny took her money and said, "Sometimes I think I should remove that song from the playlist."

"I know what you mean," Kit replied, putting her change away. "Stay out of trouble."

As usual after dark, Bourbon Street was full of tourists, many of whom were drunk, half drunk, or wanted to be drunk. But on Toulouse there was much less foot traffic. When she was about ten yards from her courtyard gate, she saw someone who'd been walking ahead of her step up to the gate and pin a piece of paper to it. Then he got a marker from his pocket and began to write on the paper.

Kit slipped up silently behind him, stepped to the side, and looked at the paper.

On it was a picture of a dog hanging from a tree. So far he'd written: WHAT WILL HAPPEN . . .

Seconds later, she put the barrel of her Ladysmith against the guy's right ear and said, "That's a .38 you feel. Drop your arms to your side and turn around slowly."

She backed up so he couldn't pull anything funny.

From the elastic band around the back of his head, she'd

already realized he was wearing something over his face. As he turned, she saw that it was a Guy Fawkes mask, the stylized smiling face of the Englishman who famously tried to assassinate the king of England in the 1600s.

"Take off the mask . . . very slowly."

In seconds, she was finally looking at the guy who'd been harassing her. Appearing to be in his early thirties, he had thin, almost manicured brows over eyes half hidden by droopy lids. He didn't seem to care that he'd been caught, because his fleshy lips were formed into an arrogant sneer.

"What's your story?" she said.

"You need to mind your own business. Let the police handle the crime in this city. Keep out of it."

"Give me your driver's license."

His sneer disappeared and his forehead became a washboard of confusion. "Why?"

"I want a souvenir of the occasion."

"Or what, you'll fire that gun? You're a psychiatrist or psychologist; I don't know which one, but either way you're too educated and civilized to shoot me. And there are people around. Look, that guy across the street is on his phone. He's probably calling 911. Shoot me, you'll go to jail."

"Let me tell you a story about why anybody decides to become a psychiatrist or psychologist," Kit said. "It's always because there's something mentally wrong with the person. They want to study human behavior to find out why they're like they are. In my case, I've always wanted to hurt people."

The look on the guy's face changed.

"So I'm thinking my gun will just go off by mistake. Oh, I won't kill you; maybe just shoot you in the foot. You might never walk normally again."

The guy dropped the mask and his hand went for his back pocket.

"Slowly now . . ."

He got out his wallet, removed his driver's license, and gave it to her.

"Okay, you can leave. But now I know where you live. If anything else happens to my car or especially my dog, God help you. Go."

The guy took off, running.

She could have held the guy for the cops, but didn't want to wait around for them to show up. If she'd done that, there'd be a report to file and a lot of her time wasted. Then they'd most likely let him go. Better he should think she was mentally ill.

Some of the people who'd seen the encounter unfold had turned around and gone back down the sidewalk. Those that continued toward their destination had done so at increased speed, keeping as far from the action as possible. The guy who'd been on his phone was still standing there.

She looked at him and waved. "Okay, thanks for coming. See you next time."

She tore the picture off the gate and picked up the mask. She then keyed the lock, and went home for the night, throwing the mask in a bin of construction debris she passed on the way.

Five miles away in the uptown section of the city, Broussard closed *The Tall Stranger,* and sat for a moment, enjoying the resolution of the story. Rock Bannon had foiled Morton Harper's plan to kidnap Sharon Crockett and keep her prisoner until he could break her spirit. Now Harper was dead and Rock and Sharon would soon be married. In a way, Broussard looked forward to the time when his memory of these stories would begin to fade a bit, when he could reread them and not remember what was going to happen next. But that day seemed far off because his memory was as sharp as ever. And right now, it took him back to his conversation with Julien a few hours ago.

Julien believed that death was a door leading to a better existence. That and his refusal to go into hiding made Broussard wonder if Julien had decided he'd rather be dead than alive. Surely not. Even though he didn't show it externally, it was probably just despair over the loss of his daughter, granddaughter, and father talking. Who wouldn't be depressed after something like that? Broussard too felt those deaths deep in his bones.

Beside him his phone rang.

A familiar number . . .

"This is Andy."

"I'm gettin' the feelin' you worryin' about someone," Grandma O said. ". . . Maybe two people."

"I am."

"An' you should be. Dis could be a bad night for 'em. Jus' thought you might want to tell 'em."

Broussard lived daily by scientific principles: Some types of bullets tumble through even the soft parts of a body, others pursue a straight course unless deflected by bone. A burned body with no soot in the lungs means the deceased was dead before the fire. Pooled blood that doesn't blanch with pressure, if found on the buttocks and back of a murder victim face-down in a field, means the body had been moved hours after death. So at first it had been difficult to accept the fact Grandma O sometimes functioned outside those rules. He didn't know why or how, but he'd seen too many examples of it through the years to ignore her when she expressed concern over something. Now, he lived with an uneasy compromise between science and whatever it was that lay behind her abilities.

"Thanks for the advice," he said.

"You' welcome."

As he hung up, the ormolu clock on the mantle began to ring out the time: 11:00. The antique timepiece was a death clock, given the name because the process by which it had been gilded used mercury, a toxic metal that regularly shortened the lives of those who worked with it. Ordinarily, he wouldn't have thought much about the fact it had sounded off right after he'd spoken to Grandma O, but the thing hadn't worked for over a year. Had she somehow been responsible for making it ring? Was it the exclamation mark on her warning? Whatever the cause, he got up and headed for the garage.

Twenty minutes later, Broussard pulled to a stop in the street outside Julien and Leona's home. Inside the house, Broussard saw Julien quickly pass by the open space between the swagged drapes in the front window, apparently to switch off a light, because a second later, the room went dark.

Now that the neighbors were no longer at work, the street was lined with cars, so that the closest parking space Broussard could find was three houses down. Sliding from behind the wheel with surprising dexterity, he left his T-Bird and walked back to Julien's home.

After a short wait, Broussard's finger on the bell brought Julien to the door. Happily, the old philosopher wasn't in his pajamas.

"Andy . . . What's going on?"

"I just saw you walk past the front window. After what we talked about earlier today, I thought you might be more careful."

"Did you really think that?"

"To be honest, I hoped it, but didn't believe it. Do you

own a gun?"

"No, do you?"

"We're not talkin' about me."

"Sure we are, by mentioning you, I added you to the conversation."

By now it was obvious Julien wasn't going to invite him inside. "I want you and Leona to come and stay with me for a few days."

"Look, I appreciate your concern, but we've already discussed this. You know my feelings."

"For a genius, you can be really dense."

"Have you ever convinced someone of your views by insulting them?"

"I'm just worried about you."

"I hereby absolve you of that responsibility."

"You don't get to do that. Only I can."

"I need to look over a lecture I'm giving tomorrow. Thank you for coming. We'll talk again another time."

Julien then shut the door.

As Broussard reluctantly turned and headed back to his car, he heard the click of a lock behind him. At least Julien did *that* much.

Broussard's thoughts rolled the years away. Julien . . . He'd question the meaning of life and then do something inanely stupid because he didn't stop to think ahead. He once jumped in a puddle that appeared to be only a few inches deep, then discovered it was a hole that almost drowned him. And all his life he'd been as stubborn as a doorstop about listening to what anyone said. Once on a fishing trip when he was using a jig with treble hooks for the first time, he caught a white bass. Joe told him to use the pliers to take out the hook, but Julien ignored him. The fish gave a mighty flip and one of the hooks ended up deeply embedded in Julien's thumb.

Broussard wanted to sit out front and keep watch for a while on Julien's house, but with only a distant parking space available, he couldn't. Instead, he drove around to the alley that ran behind the house and parked next to Julien's garage, by the garbage cans, not seeing that he was being as big a doorstop as Julien.

Broussard had some Tchaikovsky and Mozart CDs he could have played in the car, but didn't want to mask any sounds that might signal trouble. So he simply sat there with the engine off and windows down, listening to the crickets that started up a few minutes after he got there. About the time he realized he needed to pee, a light attached to the garage came on, illuminating the area where he sat. He heard the hinges on Julien's back door creak. Suddenly, the fence gate swung open and there was Julien, with a bag of garbage in his hand. And he wasn't happy.

He came around to the driver's window of the T-Bird.

"Damn it Andrew, you're treating me like a child. You're not my mother."

"I don't want you to get hurt."

"We've already had this debate. Now go home."

Given no choice, Broussard fired up the T-Bird, backed into the alley, and drove away.

When he got near the end of the alley he pulled onto the approach pad to another garage, took out his phone, and called Gatlin.

"Hey, this is Andy. I told Julien he and his wife could be in danger, but he won't listen . . . won't go into hidin', won't do anything. He just caught me in the alley behind his house keepin' watch on him and he ordered me to go home, which I have to do. Any possibility you could have a patrol car cruise by periodically tonight?"

"I can try," Gatlin said. "But you know we're shorthanded."

"This is important," Broussard replied. "And be sure they check the alley on each pass."

Chapter 28

The buttered English muffin halves in Kit's oven had turned a nice shade of brown. As she reached in with a case knife and flicked the first one onto a plate, her phone rang. Quickly retrieving the second half and putting the plate on the counter, she grabbed her phone. It was Gatlin.
"This is Kit."
"You might want to come down to headquarters ASAP."
"What's happened?"
"That guy you trailed yesterday trying to get a DNA sample . . . He was pulled in last night on a peeping Tom charge. He's gonna be arraigned in about three hours. Judge could let him go ROR. We need to have a talk with him before that happens."
Kit knew that ROR meant released on his own recognizance, no bail set. "Be there in twenty minutes."

"Down here," Gatlin said, leading the way to one of the Homicide squad interview rooms. "Let me do the talking."
They found Jes Deleon slouched in a straight-backed chair. He was dressed in a black hoodie and black jeans. The sneaker on the foot she could see didn't appear to have any blood on it. The room was oppressively hot.
Gatlin pulled out the only other chair on the near side of the table and sat down. "Mr. DeLeon, I'm Detective Gatlin and this is Detective Franklyn. I believe you two have met."

"Yeah, she was following me the other day. And she wasn't very good at it. You still think I hurt Betty Bergeron?"

"Let's not worry about that right now," Gatlin said. "What were you doing last night when the officer arrested you?"

The room was so hot, Kit's scalp began to sweat. She also saw that above his shirt collar, Gatlin's neck was getting red

DeLeon shrugged. "I was looking in someone's window."

"Were you aware that's a crime?"

"Didn't think much about it."

DeLeon's forehead was wet with perspiration.

"Is that generally how you behave . . . just do whatever you feel like?"

"Pretty much, except I don't hurt people."

"You don't think invasion of privacy hurts people?"

"How could it?"

Gatlin looked at Kit. "Tell him."

"People have to feel safe somewhere," Kit said. "That's what home means to most of us. When you violate that, especially if the victim is young, they may never be able to form close relationships in life. To destroy a person's ability to trust another is a horrible thing to take from someone."

"Boo hoo," DeLeon said.

Kit felt like slugging him.

"Jesus, aren't you two, hot," DeLeon said, wiping the sweat from his forehead. He tore off his hoodie and put it in his lap. Kit instantly noticed that he had four deep scratches on his neck, all of them crusted with dried blood.

"Where'd you get the scratches?" Gatlin said.

"I don't remember."

"Betty Bergeron scratched her killer. That's why I asked."

"I didn't hurt her."

"Does that mean you killed her quickly, so she didn't feel any pain?"

"It means I didn't do anything to her."

"I know how women can be. Sometimes they say things that can make you so angry. Is that what happened?"

"No."

"I'm sure you didn't mean to hurt her. It was more like an accident. I could understand that. And I think a jury could too."

"Do you ever pay attention when other people talk?"

"Go ahead and talk. I'll listen."

"Forget it."

"Okay, tell you what. You say you're not responsible for Betty's death. There's a way you can prove it."

"I don't have to prove it. I know the truth."

"I hate to say this, but there are lots of innocent men in prison. I'm sure some have even been executed for crimes they didn't commit. A lot of the innocent ones have been saved by reexamining old evidence with the new DNA techniques. Why not save yourself a lot of trouble by giving us a DNA sample right now."

Kit held her breath to see if Gatlin would be more effective than she had been asking DeLeon the same question in Audubon Park.

"I want a lawyer."

Gatlin shoved his chair back and stood up. "Do you have one or you want the court to appoint one."

"The last thing you said."

"Someone will be here in a few minutes to take care of it."

Outside the interview room, Kit and Gatlin headed for his desk.

"Why'd you turn the heat up like that?" Kit asked. "Couldn't you have just forced him to take off the hoodie?"

"Didn't want to take any chances with some judge deciding that the misdemeanor he'll be charged with disallowed any degree of forced disrobing. Now, along with what you've learned about him, those scratches should allow us to get a court order for a cheek swab."

"Was he carrying a cell phone?"

"Yeah, but it wasn't the burner we're looking for."

"Where are we on location tracking for the burner?"

"Right where we started, which is nowhere. The phone only made calls to Betty and only received calls from her. And it never moved from one general area. Maybe didn't move at all."

"So where's it located?"

"Can't really tell. I said 'general area' because it apparently doesn't have a GPS chip. That means any location data was derived from cell tower triangulation when calls were made or received. And it's now been turned off, probably thrown away."

"That's some careful planning."

"On each end – both Betty and whoever – No point though in dwelling on what can't be changed."

He was right. But Kit was still very disappointed. "Okay, back to DeLeon. If we can get a court order for a swab, could we also get a search warrant for where he lives and for his phone tracking data?"

"Wouldn't surprise me."

Kit reached in her handbag. She withdrew something and handed it to Gatlin. "Before I forget."

"What's this?" Gatlin said looking at it.

"The driver's license of the guy whose been harassing me for filling in as a detective."

"How'd you get it?"

"Sort of took it from him at gunpoint."

Gatlin stopped walking. "This is a story I *gotta* hear."

When she finished telling what she'd done, Gatlin said,

"And this was in front of witnesses?"

"A few."

"Anybody call it in?"

"Nobody's contacted me about it."

"Okay, I'll take care of it. I'll also find out why this guy's been targeting you. But next time . . ."

"I don't think there'll be a next time. At least not with him."

Chapter 29

"Here's something we need to take," Kit said, coming out of DeLeon's bedroom closet with a pair of sneakers.

"Any obvious blood on them?" Gatlin asked from where he was searching the drawers in DeLeon's dresser.

Needing better light, Kit went to the window. "Doesn't look like it."

"Crime scene got some excellent samples of the tread pattern on the killer's shoes from the scene at Betty's parents. Even if there's no blood, a tread match would be a major discovery."

Kit slipped the shoes into a paper evidence bag and put the bag in one of the cardboard evidence boxes they'd brought. After the interview with DeLeon, they'd also taken possession of the shoes he was wearing. Even as Kit and Gatlin searched the apartment, the crime scene team was crawling over DeLeon's car, looking for traces of Paul and Acadia Bergeron's blood or any evidence that Betty had been in it.

Finished with the dresser, Gatlin shut the bottom drawer and said, "I'm gonna check the next room."

If DeLeon was their guy, the clothes he was wearing when he killed the Bergerons would have been covered with blood. Even though it didn't seem likely he would be so stupid as to keep those clothes, Kit returned to the closet and one by one removed the shirts and pants hanging there, taking each item to the window, where she looked for evidence of incriminating stains. She didn't find any.

There were two small cardboard boxes on the closet shelf. She pulled down the first one and looked inside.

What the . . . ?

It held a dozen or so plastic bags each containing a single object. She took the box to the window and put it on a nearby table. The first bag she removed held a cameo broach, the next one, a charm bracelet. Each of the others contained another small piece of jewelry.

She returned to the closet for the second box. Even in the dim light she could see that the bags in this box each contained a small wad of hair.

She quickly left the room and went down the hall, where she found Gatlin rummaging through a closet in the next room.

She hurried over to him. "Look at this."

Gatlin pulled his head out of the closet and turned around. Seeing the box, his expectant expression downshifted to one showing only mild interest. "I was hoping you'd found a baseball bat." But when he saw the bags of hair in the box, his bushy eyebrows arched upward and he reached for his phone.

"Andy . . . Philip. Did you check on Julien this morning?"

He'd put the call on speakerphone so Kit heard Broussard say, "Called him this mornin'. Wife said he'd just left for work."

"That's good. Maybe we're wrong about him being in danger."

"Too soon to relax about that."

"Relaxing isn't on my schedule just now. Say, you probably didn't notice when you did the post on Betty Bergeron, but could you check and see if any part of her hair looks like a piece has been chopped out?"

"Don't have to check. I already know. So any hair you've found isn't hers, unless it's only a few strands."
"Well, it's more than that. What about her parents?"
"C'mon Phillip . . ."
"I know, desperate question. But I could use some cooperation here."
"Where are you?"
"Still at DeLeon's place. He's a nut job of some type. I just can't be sure yet he's *our* nut job."
"You drop his saliva sample off at Tulane?"
"Right before we came here."
"Who'd you give it to?"
"The guy you told us about."
"Directly to him?"
"Handed it to him myself."
"He say when he'd do it?"
"Not exactly. 'Soon' was all he said. Remind me, I've got it written down, but what was the blood type of the person whose skin was under Betty's nails?"
"Type A."
"Think the guy at Tulane would be upset if I called and checked on it?"
"I'm sure he wouldn't"
"Anything of interest show up during the post of Betty's parents?"
"She had ovarian cancer that had metastasized to her liver. Probably didn't have more than six months to live."
"Poor woman . . . Think she knew about it?"
"Odds are she didn't."
Gatlin made a mental note to schedule a complete medical physical ASAP. But even as he thought about it, he knew he'd never follow through. "When I get DeLeon's blood type, I'll let you know."

He ended the call then scanned his contact list for the Doc at Tulane. Finding the number, he punched the green phone icon.

One ring . . . two . . . three . . . "This is Dr. Cummins."

"Detective Gatlin calling. I don't mean to bother you but . . ."

"No bother detective, that sample you gave me tested as type A."

"That's it then," Kit said. "We've got him."

Chapter 30

"I agree with Phillip," Broussard said, after taking a sip of iced tea. "It's not certain that DeLeon is our guy."

Kit's mouth dropped open and she huffed in exasperation. "Okay, I know we didn't find the murder weapon and so far, neither the shoes he was wearing when he was arrested, nor the ones I found in his closet match the bloody footprints, but he had scratches on his neck, he was in the bar where Betty worked the night she was killed, and his blood type matches the killer's."

"About that blood type," Broussard countered. "It's present in about 40% of the population. From the objection you made a few days ago when I proposed checkin' the tissue under Betty's nails for blood type, I'm sure you knew that."

"So," Grandma O said, the rustle of her taffeta dress announcing her arrival before she spoke. "What you chatterboxes havin' for lunch?"

"Crawfish salad," Kit said, "with Oustellette dressing."

Nodding in agreement that she'd made a fine choice, Grandma O looked at Gatlin.

"Debris po'boy and alligator chili."

"What about you, City Boy?" Grandma O said.

"Think I'll eat light today; Crab and shrimp gumbo . . ." he held up a stubby finger, ". . . a bowl not a cup, a muffaletta, and a double order of honey cornbread."

Grandma O looked down her nose at him. "You prepared

to eat all dat, I hope."

Broussard cupped his ponderous belly. "How can you possibly ask me that?"

"Jus' checkin'." She cocked her head. "Anything happen las' night you wanta tell me about?"

"Everything turned out fine."

"Well, my timin' might have been off a little." She turned to go then spun back toward them. "An' about dat killer who left da bloody footprints, don' you ignore what Kit's tellin' you."

"Were we talking that loud?" Gatlin said, looking around to see who was nearby.

"Don't worry about it," Broussard said. "In here, she knows everything."

"What did she mean 'her timing might have been off'?"

"She called me last night warnin' that I should keep an eye on the people I was worryin' about." In response to Gatlin's puzzled look, Broussard added, "Julien and Leona."

"How'd she know about them?"

Broussard shrugged.

"What's the main reason you two are not sold on DeLeon?" Kit said.

Gatlin continued staring at Broussard for another few seconds, trying to make sense of Grandma O's phone call, then turned to Kit and said, "Motive. I can see how an argument between Betty and DeLeon could result in her death, even though I still don't know why she would have voluntarily gotten into his car at the dollar store. But let's say, I give you that. I think we all believe Betty's killer also murdered her parents . . ." He paused. Sensing he was checking to see if she agreed, Kit nodded. He then looked at Broussard, who did the same. Shifting his attention back to Kit, he said, "Okay, why'd he do *that*? And Andy thinks Betty's killer also did Uncle Joe."

"Excuse me," Broussard said, "but after Betty's parents were killed, you wanted on that same horse."

"Okay . . . okay. The point is, what's the connection between DeLeon and Joe?"

"Just because we're not smart enough to have figured out the motive doesn't mean we're wrong about him," Kit said.

"Don't misunderstand me," Gatlin said. "I'm not convinced he's the wrong guy. But it's gonna take weeks for the DNA results to come back. So I don't want to just sit around and ignore other possibilities. And I've got two that are under my skin. One is Howard Karpis, the guy that threatened to kill Uncle Joe after Joe fired him."

"And he lied to you when he said he was fishing somewhere else the morning Joe was killed," Kit said.

"That's not all. When we were talking about Joe being killed, Karpis mentioned Deuteronomy 5:9. I made a note of that after I finished talking to him, but didn't give it any thought until Betty's parents were killed." Gatlin took out his little black detective notebook, turned to a page in the middle, and said, "Either of you know the passage?"

Kit shook her head.

Then Broussard said, "Thou shalt not bow down thyself unto them, nor serve them: for I the Lord thy God am a jealous God, visiting the iniquity of the fathers upon the children unto the third and fourth generation of them that hate me."

Gatlin's face fell. During any investigation when the assembled facts had accumulated to a significant tipping point, each of them wanted to state the conclusion before the other. In this case, Gatlin had been sure he had the upper hand.

"How the hell did you know that?" Gatlin said, his rare use

of a curse word showing how upset he was.

"My grandmother was a big fan of me learnin' the more popular biblical passages."

"Well, you could have at least paraphrased it instead of quoting it word for word. Anyway, there's the motive we been missing."

"That's a major case of hatred," Kit observed.

"He has a history of that kind of thing," Gatlin said. "Years ago he served ninety days in jail for assaulting the other driver when the two of them had a minor traffic accident. Then had to attend mandatory anger management classes."

"When you two spoke did he have any scratches on him?" Broussard asked.

"A couple on his arm."

"He sounds plausible to me," Broussard said.

"Me too," Grandma O said, steaming over to the table with a big tray holding their food.

"Hey," Kit said to Grandma O. "I thought you were on *my* side."

"Chil', the truth don' have sides."

While they all ate, conversation flagged as each of them spun mental webs around the various facets of the four murders, hoping to collect them into a unifying explanation. Finally, when the meal was over Broussard said, "What are you two gonna do now?"

"While I was obtaining the search warrant for DeLeon's place, I also got one for Karpis's house and truck and for a cheek swab. Just too many questionable issues about Karpis's behavior for a judge to ignore."

"Did you ever get his phone records?" Kit asked.

"Yeah, but they didn't show anything. He didn't make any calls during the time he was supposedly fishing on Saturday morning or any time around Betty's death. And there was no tracking data for those periods either. Must keep his phone off most of the time or has it set not to track."

"Any cell tower calling data for the night Betty's parents were killed?"

"Didn't know about them when I subpoenaed his records. For whatever it's worth, I'll send another request."

"How are we going to do a decent job searching Karpis's truck?" Kit asked. "I mean, suppose we see a stain in it we think is blood. What then?"

"We'll look at the crime scene techs who are going with us in their van and say, 'Is that blood?'"

After they'd all paid and were headed back to their cars, Grandma O pulled Broussard aside, "I think you should check again on dose people we talked about las' night."

Broussard nodded. Grandma O wasn't the kind of person who took it lightly if you disagreed with her about anything. Sometimes when Broussard nodded at what she'd said, it wasn't because he agreed with her, it was just designed to keep her calm. But in this case, he was already so edgy about Julien and Leona he fully intended to take her advice.

Broussard slowed his T-Bird to a crawl as he passed the house that looked like a museum. From the front, nothing seemed out of place. Resisting the urge to just go up to the front door and knock, he continued down the street, made a right turn, and entered the alley behind Julien's house.

A few heartbeats later, as he approached the couple's garage, he saw that its door was open. Julien had left for work hours ago. Why would the door still be open, making the contents of the garage available to anyone who felt like taking something?

Dreading the next few seconds, Broussard drew even with the garage interior.

Oh-oh. Both cars were still inside.

Without bothering to pull into the alcove by the garbage cans, Broussard cut off the T-Bird's engine and oozed from behind the wheel. He hustled around the front of his car and stepped into the garage's dim interior. Two steps more into the space between the two vehicles and he saw what he'd hoped wouldn't be there. On the garage floor, sticking out from in front of the SUV on his right he saw a pair of trousered legs.

Moving forward, his eyes now growing accustomed to the poor light, he saw Julien lying on his back, rivulets of drying blood running onto the cement from a bullet hole in Julien's forehead, one through his left cheek, and another through the bridge of his nose. Clearly, those three shots had been enough to end his life. But his killer hadn't been satisfied, for the region of Julien's pants that covered his groin was also soaked with blood.

Chapter 31

"How do you see it happening?" Gatlin asked, while the crime scene team was finishing up their documentation of the carnage in Julien's garage. Standing beside Gatlin, Kit listened attentively to what Broussard would say. They had been summoned back to the city by Broussard's call before they'd even reached Howard Karpis's home.

"I think the killer was waiting behind one of the garbage carts in the alcove," Broussard said. "When he heard the garage door open, he darted around the corner, ran past the car on the left, and hit Julien with one of those shots to the head just as Julien shut the backyard door behind him."

"Yeah, I saw that bullet hole in the door," Gatlin said.

"Julien must have done a pirouette to the left and collapsed in front of his car. The killer then moved in and most likely emptied his gun . . . two more rounds in Julien's head and the rest into his groin."

"Pretty brassy to do it in daylight right where anybody going down the alley could see him," Gatlin said.

"We're about in the middle of the block," Kit said. "Could be he figured odds were good that anybody leaving their garage would take the shortest route to the street and wouldn't pass by." She looked at the garage on the opposite side of the alley. "But that one could have been a problem."

"Anybody would've come out of there at the wrong time, they'd be dead too," Broussard said.

Gatlin rubbed his face, fuzzing his eyebrows with his big hand. "All the casings littered over the floor say he was using a semi, most likely with a suppressor on it."

"Guy has access to a lot of weapons," Broussard said.

Gatlin nodded. "Like someone who owns a gun shop."

"Julien's brother, Lewis?" Kit said.

"Yeah."

"What would be the point?" Kit asked. "You got interested in Lewis when you found out he needed money and would get a quarter of Uncle Joe's wealth. Now, won't Julien's share go to *his* estate?"

"Depends on how the will is written and whether probate has already occurred," Broussard said.

"Something we definitely need to know," Gatlin replied.

"Let's say Julien's share *would* be divided among the other heirs," Kit said. "We all agreed earlier that Julien was in danger from whoever killed Uncle Joe, Betty, and Betty's parents. How does *that* fit with a financial motive?"

"Work in progress," Gatlin said. He looked at Broussard. "How's Julien's wife doing?"

"Not well. Her sister's in there with her now."

"How about *you*?" Kit asked.

"We knew this was gonna happen and still couldn't stop it. I'm upset."

"You tried. He just wouldn't cooperate," Kit said.

"I should have found a way to convince him."

"Stop it. What you're doing is natural but that kind of thinking destroys people who've suffered a loss."

"I'm not gonna be destroyed, just unhappy for a while . . . Maybe a long time."

"All the dots are now connected," Gatlin said. "Should mean the killer is satisfied."

"Unless we don't understand the point of it all," Broussard

replied. "And of course we *don't*."

"On the bright side, we know almost to the minute when it happened," Gatlin said.

Broussard made a sour face. "I'd call it useful, not bright."

"Sorry, I was just thinking how I'll be able to pin our suspects to the wall when I ask 'em where they were when Julien walked out here this morning. But I see your point. I wasn't trying to minimize the gravity of it all."

"I know."

When the crime scene investigators were finished and after Broussard, Gatlin, and Kit had a chance to see all the details of the tragedy for themselves, there was general agreement among those with the appropriate knowledge of firearms that Julien had been killed with a 9mm semiautomatic handgun equipped with a screw-on suppressor.

Able to contribute nothing more by hanging around, Broussard said, "I'm gonna head to the morgue and get ready to receive him."

Gatlin nodded and looked at Kit. "We need to maximize our efforts. I'll go with the crime scene techs to serve the search warrant on Karpis, while you canvass the people who have garages on the alley."

"Most of those who would have seen anything are probably still at work," Kit said.

"I know," Gatlin said. "Places where someone *is* home, ask your questions then leave your number for whoever's at work to call you later if they have anything to tell us. If you get a description of the killer or the vehicle that was most likely parked in the alcove out there this morning, call me. After you finish here, see what you can find out about those aspects of Uncle Joe's will we discussed."

Two hours later, as Broussard slipped on a pair of rubber gloves, he thought about the professional relationship he'd had with death for nearly four decades. In all that time he'd never done an autopsy on someone he'd known and spoken to mere hours ago. He'd let his assistant examiner, Charlie Franks, do Uncle Joe, but he felt that having failed to protect Julien, he could at least personally see him through this penultimate indignity, his final insult being ministrations of the undertaker.

Broussard crossed the room and approached Julien's naked body. Cleaned of the blood that had stained his skin, Julien's wounds stood out in stark relief against his death pallor. There were three in his head, one in each of his testicles, and one in the glans of his penis. There would be no bullets to recover from the body, because all had made through and through wounds, one lodging in the door of the garage, the others, flattening against the garage floor.

The three shots to Julien's head surely had been enough to kill him. It seemed obvious that the shooter had kept firing because he was enraged at Julien for some reason. But why aim for the groin? To humiliate him by emasculation?

His eyes traveling from Julien's groin upward, Broussard saw the likely reason that as a kid, Julien would never let anyone see him without a shirt. He had an extra pair of rudimentary nipples complete with areola, one on each side, below his normal pair. Other than being a fairly common congenital condition and obviously causing Julien embarrassment, they had no medical significance. But the vertical scar extending along the skin over Julien's sternum was another matter. He'd obviously had coronary artery bypass surgery.

Broussard inspected the inner part of Julien's leg on both sides. Then he looked at Julien's wrists. The absence of scars in those four locations meant the surgeon who'd done the heart operation had not taken a piece of replacement vessel from any of those places but had probably used the internal mammary arteries in the chest.

Broussard shook his head. While Julien was being subjected to major surgery, Broussard had no idea what his old friend was going through. And that just didn't seem right. Then his mind shifted to another track. There was evidence that cardiovascular disease had long-term effects on cognitive function. Was that why Julien had ignored the danger he was in when it was explained to him?

Broussard's eyes moved upward to Julien's mouth, which was slightly open. For the first time, he noticed something inside, pushing against Julien's lips. After a quick trip to a nearby drawer for a hemostat, he returned to the body, pulled down on the mandible, and inserted the open jaws of the hemostat into Julien's mouth. Getting a firm grasp on the object, he pulled out a foil-wrapped condom.

Chapter 32

Search warrants must contain a list of items that are being searched for. Gatlin got a delayed start on his trip to serve Karpis because he wanted to update that warrant to include any 9mm semiautomatic or sound suppressor he might find in Karpis's possession. It also was extended to cover any 9mm ammunition that Karpis might have, whether in a weapon's magazine or a box on a shelf.

Because he was occupying the time of a crime scene team and it would be a long drive to where Karpis lived, Gatlin arranged for a patrol car from the Jefferson Parish sheriff's office to first do a drive-by to make sure Karpis was home.

From his previous trip, Gatlin remembered that Karpis's place was just around the bend ahead. At that moment, he got a phone call. Without bothering to check caller ID, he snatched his phone out of the holder on the dash and answered. "Yeah, Gatlin here."

"It's Kit. Found someone who remembered seeing a black pickup parked in the alcove by Julien's garage this morning."

"Before or during the murder?"

"She was sure Julien's garage door was closed . . . so it was before."

"She see anybody in the truck?"

"She didn't remember and no, she doesn't recall the license number or know the make or model."

"Okay, thanks. I gotta go."

Black . . . Like Karpis's truck. He'd already included the truck in the search warrant, thinking maybe they'd find evidence that Betty Bergeron had been in it, or possibly find traces of her parents' blood tracked into it on Karpis's shoes after he'd killed them.

As he rounded the bend and saw Karpis's driveway, Gatlin nodded with satisfaction and thought, *I'm just too good to be a mere mortal.* The Jefferson Parish patrol car that had earlier checked to see if Karpis was home and which Gatlin now wanted with him, was coming toward Karpis's drive from the opposite direction.

In the drive he saw Karpis's pickup and behind that, a red late model mustang.

The cops let Gatlin and the van behind him head in first. With no more room in the drive, the cops parked on the shoulder. As they all got out of their vehicles, the door of Karpis's house opened and a slim blonde with hoop earrings and dressed like that gal who played the female lead in *Grease* came onto the porch, Karpis close behind.

"What the hell is *this*?" Karpis yelled from the porch.

"Search warrant," Gatlin said, holding up the document, "for your truck and house."

"You're blocking my girlfriend's car and she needs to leave," Karpis said.

There looked to be about twenty years difference in age between Karpis and his girlfriend. If Gatlin cared, he might have mentioned to Karpis all the cases he'd worked in which much younger women take a lover their own age and then the two of them end up killing her sugar daddy. But that was Karpis's problem, and depending on how the search went, maybe one he wouldn't have to worry about.

"There's room for her to get out by going around us,"

Gatlin said. "But I'd like her to stay a minute."

"I don't think so," Karpis said, ushering her down the porch steps and toward her car.

"A man named Julien Broussard was shot to death this morning around 9:00 a.m." Gatlin said. "He was Joe Broussard's son. Where were you when that happened?"

Gatlin saw the girl give Karpis a questioning look.

"I'm not answering any of your questions today," Karpis said. "It doesn't mean I know anything about this morning. I just don't like you." He pushed the girl toward the car and opened the door for her.

There wasn't any legal reason Gatlin could detain her, so he let her go.

While the girl carefully backed her mustang down to the street, Karpis walked up and defiantly stood in front of Gatlin, hands on his hips. Though Gatlin was at least three inches taller than Karpis, the cops from the patrol car stepped closer to the pair in case Karpis turned physical.

"What's the probable cause for the warrant?" Karpis asked.

Gatlin wanted to say, "your big mouth," but deciding to keep it professional, he simply offered Karpis the warrant and said, "You can read all about it in here."

Karpis snatched the document from Gatlin and headed for his truck.

"Sorry," Gatlin said, "but that's gonna be off limits to you for a while." Responding to the frustration mask that appeared on Karpis's face, Gatlin added, "Yeah, that's also something you can read about."

"So what, I'm supposed to just sit out here on the ground while you all snoop through my crap?"

Gatlin found it hard to believe this guy knew anything about oil exploration. But, considering he'd been fired for not finding any, maybe he didn't. "You could have sat in your girlfriend's car if you hadn't let her leave."

When Gatlin had submitted his paperwork to the judge for expansion of the search warrant, he had briefly considered adding a request for collection of gunshot residue from Karpis's hands. Ultimately, he decided to skip a residue test because contamination of the labs analyzing the collected material had become a big problem. Even the FBI had stopped doing the analysis, something any decent defense attorney would know. But he *had* convinced the judge to include a cheek swab in the warrant.

"I'm gonna need to frisk you for weapons," Gatlin said. "So if you'll just step over to my car, lean forward, and put both hands on the top."

Eyes blazing, Karpis said, "I don't think so."

"Look, Mr. Karpis. You don't have to like me, or what's happening. If I were you, I'd probably feel the same way. But you're outmanned here. The three of us . . ." He motioned to the two cops, ". . . are all bigger than you are, and they've got Tasers. So respect yourself enough not to make us use force to accomplish any of this. We don't want to do that."

Gatlin could see by the subtle way the bonfire in Karpis's eyes began to subside that he was thinking it over. Finally, the set to his chin softened and he nodded. With Gatlin and the two cops following, Karpis walked over to Gatlin's car and took the position.

Gatlin did a quick but thorough pat down then said, "Okay, you can turn around."

With Karpis now facing him, Gatlin said, "That warrant also gives us the right to do a cheek swab. Will you cooperate?"

Karpis hesitated.

"It's not a trick question," Gatlin said. "By agreeing, you're just saying you won't resist."

Karpis nodded again.

Gatlin motioned to the crime scene techs, and one of them came over carrying a plastic box that looked like it might have fishing lures in it. Because the guy was shorter than Karpis, Gatlin said, "Just hand me the swab."

The tech put his tackle box on the ground, briefly fiddled around inside it, then removed a long plastic rod from a paper sheath and handed the rod to Gatlin.

Gatlin turned to Karpis, "Okay, open. This won't take long."

Using the end of the rod that had a toothbrush-like piece of cotton on it, Gatlin rubbed it over the inside of Karpis's cheek for about 10 seconds, glad the swab had such a long handle. Satisfied that he had what he needed, Gatlin removed the swab from Karpis's mouth and handed it to the tech, who carefully put the toothbrush end into a plastic vial containing saline, and detached that part from the handle with the plunger on the other end.

"Okay, one more and we're done," Gatlin said to Karpis.

Karpis scowled. "Earlier, you said *a* cheek swab. That means one."

"Today, it means two," Gatlin said, taking the second swab from the tech.

"Okay, that's it, you can relax." Gatlin said ten seconds later, handing the second swab to the tech. "Now, where can you sit? He looked around. "Under that tree . . . or . . . in the back of the patrol car."

"I'll take the tree."

While Gatlin headed for Karpis's house, the crime scene techs went to his truck. The two cops drifted back to their patrol car, where one got in the passenger seat and began to play with his cell phone. The other one took up a position leaning against the car's front fender, passively accepting his role as watchdog in case Karpis decided to get aggressive.

Gatlin went up the steps to Karpis's house and stepped inside, finding himself in a room covered with knotty pine paneling. All the furniture was rustic stuff, not banged together by some clod, but beautifully crafted. Gatlin particularly admired the coffee table, which had an amazing piece of walnut burl wood for a top. The sofa had stumps of polished walnut for its four legs and stout tree branches for all the rest. The cushions were decorated with Native American designs, or maybe it was something else, Gatlin didn't know much about things like that. Whatever is was, the rug had the same feel to it. All around the room the walls were decorated with color photographs of oil rigs like those he'd often fished around in the gulf, making Gatlin wonder if Karpis had discovered the oil they were pumping. Remembering he wasn't there to gawk, he headed for what looked like a closet.

Outside, the crime scene tech that everyone called, Bluefin or sometimes just Blue, because he always had a tuna sandwich for lunch, noticed a reddish brown stain on the driver's carpet in Karpis's truck. Using a scalpel, he cut out a small section of the stained fabric and took it to the lowered tailgate of the truck. There, he got out a dropper bottle of phenolphthalein, the reagent he'd occasionally add to a detective's coffee to give the guy the runs if he didn't like him. He put a drop of the reagent on the piece of carpet, then quickly followed with a drop of hydrogen peroxide. The carpet promptly turned pink, proving that the stain was blood. Was it human? No way to tell in the field. He'd have to take a bigger sample back to the lab and do another test.

Back in Karpis's home, having found nothing of official interest yet, Gatlin walked into the master bedroom and whistled at the gorgeous king sized bed, which had a magnificent piece of walnut burl for the headboard, and another at the foot. The bedclothes were a mess and Gatlin now caught a distinct whiff of semen and lady secretions, his knowledge of the latter of course, drawing only on distant memories.

Wrinkling his nose at the odor, he went to the closet and began to prowl through the contents. He emerged five minutes later with nothing to show for his trouble. And so it went for another fifteen minutes. Then, at the back of the house, he entered a room that was paneled like all the others, but on the far wall was a huge picture of Joe Broussard, which looked like a color photo of an oil painting. And it was full of holes.

Looking to his right, Gatlin saw a comfortable looking red leather chair. On the tree-branch table to the right of the chair was a 9mm semiautomatic.

Chapter 33

"A condom?" Gatlin said. "In his mouth? Wrapped or unwrapped?"

"Wrapped," Broussard said, shaking his head at Gatlin's question.

They were all sitting around the conference table in the room next to Broussard's office.

"Coupled with the shots to Julien's groin, looks like the killer's motive involves some sexual issue," Kit said. "The only relevancy I can think of is maybe the Deuteronomy quote from Karpis. That had to do with family lineage and reproduction."

"Not sure that's it." Broussard said.

Kit's brow furrowed. "Well, what then?"

Believe me, if I knew, I'd have told you already."

"Speaking of Karpis, I found a 9mm semiautomatic at his home," Gatlin said. "He was using a big picture of Uncle Joe on a homemade bullet trap for target practice. I took the gun and a box of rounds I found there over to the NOPD firing range to see if they can match breech marks the gun makes to marks on the casings from Julien's garage. I also stopped by Tulane and dropped off a saliva sample I took from him." He focused on Kit. "Find out anything about how Julien's death will affect distribution of Joe's estate?"

"I did. Dr. B gave me the phone number of Joe's executor, his daughter, Amelia. The will states that any of the four beneficiaries who die within 120 hours of Joe's death will be considered to have predeceased him and that beneficiary's portion would be shared among the other three."

"That seems weird," Gatlin said.

"I did some research on it. A hundred and twenty hours is the number used in what's known as 'The Uniform Simultaneous Death Act,' which says that if two people die within 120 hours from each other, each is considered to have predeceased the other. The act was created primarily to deal with couples that both die in a car or plane crash but it can't be determined who died first. It provides a way to settle squabbles over who gets the money. It would go equally to claimants on both sides."

"What does that have to do with this case?" Gatlin said.

"I was just explaining where the 120 days came from. In Joe's situation, the lawyer who drew up the will was trying to simplify estate administration by preventing money from being transferred twice. Two transactions would increase legal expenses and double the taxes on the estate."

"I don't care about any of that," Gatlin said. "What's important is, did Lewis know that provision was in there?"

Kit said, "Amelia didn't want to tell me this, but on Sunday afternoon, the day after Joe was killed, Lewis came by her house and asked to see the will."

"She never told me any of that," Broussard said. "And we had discussed the will and Lewis's financial problems that mornin'. So when I spoke to her again on Monday, she could have mentioned it."

"Put yourself in her place," Kit said. "To tell either of us the things she did must have made her feel like she was selling out her brother."

Broussard nodded. "I'm sure you're right."

"Crucial point in all this is that Julien was killed within the

120 hours mentioned in the will," Gatlin said. "So Lewis benefits."

Johnny Cash and "Ring Of Fire" suddenly filled the conference room. Gatlin pulled out his phone and looked at the caller ID. Switching on speakerphone, he answered. "Gatlin."

"This is Dr. Cummins at Tulane. I've got the typing results on that sample you dropped off an hour ago."

He was referring to the one from Howard Karpis.

"Good. What did you find?"

"I'm afraid the results were inconclusive."

"Why's that?"

"The test involves an antibody against either the A, B or H blood proteins. We dry several tiny spots of the sample on a piece of nitrocellulose then treat those spots with each of the three antibodies. If the sample only binds the antibody specific for the A protein, then the blood type is A. If it binds only anti B, the type is B. If it binds both anti A and anti B, it's type AB. If it binds only anti H, it's type O. The most recent sample you left didn't bind any of our antibodies."

"I don't understand. Aren't there only four possibilities?"

"If it's a *blood* sample, yes. But not necessarily for saliva. Are you familiar with the secretor vs non-secretor concept?"

"I am, but it wouldn't hurt me to hear it explained again."

In about 80% of the population, their blood group proteins aren't found only on their red blood cells, but are also secreted into their body fluids, like saliva. But 20% aren't secretors. The subject who provided the saliva sample we just tested is apparently a non-secretor."

"So he *could* be *any* of the four primary blood types."

"Yes."

"Are non-secretors more likely to have one blood type over another?"

"Well, based on the percentages of the various blood types in the population and the fact type O has the lowest percentage of non-secretors, I'd put my money on type A."

"Okay, thanks for doing that." Gatlin put his phone away and looked at Broussard. "That sample from under Betty Bergeron's nails . . . Would we consider that as secretor or non-secretor-derived? Because if it was secretor-derived, we can eliminate Karpis as her killer."

"No way to tell," Broussard said. "There were probably some red blood cells in there as well as the fluid parts of blood."

"So we can't exclude him based on his secretor status," Gatlin said. "Which still leaves us with the most likely possibility that he's blood type A, and therefore remains a viable suspect."

"We need to get a blood sample from him," Kit said.

"Based on what we have now, I'll never be able to get a warrant for one."

"That's ridiculous."

"A blood draw is an invasive procedure. It falls into a different category than a cheek swab. I know these judges. They'll say a DNA profile is the ultimate way to determine guilt in Betty's murder and we can get that from the cheek swab we already took. But even his DNA won't prove he killed Joe. We need something else, like the ballistics results from the gun I found. We get a breech match, I'll arrest him."

Shortly after Kit and Gatlin left, Broussard received a call from the main office on the floor below saying there was a man named Lewis Broussard asking to see him.

Not letting his surprise show in his voice, Broussard said, "Send him up to the conference room."

A few minutes later, dressed in his Marksman Arms work outfit, Lewis walked into the meeting room, where Broussard welcomed him with a hearty handshake.

Broussard gestured to a chair near the head of the table. "Have a seat."

While Lewis got settled, Broussard took the facing chair on the other side and said, "It's been a long time since we've talked."

Hands folded on the table, Lewis said, "Hard to believe we grew up together . . . I mean because we've both done so much since then. Look at you, Chief Medical Examiner."

"Never figured you for a career military man."

"Why not?"

"As a boy, you were very sensitive. Remember what you did when you saw that kid down the street burning ants with a magnifying glass?"

"Did I smash the glass?"

"Yes you did."

"The military doesn't just consist of insensitive louts," Lewis said, indignantly.

"I'm sorry. I didn't mean to suggest that. I was —"

"You of all people should know that some lives need to be forcibly terminated." Realizing what he'd just said and the implications it had for him as a possible suspect in his father's murder, Lewis batted at the air. "You know what I mean . . . purveyors of evil and those who serve them."

Silence hung heavily in the air for a few seconds then Lewis said, "I understand you were talking to my father when it happened."

"That's true."

"I assume you've spoken with that detective who came to see me and therefore know about my financial problems."

"It's been discussed."

"When you were talking to my father, did he say anything about that? My sister Amelia knows, but promised she'd never mention it to him."

"Even if he knew, why would he say anything to me about it, which he didn't by the way."

"I just wanted to be sure."

"Why didn't you tell him yourself? I'm sure he would have helped you out."

"You didn't know him. He would have viewed my problems as a sign of weakness. And would have told me to clean up my own mess. That was one of his favorite expressions. He certainly said it to me enough growing up so I didn't need to hear it again. He respected me for being a marine captain. And I was *not* going to tell him anything that would devalue that."

Lewis looked down at the table. "This was a mistake . . . coming here . . . worrying that you two talked about me – self-centered bullshit."

He pushed his chair back and stood up. "Thanks for seeing me."

Then he was gone.

Left to reflect on their conversation, Broussard mostly remembered Lewis's comment about some lives needing to be forcibly terminated. Was this something Gatlin should know about?

He ruminated on it for nearly a minute, then decided that considering the context, He wouldn't bother passing it along.

Chapter 34

Kit woke the next morning with Fletcher's nose in her armpit. Gently disengaging herself from him, she slid her feet over the opposite side of the bed and sat for a moment, getting her mind in order. She glanced at the clock; 6:14 a.m. She reached over and shut off the alarm before it could ring. She now had no idea who had killed Uncle Joe and the others. Maybe they were wrong about one person being responsible for it all. But she wasn't going to think about any of that for the next hour.

She rounded the bed, lifted Fletcher to the floor, and pulled open a dresser drawer to get her jogging clothes, which consisted of a sports bra, a pair of loose shorts, a long Tulane T shirt, athletic socks, and running shoes. The T-shirt served three purposes. It covered her breasts and her butt, none of which she wanted on display, and also concealed her jogging holster, which firmly held her Ladysmith, her keys, and her phone.

She fed Fletcher, but skipped any breakfast for herself, having learned from experience that running immediately after eating is a bad idea. Fletcher had to stay home because terriers in general would rather smell *anything* than trot along beside you. And he got plenty of exercise through the day going up and down the steps to her apartment. Even so, after her run, she'd take him for a smell around the block.

Reaching her courtyard, she looked up and saw a sky

littered with gray clouds that didn't appear dark enough to worry about. She disliked running on the sidewalk. You could never tell when someone might lurch out at you from a doorway. So, a moment later, when she emerged onto Toulouse, she glanced to her right, made sure there was no traffic coming, then stepped into the street and took off. Heading in the direction of the Mississippi River, she ran close to the left hand curb, where no parking was allowed.

By the time she reached Royal Street and turned left, she was loose and comfortable and moving well. Whenever she was in the quarter she kept her mental state on yellow alert, not white like the blonde she saw jogging a few yards ahead, who, judging by the earphones blocking her hearing, was apparently afraid to be alone with her own thoughts for even a few minutes.

Earlier, back on Toulouse, Kit had noticed a guy dressed in dark blue shorts and a light blue T-shirt leaning on a building across the street. He too, was wearing earbuds and appeared to be picking out some tunes on his phone. Shortly after she'd started running she'd heard his footsteps as he began to jog along the opposite sidewalk. There was nothing alarming about the guy's appearance, but being in the habit of keeping track of her surroundings, she occasionally glanced behind her to see where he was. That's how she now saw him join her on Royal.

Kit and almost everyone else who jogged in this area of the Quarter included Jackson Square as part of their itinerary. At the next intersection, the blonde headed for the Square by taking St. Peter Street. Preferring a different route, Kit stayed on Royal. So did the guy in blue.

Half a block further down Royal, Kit turned into Pirates Alley, a traffic-free passageway about three sidewalks wide that ran along the wrought iron fence surrounding the back courtyard of the St. Louis Cathedral. She wouldn't have become alarmed even if the guy in blue had done the same, but he didn't.

A few minutes later, she emerged from Pirates Alley onto the promenade in front of the cathedral. The cathedral and the square with its huge bronze statue of Andrew Jackson on his horse, Duke, is the most photographed site in the city. Later in the day, the place would be filled with tourists and artists. But this early it was populated mostly by joggers and pigeons.

She quickly went up the steps to the square and followed the outermost circular walkway until it brought her back to where she'd entered. She then headed again to Pirates Alley for the return home. Alert as she was, she was not aware that far to her right, the jogger in blue was watching her intently from behind some shrubs on the edge of the square, near the Pontalba apartments. And he was no longer listening to music, he was talking on his phone.

Halfway down Pirates Alley, Kit glanced to her left, toward Cabildo Alley, the shortcut to St. Peter Street. Seeing nothing of interest, she again turned her eyes forward. As she did, a figure dressed in black and wearing a Guy Fawkes mask stepped into view from the sidewalk on Royal. He was cradling her dog, Fletcher, in one arm. His opposite hand was holding a big knife to Fletcher's throat.

Chapter 35

Kit was consumed with anger at seeing her little dog in danger . . . and from the same guy she'd warned earlier. Stripped of reason by the situation, she pulled up her shirt, grabbed her Ladysmith, and put on a blast of speed to reach the masked creep before he could do anything that might make her kill him. But before she could take two steps, he turned and disappeared down Royal, her view of him blocked by the buildings lining the walk.

Two more strides and something caught her foot. With the sickening knowledge that she couldn't stop herself, she pitched forward onto the pavement, the force of the fall causing her to drop the Ladysmith, which clattered away from her. Before she could even begin to get up, two men also dressed in black and wearing Guy Fawkes masks, came running out of Cabildo Alley. The first one to reach her bent down and jammed a stun gun into her back. Jolted nearly senseless by the charge of electricity that ripped through her, she couldn't do anything to protect herself.

The guy with the stun gun then kicked her in the side, muttering, "You were warned, but wouldn't listen."

The other guy now kicked her in the ribs from her other side, growling, "Mind your own damn business."

Through sheer force of will, Kit rolled over and grabbed the first guy's foot as he tried to strike her again. She pulled his captured leg far enough toward her so she could get her own foot below his crotch. Then she jackhammered him in the balls, the effort of all this encasing her battered torso in a cage of fire.

Howling, the attacker with the crushed scrotum toppled to the pavement. As he did, the second guy gave her another shot in the ribs.

Pain and shock stole her ability for further resistance.

Glaring at her with feral hatred, the guy she'd slammed in the crotch struggled to his feet. To get better leverage, the other one moved back, then lunged at her, one leg already swinging forward . . . more punishment coming. Her eyes focused on the blunt toe of his boot. She couldn't stop him, but she wouldn't make a sound. She'd absorb the blow without giving them any hint of how much they'd hurt her.

Suddenly, she saw a blur swing past her. It hit the guy standing over her in the side of the head and he fell back against the wrought iron fence behind him. In that moment, she saw that the blur was a two by four. And then, her two attackers were gone.

She heard the clatter of the two by four hit the pavement. Someone knelt beside her. A face came into view; Zachery LeBlanc, founder of the construction firm working in her courtyard.

"Do you need an ambulance?" he said, softly.

"I don't know."

"What all did they do to you?"

"Hit me with a stun gun and kicked me in the ribs a couple times."

"You're obviously coherent. If your ribs aren't broken, you probably don't need an ambulance. I've had broken ribs and I know what to look for, but I'll have to touch you."

"Go ahead."

LeBlanc straddled her, put his rough hands under her

T-shirt, and carefully ran his fingers over her ribs. Gentle as he was, even that hurt.

"I don't feel any bulges," he said. "So my opinion is . . . no breaks. But hey, I'm just a workin' stiff. What do you think, ambulance or not?"

"No ambulance."

LeBlanc stood and held out both hands. "Ready to get up?"

Kit nodded and grabbed on. With LeBlanc's help she sat up, the effort sending a barrage of 911 calls to her brain.

"All the way?" he asked.

Kit nodded and he pulled her to her feet, where she kept hold of his hands, waiting for her shaky legs to calm down and the fresh bloom of pain in her chest to fade. "I don't want to spend two hours in an emergency room either. Could you just take me home?"

"We should call the cops and stay here until they come. Then I'll take you."

Kit didn't want to hang around, but the bastards had Fletcher. She had to do all she could to help him. And that meant doing what LeBlanc said. "I agree."

"I'll call," he said, still holding both her hands. "Okay for me to let go?"

Her legs felt stronger now and the pain from being kicked had subsided to rhythmic jolts only when she inhaled. Nodding in answer to his question, she withdrew her hands.

While LeBlanc got on his phone, Kit began to feel a throbbing sensation in her knees. Looking down, she saw bloody scrapes on both of them.

"They're on the way," LeBlanc said. "Stay right there."

He took a few steps toward Royal Street and scooped up her Ladysmith. Returning to her side he held it out to her.

Fully aware that the principles of crime scene analysis

dictated that the gun should have remained where it had fallen, Kit found that she didn't really care. She just wanted it back. So she took it, offered her thanks, and shoved it into her jogging holster. Then she looked to see what had caught her foot and made her fall.

A few feet back in the direction she'd come, she saw a black rope lying across the pavement, one end tied to the base of an ornate street lamp next to the cathedral, the other lying free just inside the entrance to Cabildo Alley. Now the whole plan became clear. Fletcher had been the bait, drawing her attention upward to keep her from seeing the rope.

"C'mon," LeBlanc said. "Let's wait in my truck."

He ushered her back to Royal Street, past a couple of gawkers, and into the passenger side of his truck, which was parked at the curb.

When LeBlanc was seated behind the wheel, Kit said, "How did you know what was going on?"

"I saw this guy with a mask holdin' a dog, like he was showin' it to someone in the alley, then he took off. It seemed so odd, I just looked down the alley as I was passin'. I didn't know it was you, but it was clearly somebody needin' help."

"Lucky for me you were here."

"I was takin' some lumber to the job at your place. I know the rules are no work until 8:30, but I wasn't gonna actually do anything noisy this early, just deliver."

"You don't owe me *any* explanation," Kit said.

"The masks those guys were wearin'... I saw one just like it in the trash at your place."

He paused, his comment obviously an invitation for her to explain why that should be.

"There's a lot to that story, and I don't feel like telling it right now."

"I understand."

It took about 15 minutes for the cops to get there and another five for Kit to tell them what happened. Then LeBlanc drove her home.

When they reached her courtyard door, there were no legal parking places available nearby. LeBlanc pulled to the curb on the illegal side of the street and got out. He came around, helped her down, and saw her to the door, where she said, "I can make it. You go ahead and drop off the materials you brought."

"If you're sure . . ."

"I am."

While LeBlanc went back to the truck, Kit let herself in and slowly walked through the wisteria-topped passageway, the pain in her ribs and the knowledge that Fletcher would not be there to greet her, making each step a vexing ordeal.

Finally, she reached the opening to the courtyard. Dreading the moment when she would see the empty enclosure where Fletcher always waited for her appearance with his tail and ears standing straight up and his mouth open in anticipation, she paused to get control of her emotions. Then she stepped around the corner, and . . . there was Fletcher, perfectly normal and safe.

Chapter 36

"How you feelin?" Broussard asked, looking down at Kit lying on her sofa.

"Stupid," she replied, gingerly repositioning a bag of frozen peas on her left ribs and another on her right side. "To keep from being predictable, I've been thinking I shouldn't go the same route every day when I jog. But I like that way. I didn't want to change it."

"I have to say I feel responsible for this," Gatlin said, standing beside Broussard.

"Please stop hovering," Kit said. "Sit down."

Broussard headed for the big upholstered armchair she'd bought just for him when she'd first moved in. It was the first time she'd needed it. As soon as the old pathologist's rear hit the cushion, Fletcher jumped into his lap.

Embarrassed, Kit shouted, "Down boy." It not only hurt to move, it hurt more to shout.

"He's fine," Broussard said, scratching Fletcher's chest.

Gatlin sat in the narrower version of Broussard's chair.

"Can I get you anything?" Teddy LaBiche said. He'd arrived ten minutes earlier, setting out from Bayou Coteau right after Kit had called him and explained what had happened. He'd made the trip so fast his shadow was still trying to catch up.

Outside, the LeBlancs were doing a lot of sawing, which made conversation difficult.

Broussard and Gatlin both waved off Teddy's offer of something to drink. With nothing for him to do, Teddy pulled a chair over from the counter between the kitchen and the living room and joined the group.

"I should share some of the responsibility for what happened," Broussard said. "I didn't have to let you work for Philip."

"Please, this paternalism is suffocating me."

"We're just sorry you were injured," Broussard said.

"Let's only blame those actually involved. Any progress in finding them?"

"LeBlanc said you kicked one of them in the crotch," Gatlin replied. "We're checking emergency rooms for anyone who came in this morning with injured nuts. So far, nothing."

Shifting one bag of peas to another spot, Kit said, "They were all wearing masks like the guy I caught at my gate. So they either know him or he was one of them."

"He wasn't one of them," Gatlin replied.

"How do you know?"

"He spent the night in jail waiting for arraignment this morning on vandalism charges for what he did to your car."

"Who is he? I mean I know his name, but where does he fit in?"

"He's a cop groupie."

"There are male cop groupies?"

"That's what I call them. Your guy flunked out of the academy and thinks that by giving you a hard time for filling in, he'll ingratiate himself with the department and they'll give him another chance."

"What about the others?"

"Haven't caught 'em yet, but probably more of the same."

"'My guy' as you called him, has to know who they are."

"Soon as I leave here, we'll be having a talk about that."

"Heard anything from ballistics on Karpis's gun?"
Gatlin sucked on his teeth. "Not a match."
"So where does *that* leave us?"
"Lacking good fortune," Gatlin replied. Then, responding to Kit's puzzled look, he added, "Replace that with any crude cliché that occurs to you. He could still be our guy. How dumb would he have to be to leave the murder weapon right out in plain sight."
"What about Lewis Broussard?"
"Still in the picture. I need to see him too."
"You've got a lot to do. I should be helping."
Gatlin got out of his chair. "Take it easy for a day or so, then we'll see."
Over in the big chair, Fletcher was licking Broussard's beard. Seeing Kit watching them, Broussard said, "I want to think he likes me for who I am, but I'm worried it has somethin' to do with what I had for breakfast." He stood and gently put Fletcher on the floor. Gesturing to the little dog he said, "If he ever needs references for a job lickin' folks, let me know."
"Thanks for coming by," Kit said, staying on the sofa. "I'll be a better hostess next time."
Teddy got up and saw them to the door. Before leaving, Gatlin said, "Your courtyard gate wasn't locked. I'm not comfortable with that. I think the guys who assaulted you now believe they've made their point, and we'll get 'em pretty quickly, but it still might be a good idea to keep that gate locked."
"It's not practical with the workmen coming and going," Kit said. "Besides, Teddy's got his gun and I've got mine. Them coming after me up here wouldn't be a good idea."
Gatlin looked at Fletcher. "Too bad your little dog is so friendly. He didn't even bark at us when we came into the

courtyard."

"No one has ever been mean to him. He trusts everybody. I think until you catch those guys, I'm going to keep him inside."

As the two men left and Teddy shut and locked the door behind them, Fletcher darted for the doggy door to follow them down the steps. But Teddy caught him before he could escape. He carried the animal over to Kit and put him on the floor beside the sofa. "It's just for a little while, big boy," Teddy said, rubbing the dog's snout. "You'll be able to go outside again very soon." Teddy then went back to the doggy door and locked it.

"That was good of them to check on me," Kit said when Teddy came back to the sofa. "They're both sweethearts, but don't ever tell them I said that. Mind if I take a little nap?"

"Not at all."

"What will *you* do?"

Teddy shrugged. "Probably go through your lingerie drawer."

Despite the continuing whine of sawing from outside, Kit quickly fell into a sound sleep.

While Kit dozed, Teddy went to her study, sat down at her computer, and accessed his own computer at home. For the next two hours he caught up on his huge backload of e-mail correspondence, much of it involving edits on legal documents involving his real estate holdings throughout the state. Finally finished with all that needed his attention, he tapped into the surveillance cameras around his alligator farm, made sure everything was in order, then wandered back into the living room, where Kit was still asleep. And there was Fletcher, right where Teddy had left him, also sleeping

While watching Kit's rhythmic breathing, he noticed that he could now hear it too. Then he realized why. No saw noise. Curious about how work was going next door and wanting to thank Zach LeBlanc for helping Kit, Teddy slipped out of the apartment and headed downstairs.

Across the courtyard, in front of the wing being renovated, there was a pair of sawhorses with a 4x8 piece of plywood on them. Scattered around the area were many cut-off pieces of plywood and lots of sawdust. On the ground nearby, was a Skilsaw. But no LeBlancs

From the looks of it, all the outside brickwork on the wing being renovated had already been done. The roof also looked new. Like the wing Kit lived in, there were three apartments down and three up. Currently there were no outside stairs to the second floor. The work being done today must be taking place downstairs.

Teddy walked over to the site and paused, listening for any noise that would tell him which of the three apartment doors would lead him to somebody. But all was quiet. Guessing, he stepped up on the porch and chose the closest apartment.

Inside, he found Zach LeBlanc, lying sprawled on the newly installed plywood flooring, blood from his head soaking into the wood.

Chapter 37

Broussard knelt and looked closely at LeBlanc's head, which appeared to have five round holes in it, all delivered from behind. Gently lifting LeBlanc's head, he saw no penetrating damage in the underlying floor, meaning the slugs that killed him were still inside his skull.

But there was something peculiar about those holes. Using a gloved finger, he moved a lock of LeBlanc's hair to the side and played the beam of his penlight onto one of the wounds while he used a Q-tip to remove the clotted blood filling the hole. Just below the surface he saw a dull metallic reflection.

Of course . . .

He turned, leaned down, and played the beam of his penlight on the tip of the object that lay on the floor two feet away. And found what he was looking for.

Grunting at the effort, Broussard stood up. "Never saw it comin'," he said to Gatlin. "Makes me think he was kneelin' when it happened."

"No shell casings anywhere, so it wasn't a semi auto."

"Not unless it shot nails."

Gatlin looked shocked. "You got to be kidding."

"Yeah, I'm a great kidder at crime scenes."

Gatlin gestured at the nail gun Broussard had just examined. "That one?"

"Had to be. There's blood on the tip."

From the courtyard they heard a loud voice say, "I'm his son. I deserve to know what's going on."

Broussard and Gatlin went outside and walked over to the two patrolmen who were keeping Remy LeBlanc from moving freely. Remy was holding a plastic encased saw blade in one hand and in the other, a takeout bag from Hot Diggity Dog, a restaurant a few blocks down Toulouse. Broussard put his chubby hand on Remy's shoulder. "I'm sorry son, but your father's dead."

Remy's eyes widened and began to jitter from side to side. His head soon began to do the same thing. "What happened? He couldn't have fallen, we were only putting the subfloor down."

"Someone shot him in the head with a nailing gun."

Remy's mouth gaped open. "Oh my God. Who would do something like that?"

"We don't know yet."

"I gotta see." Dropping the saw blade, Remy pushed between Broussard and Gatlin and headed for the apartment.

Fearing that he'd contaminate the crime scene Gatlin went after him. "You have to stay out here."

Gatlin caught him at the doorway, where Remy took a quick glance inside, then turned and said. "Are you sure he's . . . gone? Did you check?"

"We checked," Gatlin said, leading him off the porch. When they were both back with Broussard, the old detective said, "You were here with your father this morning?"

"Until about eleven. We needed a sharper saw blade and didn't have it in the truck. I went to the shop and got that one." He pointed at the blade he'd dropped. "On the way back I picked us up some lunch." He showed them the sack he was still holding. "Dad loved their NOLA dogs, the ones topped with crawfish." Eyes tearing, he ground his teeth and screamed, "Who would *do* this?"

He threw the bag of food into a nearby pile of sand then walked over and kicked the bag. He spun around, dropped his butt into the sand, and sat there, elbows on his folded knees, hands behind his neck.

Gatlin motioned for the crime scene techs. "The nail gun behind the victim was the murder weapon. Do your thing and get us some prints."

Despite her bruised ribs, when Teddy had told Kit what he'd seen, she'd dragged herself off the sofa and gone down into the courtyard, where she now stood with Teddy and Nolen Boyd, owner of the property. She had a brief verbal exchange with Boyd, then just as she was about to walk over to Broussard and Gatlin, they came her way.

"There are two surveillance cameras out front," Kit said to Gatlin "Together, they cover the street in two directions. One of them is sure to have caught the killer as he came into the courtyard."

"Exactly what I wanted to talk about," Gatlin said. He looked at Boyd, who, as usual, was wearing a floral Hawaiian shirt, cargo shorts and flip-flops. "Both those cameras in working order?"

"Yeah, but I can't vouch for the recorders," Boyd said, his small mouth a sputtering vent in his mud pot face.

Boyd was a great photographer, capturing images that created emotion in everyone who viewed them. And that seemed odd to Kit, because from the time she worked for him as a clerk she'd learned that he saw life only through a lens that focused on himself. Right now, she imagined that he was wondering if Zach LeBlanc's death meant he'd have to find someone else to finish the rear wing renovations. In contrast, because of how kind LeBlanc had been to her that morning when she'd been attacked, Kit felt that she'd lost a friend.

"Let's take a look at those recorders," Gatlin said.

"We can go in the back entrance," Boyd said, heading for a small porch covered with a tan awning.

Gatlin looked over to check on Remy. Seeing that he was now lying on the sand with his eyes closed, Gatlin followed Boyd, Broussard close behind. Figuring that this very much involved her, Kit took Teddy's arm and they brought up the rear.

Nolen unlocked the back door and led everyone through a framing workshop into a large storeroom with lots of cardboard boxes on metal shelving. Against the right wall was a long wooden table containing three recorders. Fixed slightly above eye level on the wall behind the table were three flat screen monitors. Two of the monitors were showing real time images of the street. The other displayed the counter out front with the cash register.

"Let me see what you picked up toward the river end of the street first," Gatlin said. "Play it forward starting at 10:45."

Boyd stared at the recorders helplessly for a few seconds. "Hell, I don't remember how to work these things."

"They're the same make and model we use at the farm," Teddy said. "I can do it."

Everyone stepped aside so Teddy could reach the equipment.

He punched a few buttons on the recorder that matched the appropriate monitor, and that screen went blank. He hit another button and the image came back, now showing the requested time in the upper right corner.

"Can you fast forward it now?" Gatlin asked.

Teddy hit yet another button and the people on the street and the traffic began to move faster. In the corner of the monitor the time sped by: 10:46 . . . 10:49 . . . 10:54 . . . 11:05 . . .

"Normal speed," Gatlin said. "That's Remy leaving."

There had apparently been no place for Remy to park his truck nearby, so they all watched him walk down the block. This event was interesting only because it established the time that his father had been left alone.

"Okay, speed up again," Gatlin said.

For the next few minutes, they all watched nothing of interest happen in quick time. Then far down the street a dark figure came into view. "Normal speed," Gatlin said.

Over the next few seconds, they saw someone wearing a Guy Fawks mask and what looked like a long raincoat head for the courtyard door.

Chapter 38

Just before going into the courtyard, the miscreant who had obviously killed Zach LeBlanc looked across the street and gave someone out of frame a thumbs up.

"He had a spotter," Kit said. "To let him know when Zach would be alone. And I bet they had one this morning too when I went jogging."

"Looks like retribution for Zach helping you," Gatlin said. "But murder is a big step up from assault. When I talk to the guy who was harassing you, the stakes are now gonna be a lot higher." Then, to Teddy, he said, "Let's see how long he was in there . . . fast time."

They all watched the monitor until the man in the mask reappeared.

"Now normal time."

The killer walked back the way he'd come, not running, just moving at a steady, purposeful pace. Everybody watched the monitor until the killer moved out of camera range.

"We need a copy of what we just saw," Gatlin said. "Anybody got a flash drive?"

Teddy reached in his pocket. "I do."

"You know how to . . ."

"Won't take but a minute or two."

"This guy we just saw couldn't have come from nowhere," Broussard said. "We should be able to use all the surveillance cameras in the area to track him back to where he first hit the street."

"That's what we need to do," Gatlin replied. "And try to find out where he went after the murder. But it's gonna be a big job."

"I'll do it," Kit said.

Gatlin shook his head. "You're in no shape to do *anything*."

"When you came to see me this morning you both said you felt responsible for what happened to me in Pirates Alley. Now I feel that way about Zach's death."

"You wouldn't let us take responsibility for *you*," Broussard said. "Now you want to do it for Zach?"

"Okay, I'm inconsistent. But I won't have to do it alone. Teddy can help."

She looked at Teddy, who said, "I'm in."

"Look, you all can stay here as long as you like," Boyd said, "But I'm going back out front and open up again for business, if that's all right."

Gatlin waved him away. "Go ahead."

Nolen left and shut the door behind him.

"If you feel up to checking those cameras, do it," Gatlin said. "But you need to know some things first."

Then Broussard's phone rang. "I'll take this outside."

While Broussard was on his way out, Gatlin said, "None of the cameras in the Quarter belong to the NOPD. The city couldn't afford to buy its own system. So they're all private. That means there's no central facility where you can tap into the footage from any of them. Most of the owners have registered them with the department and given us contact information in case we want copies of anything they've recorded. I can give you access to the database of contact information, but you'll have to talk to each camera owner and find out for yourself if their cameras saw anything useful."

He took out his little black book, scribbled something in

it, then tore out the page and gave it to Kit. "That'll take you to the contact file."

"I've got the copy of what we just saw," Teddy said, holding up his flash drive.

"Put the system back on real time and let's get out of here," Gatlin said.

Outside, Broussard approached the group. "I gotta get back to the morgue. I called our transport service and they're on the way. When they get him loaded, just send him on. See y'all later."

As Broussard started walking toward the passage out of the courtyard, the group saw Remy LeBlanc approaching. "My mother needs to know what happened," he said to Gatlin. "So I'm heading out to tell her."

"You okay to drive?" Gatlin asked.

"I have to be, don't I?"

"I guess so. Could you give me your mother's phone number and address?"

Remy nodded and recited the requested information. Gatlin scribbled it in his book then said, "Yours too. And the phone number and location of the shop."

When that was all recorded, Gatlin said, "You go on now and see your mother. Again, I'm real sorry for all this." After a few seconds of watching Remy shuffle toward the exit, He looked at Teddy. "That video copy you just made, I'll get it from you later. Now you two better get started checking those other cameras."

"We're on it," Kit said.

While Kit and Teddy went back to Kit's apartment, Gatlin took a last look around the scene.

Earlier, when they'd all watched the video replay of the killer's approach to the courtyard gate, he was already on

Toulouse when they first saw him. As he'd retreated back down Toulouse, the camera lost him before he reached Royal Street. So as Broussard and Gatlin had pointed out, they didn't know where he came from or where he went. Kit and Teddy arbitrarily decided that their survey should include the next block of Toulouse beyond the Royal Street intersection as well as one block in each direction on Royal.

The camera registration database would tell them the address of places that had cameras. But they didn't know the street numbers on the buildings included in their survey. So after Teddy made a quick sketch of their target area, Kit logged onto the street view function of Google maps and helped him put addresses at strategic points on his sketch.

Now they were ready for business.

Locating the registration address of the closest cameras to those on Nolen's shop, Kit picked up her cell phone then looked at Teddy. "We don't want copies of a lot of video footage that's useless. And I don't want to go and personally review footage to decide if it *is* pertinent."

"Just tell whoever answers that we're looking for any footage that shows a guy dressed like our killer. Give them the time frame and see if they're willing to review the records themselves and let us know if they see him."

"That should work."

Teddy now became pessimistic. "*If* we can count on camera owners to cooperate."

"They already agreed by signing up for the registry."

"People don't always honor their promises."

"Next you'll be telling me copper bracelets don't cure arthritis."

Not surprisingly, only about half the registry phone numbers they called were answered by an actual person. Of those, most agreed to check their footage ASAP. But then Kit and Teddy sat there with no return calls for more than 30 minutes.

At 2:34, they got their first response. Kit put her phone on speaker so Teddy could hear. "Detective Franklyn speaking."

"I'm the owner of the cameras at 709 Toulouse," a female voice said. "My system saw your subject come onto Toulouse from the St. Peter direction of Royal Street at 11:28. Then at 11:37, he came back and turned onto Royal in the same direction he originally came from."

Teddy put a plus mark on his sketch at the caller's approximate location, then added an arrow that curved onto Royal.

"Thanks, that's very helpful."

"What did this person do?"

Kit hesitated a moment, trying to decide if she should disclose the truth. Concluding that it couldn't do any harm, she said, "He's wanted for murder."

"Is there a reward for information like I just gave you?"

"Only the knowledge that you've been a good citizen."

"When you were a kid, ever get a box of cracker jacks that didn't have a prize in it?"

"I don't think so."

"Lucky you." Then the caller hung up.

"She sounded nice," Kit said to Teddy.

Six minutes later, they got another call, this time from an address half a block down Royal in the wrong direction. Naturally, those cameras had seen nothing useful.

The next call came from a Toulouse address nearer the intersection with Royal than the previous caller. One of that caller's cameras had also seen the killer turn onto Royal. Teddy put that camera on his sketch.

Feeling as though the two Tylenols she'd taken earlier were wearing off, Kit went into the bathroom and swallowed another.

There ensued a quiet interval that lasted so long, Kit took the opportunity to sit down, close her eyes, and relax. Teddy got on the floor and began to play with Fletcher, who was delighted with the attention. Finally, when both of them grew tired of their game, Teddy stood up, checked his watch and looked at Kit. "Are you hungry?"

"I little," Kit said. "We could go over to Bunny's and get something."

"Let's do that, right after I take Fletcher out for a nature break."

Five minutes later, with Fletcher safely back in the apartment, Kit got another response just as she and Teddy stepped onto Toulouse. This caller was a male. "That guy you're lookin' for, my cameras spotted him gettin' *out* of a yellow cab on Royal at 11:25. Then he came back and got *in* another yellow cab at 11:40."

"Could you see the number on either of those cabs?" Kit asked.

"Hold on."

Apparently the guy was looking at the footage again. After a few minutes he said, "Sorry, no number on either of 'em."

"Would you mind if we came over and watched the footage ourselves?"

"I've got somethin' else I have to do. How long would it take you to get here?"

"We're in the area now. What's your address?"

"Must have been a gypsy cab both times," Gatlin said.

"That's what we thought too," Kit said into her phone. She and Teddy had just finished reviewing the videos from the last caller's cameras and they were now standing at the corner of Toulouse and Royal with Gatlin on speakerphone.

"And you couldn't see even a couple numbers on either cab's plates?" Gatlin asked.

"Sorry, no. Could we put out a plea on TV for whoever picked the guy up to contact us?"

"Not likely someone operating an illegal cab will want to call any attention to himself. Find any cameras that showed who the killer was signaling to across the street when he first arrived?"

"I checked that, but there aren't any in the right spot. How about the guy I caught at my gate . . . Interviewed him yet?"

"We're waiting for his lawyer to arrive. Look, you've done enough for today. We'll talk again tomorrow. By the way, there's going be a memorial service at 9:00 a.m. tomorrow for Uncle Joe at that big Catholic church on St. Charles. I think we ought to go to support Andy . . . and his uncle. But it's up to you."

As they continued on their way to Bunny's Bar and Grill, Teddy said, "What do you think about that memorial service – going, I mean."

"Don't see how I can refuse, not that I'd ever do that."

"I agree. We should go."

A few minutes later, as they were about to step through Bunny's front door, Kit got another call. She forgot to put this one on speakerphone, so Teddy could only wonder about who it was.

The call didn't last long and when it was finished, Kit said, "That was something I need to tell Andy about. The jukebox inside is always so loud, it'll be easier to do it out here. Go ahead and get us a table and I'll be right there."

While Teddy took her suggestion, Kit navigated to Broussard's number and punched the call button.

In the medical examiner's office, Broussard looked over the

autopsy report on Zach Leblanc one more time. Convinced that it was complete, he signed off on it and leaned back in his chair, wishing he had a catfish po'boy or a bowl of Grandma O's jambalaya. And he'd already had a big lunch. But until he'd solved the puzzle of all the dead Broussards, no amount of food would satisfy him. It wasn't just the elusive identity of the killer that was forcing his skullduggery neurons into overdrive. It was also motive.

Despite that Deuteronomy reference Karpas made, it was hard to believe he could have been so angry at Joe for firing him that killing Joe wouldn't have been enough. And if it *was* Kapas, why the condom in Julien's mouth? That sort of fit with the Deuteronomy connection but it didn't feel right. Then there was Deleon. Whoever killed Betty was obviously furious at her, but her death appeared to be a spur of the moment action arising from something that happened after she got in that car at the dollar store. She had apparently rejected DeLeon's attentions on at least two occasions. So yes, he could have been furious at her. But why would she get in a car with him? That suggests it was someone else she provoked. For what reason? As for Lewis, even if he did kill Joe and Julien, he had no motive whatever to go after Betty or her parents. And then today . . . Zach LeBlanc. He wasn't even part of the lineage from Joe to Betty. But he *did* have Broussard blood in his veins.

The old pathologist's stomach rumbled like a storm rolling in over Lake Pontchartrain. Should he even be cluttering the big picture with LeBlanc? No. They'd seen *his* killer . . . part of that weird bunch that was harassing Kit. He reached for a lemon ball in the big bowl of unwrapped ones on his desk, then, realizing that a little candy like that, or even two of them wouldn't stop the noise in his stomach, he pushed his chair back, intending to go down to the vending machine in the basement and get something more substantial.

But before he could stand up, his cell phone rang, a call from Kit.

He punched the button and accepted the call. "Detective Franklyn . . . Hope you're about to say you know where to find Zach LeBlanc's killer."

"Hit a dead end I'm afraid. He got away in a gypsy cab. I wanted to tell you about a call I just got from Dee Evans, Betty Bergeron's apartment mate. She was straightening up Betty's room and knocked off Betty's big desk calendar. Under it was a Post-It with the name, Belle Broussard, on it. Mean anything to you?"

Broussard felt his brain take a deep breath. "It's a family name from long ago . . . someone who died young, shortly before I was born."

"Who was it?"

"My sister."

Chapter 39

"She died when she was seven," Broussard said to Gatlin, relaying by phone what Kit had just told him. "I wasn't born until two years later. So I didn't know her. My parents never spoke much about her, but they did say she was killed in a traffic accident . . . apparently a truck hit her while she was ridin' her bicycle. Other than my parents, the only relatives I can think of who were around when she was alive were Uncle Joe and his wife, Anne. I wonder if Betty got my sister's name from Joe."

"When I was talking to Joe's bodyguard I asked him about any recent visitors Joe might have had," Gatlin responded. "And he said, two weeks before Joe was killed, a pretty young blonde woman came to the house. Said she was a relative named Elizabeth."

"I'll bet that was her. But what was the point of their conversation?"

"Afraid you're gonna have to figure that one out yourself. I gotta get back to my interview with the guy Kit caught at her gate."

"You haven't broken him yet?"

"Hard to use a rubber hose on somebody when their lawyer is standing right there."

After that call, Broussard sat for a moment, wondering who he could call that would be able to talk to him about his sister and answer the questions he now had about her. Before he came up with any likely names, his phone rang again.

Glancing at the caller ID, he flinched. This could be uncomfortable. "Hello Amelia."

"You didn't have time to call and tell me about Julien? I can't believe you would treat me like that."

"You're right. But believe me it wasn't because I was tryin' to ignore you, it was because all my thoughts have been directed toward helpin' Julien or at least as much as I can now . . . and Joe, and Betty, and Betty's parents."

There was silence on the other end of the phone, then Amelia said, "I can't believe what I just said to you. I am so sorry."

"Forget it. We're all under a lot of stress."

"So many of our family members . . . Dead . . . What's happening Andy?"

"Wish I knew." This would have been a good time to tell her about Zach LeBlanc, but he just didn't feel like getting into a discussion about that, especially since it appeared to be unrelated to the other deaths. He wanted now to focus only on finding the solution to this mess. And he was suddenly convinced that the key was his sister. "Amelia, do you know anything about the circumstances of my sister's death?"

"Your sister . . . I wasn't even born when that happened."

"Did Joe ever talk about it?"

"Not to me. Why do you want to know about that?"

"It could be important."

"To what?"

"Never mind. I don't mean to be rude, but I have some thinkin' to do."

"Will you be at the memorial service for my father tomorrow?"

"Absolutely."

"Would you be willing to say a few words?"

"I'd be honored."

Broussard hung up, rocked back in his desk chair, and folded his pudgy fingers over his belly. Who would know about his sister's death? He shook his head. Not likely anyone in New Orleans, but maybe . . .

He dropped his chair forward and poised his hands over his computer keyboard.

As dexterous as he was with a scalpel and dissecting scissors, he was a terrible typist, and his fingers often hit the wrong key or the space between keys. Even so, he had soon navigated to the web site for the sheriff's office in Bayou Coteau, the town where he'd lived until his parents' death.

He punched the office number into his phone and waited for an answer, which came as promptly as one would expect from such an important civil servant.

"Sheriff Guidry, please. This is Dr. Andy Broussard callin' from New Orleans."

Lawless Guidry had been elected to office fifteen years earlier, despite his given first name and habit of dressing like a member of a Hell's Angels chapter. Some say that rather than a vote of confidence in his law enforcement abilities his election was a long overdue expression of admiration for him making all state running back when he played on the Bayou Coteau fighting nutrias.

"He's on patrol, but I'll patch you through to him," the female dispatcher said.

After a few minutes of static, a voice that sounded like its owner needed a laryngeal CAT scan said, "Guidry here. Speak up or shut up."

Broussard had met Guidry years ago, so after saying again who he was, the old pathologist launched right into the reason for the call. "We're havin' a rash of murders over here and it looks like it may have somethin' to do with the death of my sister, Belle."

"Didn't know you had a sister."

"She died two years before I was born. My folks said she died after bein' hit by a truck when she was seven."

"Why'd it take 'em two more years to have you?"

"Well, you know, I never thought to ask 'em about that. And they never spoke much about Belle either. Don't even know any details of the accident, and I was thinkin' that the sheriff at the time, T. O. Neuville, would be the one I should talk to. He still alive?"

"Sort of. Had a stroke a few years ago and is pretty much an invalid. Lives with his daughter, Connie, who takes care of him."

"How's his mental state?"

"I'm guessin' he's depressed."

"You know what I mean."

"You'd have to ask Connie about that."

"She married?"

"Divorced, but still uses her husband's last name; Castille."

"Wouldn't happen to have her phone number would you?"

"Ordinarily, at this point I'd explain to you that I'm not a community bulletin board, but I remember when you was in town a few years ago and we shook hands, you had a grip on you that'd make an albino color up. Ain't many around here can match me on that score. So that buys you my respect an' the phone number you want. Hold on."

After about thirty seconds of static, Guidry came back on the line and gave him Connie's number. He then said, "How come you didn't ask me if I had Neuville's files from all his old cases? What you're lookin' for might be in there."

"Figured I'd try Neuville first and if that didn't work out, come back to you about the files."

"Yeah, well, I don't have 'em . . . lost in a flood from a burst pipe ten years ago."

"Then why'd you bring it up?"

"Wanted you to know that Neuville was your only chance . . . so you wouldn't piss it away thinkin' you had another boat in the weeds."

"Very considerate of you."

"It was, wasn't it? Good luck with whatever the hell you're doin'."

Connie Castile's voice drifted out of Broussard's phone like dandelion fuzz blowing gently on a summer breeze. After running through the necessary preliminary gab about who he was and the generalities of why he was calling, he got to the point. "Would I be able to ask your father some questions about that over the phone?"

"Do you speak Cajun French?"

"No. Why do you ask?"

"Ever since his stroke that's the only language my daddy speaks. I can't translate for you because I only know a few words. Mostly I communicate with him now by simple hand gestures and showing him objects he might want."

When it came to Cajun French, Broussard had the same problem Connie did, but he knew someone who could help. "Would it be alright if I came to see your father and I brought someone who can translate for me?"

"It's okay with me, but if daddy doesn't like either one of you, he won't cooperate. And I should warn you that even before his stroke, he didn't like *anybody*. When were you thinking of coming?"

"If I can get my translator on board, would two or three hours from now be okay?"

"Yes."

"I'll call back in a few minutes and let you know whether to expect us."

It was one thing to be in a restaurant with Grandma O and quite another to be closed up in the same vehicle with her for over two hours, mostly because her personality just wouldn't fit into a space that small. This made Broussard consider taking Teddy LaBiche with him instead. But Grandma O would surely find out about the whole trip and then be upset that *she* hadn't been asked to go. And he didn't want to hurt her feelings. So the decision was made.

Chapter 40

"Okay, I'll go," Grandma O said. "But I can't fit in one a dose hiccups you drive. We'll take my truck. An' I'm drivin'."

"I should warn you, we have to be likable, or he won't talk to us," Broussard said.

There was a pause, then Grandma O said, "You implyin' dat sometimes I ain't likable?"

"Just want you to be extra likable when we meet him."

"Don' you worry about me. I got tricks I can use on a man. I don' know *what* you're gonna do."

Twenty minutes later, Grandma O pulled up in front of the morgue in a black Ford F10 4X4. As Broussard climbed in, he thought about how every time he parked one of his T-Birds in a public lot, there was always a mountainous truck like this parked on either side of him blocking his view as he tried to leave. Settling into his seat, his nostrils were filled with the scent of gardenias, Grandma O's favorite perfume. This was a part of the equation that might have tipped his choice of a translator toward Teddy LaBiche had he remembered to factor it in. But a man who can autopsy a floater when necessary could certainly deal with a gardenia odor no matter how strong.

Grandma O glanced in the side mirror then abruptly pulled into traffic before there was room for her to do so safely, causing the driver behind her to wear out his horn.

"What you suppose *he* sat on?" She asked, oblivious to the problem.

"Probably just one of those malcontents that wants to get home alive," Broussard replied.

"I didn' know you better I'd think dat was a comment on my drivin' skills."

If it had been Gatlin behind the wheel, Broussard would have knocked that one into the river, but coming to his senses, he simply said, "I never criticize folks who are doin' me a favor."

"Suppose I was takin' you somewhere to do *me* a favor?"

"Why am I startin' to feel like a catfish fillet in one of your skillets?"

"Why you answerin' my question with another question?"

"Did I?"

Grandma O suddenly let out a cackle that rattled something on the dash. "You're slippery, I'll give you dat."

She turned on the radio, filling the cab with Zydeco music. "That station okay for you?"

Speaking truthfully, Broussard said, "It's my roots. I don't mind at all."

They were soon on I-10, heading west, the elevated highway flanked by cypress swamps, scattered clouds hanging low in the sky. A few miles further and the trees gave way to a vast plain of low vegetation surrounding interconnected bayous and lagoons. On the distant left horizon, white smoke billowed from unseen industrial chimneys and joined the clouds as though issuing from some ancient installation laboring to terraform the planet.

The watery plain continued along the highway for miles and miles, an interminable preamble to a view Broussard had seen many times in his life, but now longed to gaze upon again.

Then finally, there it was; the choppy waters of Lake Pontchartrain, which alternated in large swathes between brown and blue, the colors indicating its varying depth. Leaving New Orleans by this route reminded Broussard as it always did, that he lived in a city set apart from the rest of the country by geographical considerations as much as cultural. There, surrounded by the immense watery wilderness, he felt both humbled and special at the same time.

A short while later, as they left the lake and wild plains behind, and trees once again lined the highway, Broussard's thoughts returned to wondering how his sister, Belle, was involved in the slaughter of so many of his relatives.

Their route took them through Baton Rouge and Lafayette, then down the Southern leg of I-90, Grandma O pushing the F10 over the speed limit most of the way. Even so, they reached the exit for Bayou Coteau with the sun low in the sky. With dusk fast approaching, they traveled the next seven miles accompanied by a saw grass swamp on both sides of the road. Then Broussard saw what he'd been worried about. He threw up his arm and shouted, "Turtle."

Grandma O gently swerved the truck to miss the animal, came to a stop on the shoulder, and looked at Broussard. "Go on."

Broussard climbed out of the truck, hustled to the turtle, and picked it up. He carried it across the road and put it down on the edge of the black water lapping at the shoulder. Then he returned to the truck and got back in his seat.

"How'd you know what I wanted?" he asked, hooking up his seatbelt.

Getting underway again, Grandma O said, "Bubba's been tellin' me for years about you and turtles."

"He ever say anything about a chipmunk?"

"No."

"Good."

Soon the swamp on the left gave way to solid ground and the beginning of a line of ancient twisted live oaks that would continue all the way into town. On Broussard's side of the car, the swamp persisted until the road divided. There, a small right artery ran under a big sign for Teddy's alligator farm. From this point on, oaks now lined both sides of the main road.

For the first time since leaving New Orleans, Broussard felt the poignant emotion of returning to his childhood home. Passing an oak with a distinctive bulge on the side of the trunk facing the road, he remembered the day he'd found an almost intact shed skin of a snake hanging from one of the tree's tortuous lower branches. He'd told the boy with him, Billy Crochet, that the skin belonged to a yellow rat snake. Billy had then spit on the ground and said it was impossible for anybody to know what kind of snake a shed skin came from. Broussard had subsequently found the skin's owner under a nearby bush. And it was indeed, a yellow rat snake. Over there, Broussard remembered falling out of that tree and breaking his left little finger. Even now, the appendage still wasn't completely straight.

Minutes later, as the F10 arrived at the quaint town square with all its balconies and wrought iron railings, the antique lantern-style street lights had just come on. At that moment, the superficial memories Broussard's mind had been using to mask the ones that hurt, melted away.

"If you don't mind let's take a moment and go down there," he said, pointing at one of the streets that radiated away from the square. Sensing his melancholia, Grandma O did as he asked without comment.

The requested detour led them first to a pink-stuccoed church and then, with a prompt from Broussard, under the wrought iron elliptical arched entrance to the town cemetery.

Broussard pointed to one of three possible driving routes into the grounds. "That way."

Like New Orleans, the water table in this area was too high for dry in-ground burials. So the narrow asphalt ribbon they'd chosen wound through a marble city of the dead. Finally, Broussard said, "Stop here, just for a minute."

He got out and walked over to an arched crypt with a sleeping lamb perched on a pedestal at the peak. In carved relief across the gable was the name BROUSSARD. Those interred inside were listed in order of their deaths. At the top was his sister Belle, her short life inscribed below her name. His father was next, his name added eighteen years after Belle, when a 3000-pound cypress log rolled off one of his own saw mill trucks and crushed his car. Broussard's mother was the final name on the entry slab, killed in the same accident as his father, but dying twenty minutes later, just as the ambulance arrived at the hospital.

To one side of the entry slab there was a pedestal meant for flower vases. There being no Broussards left in town, the pedestal had nothing on it. Feeling as empty as that pedestal, Broussard moved down the line of crypts until he came to the one for The Duhon family. He stood for moment thinking about Claude and Olivia and the horrible circumstances of their deaths, which had occurred a few years earlier, when one of his most bizarre cases had reached out from New Orleans and snared them in its grip.

Perhaps it was his parents' death when he was a kid that pushed him toward forensic pathology as a life's work, a motivation to learn exactly what happens when someone you love and depend on, is simply gone in a matter of seconds or minutes. Certainly that experience at such a young age would explain the anger he felt toward the homicidal instruments of death. Natural causes . . . it's right in the name . . . natural. No one is supposed to die at the hands of another. But he also felt anger when bodies came to the morgue because of an accident, especially one caused by negligence or stupidity. In the case of his parents, the chains responsible for safely securing the log on the truck had either been the wrong size or improperly rigged. No blame was ever officially lodged against anyone. But someone was at fault.

Then there was Claude and Olivia, that wasn't natural, but who was accountable? Some would say *they* were. But maybe in a sense, *he* was.

"You okay?"

It was Grandma O standing beside him. Only then did he realize his usually organized mind had been knocked out of alignment by a toxic memory mudslide. This was why even after he retired, he could never return here to live. "I'm fine," he said. "We better get goin'."

Chapter 41

Grandma O pulled into the dirt driveway of a cottage almost completely covered with a gargantuan rose bush covered with clusters of little yellow blooms with a color so intense they could clearly be seen even in the advancing dusk.

"Somebody here got a green thumb," Grandma O said, as she unbuckled her seat belt.

A moment later, in response to Broussard's finger on the bell, a slim woman with long brown hair and a pleasant face opened the door. Her apparent absence of makeup even though she knew visitors were coming suggested to Broussard that she was a no nonsense woman who cared more about substance than appearance. In validation of that opinion, she took immediate charge of their interaction by offering her hand and saying, "I'm Connie Castille. You must be Dr. Broussard."

Her hand was warm but rough. "It's so good of you to allow us to see your father." Releasing her hand, Broussard then said, "This is my friend . . ." And there he faltered. It seemed odd that he should introduce her as Grandma O to someone neither of them had ever met before. But in all the years he'd known her, he'd never learned her first name. It seemed so ridiculous.

Sensing his problem, Grandma O edged Broussard to the side, offered her hand to Connie, and said. "Zenobia Oustellette, but you can call me Grandma O. Everybody else does."

"Well, you both better come in," Connie said, stepping aside.

Inside, the décor was like Connie herself, functional and tidy.

"Before I take you in to see him, I should explain that talking to him won't simply be a matter of translating what he says. His stroke somehow altered the parts of his brain that deal with language. Now, he doesn't even *understand* English any more. I'm not sure I made that clear when we spoke earlier. I've learned a few simple French phrases so I can take care of him, but I couldn't help you carry on a conversation. Your questions will also have to be in French. I hope that's not a problem."

Broussard looked at Grandma O, who said, "We gonna be fine."

"He's also paralyzed from the neck down on his right side," Connie said. "So he doesn't shake hands. When we go in, I'll let you explain why you're here. Be prepared, you won't have long to make him like you. " She motioned for them to follow and they all went to an adjoining room with a hospital bed facing the door.

On that bed was her father, looking right at them with intelligent eyes whose clear blue color Broussard could see even from the doorway. His paralysis didn't involve his face so there was no drooping, or any other evidence he was ill. He was old and his face was heavily road mapped, but there was still strength in it. Even before they were all inside, the old man said, "*L'enfer qui etes-vous?*"

Grandma O looked back at Broussard and translated in a whisper. "He say, 'who da hell are you?'"

Broussard had briefed Grandma O on the general reason for this visit. His plan was for her to introduce them as she saw fit, then he would begin to tell her what to say. She approached the bed and began a fluent cascade of French, speaking in a gentle tone Broussard had never heard before. Soon, he saw Neuville nod his head, apparently agreeing to something.

Grandma O had brought a huge handbag into the house with her. She now put it on the edge of the bed and reached inside. Her hand came out holding a large plastic container, which she placed on the nightstand. Another incursion into her bag produced a plastic spoon and a napkin in a zip top bag. A moment later, she guided the spoon, with a generous helping of whatever was in the container, toward the old fellow's mouth.

When he tasted what she'd brought, his eyes rolled back in his head, which apparently made Connie think he was having another stroke, because she bolted toward the bed. But before she got there, Neuville smiled, shook his head in wonder, and rattled off something in French that included the word, *fantastique*.

Grandma O gave him a second spoonful, then wiped his chin. Following another torrent of French from him, Grandma O put everything back on the nightstand and turned to Broussard. "Well, he gonna talk to me, but he say you can stay only if you can prove we're married."

Broussard's brows lifted in shock, raising his lids so his little eyes apparently doubled in size. He'd come in with a few ideas about how he might gain Neuville's favor, but this . . . What the hell . . .

Suddenly, Grandma O let out a cackle that made the windows hum. "He didn't really say dat. But he want to know what kind a Broussard you are?"

"Tell him I'm the son of Aubrey Broussard, his old fishin' buddy."

As she translated the message, Neuville nodded, then, for the first time looking at Broussard as he spoke, responded briefly.

"He say, 'Dat damn accident should never have happened'."

"I've thought about that more times than I can tell you," Broussard replied, speaking now directly to Neuville, but still in English.

Broussard waited until it sounded like Grandma O had finished translating his comment, then he said, "My father considered you the most honorable man he ever knew."

Once more waiting until that had been relayed, Broussard quickly added. "But he also told me your name should have been T.O. Birdsnest, because when you two went fishin' you fouled your line more than anybody he'd ever seen."

It was clear from the look on Grandma O's face she didn't think Broussard was helping himself by telling the old sheriff something so uncomplimentary, but she translated it anyway.

The sheriff actually laughed. Then, seemingly still in a good mood, he said something that Grandma O translated as: "Aubrey used to say dat to me all da time. Wish I was fishin' with him right now."

The old man seemed to retreat for a moment into the past, his eyes focused on nothing anyone else in the room could see. Then he looked at Broussard and spoke again.

Grandma O grinned at Broussard, showing the gold star inlay in one of her front teeth. "You did it. He say, 'You came a long way to see me. How can I help'?"

"I've been wonderin' about the day my sister, Belle, died. What can you tell me about the circumstances?"

Broussard was concerned the old guy might have at least a few gaps in his memory and that the details of Belle's death might be one of them. But without even thinking about it, the old fellow responded.

When he finished answering, Grandma O said, "Belle was hit by a truck haulin' fill dirt for a new addition to da elementary school. She was on her bike and was kinda wobbly on acounta da road wasn't in good shape. Da driver honked at her to let her know he was comin', but she jus' wobbled out in front a him."

"Was the driver cited for anything?" Broussard asked.

Grandma O passed the question along, and T.O. responded.

"Considerin' Belle's condition, it seemed like it probably wasn't his fault at all."

Puzzled, Broussard said, "What condition?"

Grandma O relayed and T.O. answered.

"She was born deaf and her eyesight was gettin' worse every year."

Good God, Broussard thought. *Could that be why Uncle Joe and . . .? No . . . it was too outrageous . . . nobody could be that deranged . . . Or could they?*

Chapter 42

Broussard was a little late arriving at the church where Uncle Joe's funeral was being held. After getting home from his trip with Grandma O to see T.O. Neuville, he'd stayed up most of the night, looking at the Broussard pedigree chart he'd made and thinking about everything that had happened since Uncle Joe had been killed. Eventually he'd fallen asleep at his desk. Though he'd dozed for only an hour, he woke twenty minutes ago with a clear mind and the belief that he knew who the killer was. Aware that Gatlin and Kit would be at the funeral, he planned to tell them what he knew as soon as the event was over.

Because he was late, the parking lot was already crowded with other mourners' vehicles. As he headed inside, he walked past a black pickup truck that drew him toward it like a magnet for chubby pathologists. Reaching the passenger side, he looked in and saw a sheet of paper lying on the seat. He shaded his eyes and leaned as close to the window as he could. The print on most of the sheet was too small to read from where he stood, but the caption was clear: Bomb At Funeral Kills 16 North of Iraq's Capital. *Oh my God.*

Running as fast as his short legs could carry him, he dashed to the church entrance. Heart thudding in his ears, he ignored the pain mushrooming in his side and stumbled up the steps and into the church. Yanking open the sanctuary doors, he stood for a moment and scanned the scene before him.

There were about a hundred people already seated, most of them in the pews near the front, a few farther back. Among those toward the rear were Kit and Teddy and Phil Gatlin. Amelia was standing behind a lectern on stage talking about Uncle Joe, whose flower-enshrouded casket sat nearby. Three pews from the front, sitting on the right aisle, was the driver of the pickup.

Unaware of how much time he had, but knowing that he didn't dare just shout for everyone to get out, Broussard's mind raced, trying to come up with a workable plan. Years ago, he'd been called to that building to examine the body of the church secretary, who had been killed during a bungled burglary. Using the knowledge of the church layout he'd seen then, he suddenly had an idea.

He ran back into the entry, went to the funeral sign-in book, and tore out a blank page. Folding the page like a letter, he returned to the sanctuary and hurried over to Phil Gatlin, where he whispered. "No time to explain. When I go through that door up there by the stage, and only then, get everybody out of here. And keep your voice down. You might have a minute to do that, maybe two. When the place is clear, call me on my phone. Got it?"

Knowing him well enough not to question his instructions, Gatlin nodded, his face already showing him poised for action.

Broussard hustled to the driver of the pickup, bent down, and showed him the folded paper while softly speaking into his ear. "I've just received a note for you from Joe. He wanted you to read it before his funeral. Let's go into the hall over there and I'll give it to you."

In the history of great plans, this one wouldn't even rate a footnote. But he didn't have time to create anything better.

The hall Broussard had gestured to was beside the stage and therefore, not far away. Everything depended on the guy doing as Broussard asked. If he balked, there was no backup strategy. He looked up at Broussard, obviously puzzled at how Joe could have sent anybody a letter after death. To help the guy make the right decision, Broussard motioned toward the door with his chin and headed for the hall.

There was another moment of hesitation from his quarry that made Broussard begin to sweat under his black suit. Then the guy got up and moved in Broussard's direction.

Broussard went into the hall first, noting with satisfaction, that the access door was quite heavy, just as he remembered it. Therefore, a moment later, when it shut behind the killer, they could no longer hear Amelia talking. That also meant the guy wouldn't know when she suddenly *stopped* talking as Gatlin cleared the sanctuary.

Facing each other, Broussard could see that the man's dark suit looked puffy around the waist, most likely because he was wearing a bomb under his jacket. Broussard also believed that there was at least one device in the sanctuary.

The guy reached out for the fake letter. Instead of giving it to him, Broussard said, "How you doin'? We haven't had any time to talk and I'm worried about you."

This was a horribly dangerous moment. The killer had his left hand in his pants pocket, so that was likely where the button was. Any attempt by Broussard to grab the man's arm might cause an immediate detonation. Even if Broussard didn't make a move, the guy might realize what was going on and decide to end it all right then.

The two men locked eyes while seconds ticked by in pregnant silence. Then the killer said, "I'm fine. I should get back inside." He reached again for the fake letter, but Broussard still didn't offer it.

"If you ever want to talk about anything, I'm always available," Broussard said. "Well, not always, but I'll certainly make time for you."

"I appreciate that. Could I have the letter now?"

"It's odd how I got it," Broussard said. "It came by e-mail early this mornin'. I don't know how Joe arranged that. He must have some program on his computer so he can delay the time e-mails get sent."

The other man's benign expression suddenly hardened. "There is no letter is there?"

Broussard hesitated before answering, trying to buy a few more seconds. Then he said, "Why'd you do it? There was no malice toward you by anyone involved. It was just biology."

Up to this point, Broussard had been circling the rattlesnake. Now he'd just grabbed it by the tail. The guy clenched his jaw and Broussard was certain he was about to scatter both of them over the hallway.

Then the man spoke, his voice loud and angry. "Biology that everybody should have known about . . . biology that never should have happened if people had been careful. Joe knew. He could have taken precautions, then we wouldn't be here. It would have been better if I'd never been born, or Betty either."

At that moment Broussard's cell phone rang. Sensing that what had just been said was intended as the guy's epitaph, Broussard rushed forward, put both hands on the guy's chest and drove him backward through a pair of double doors to another section of the hall.

As the swinging panels closed between them, Broussard turned and dove for the side door to the outside, aiming both hands for the bar to open it.

The blast from the bomb the killer was wearing tore both swinging doors off their hinges. Nearly simultaneously, it blew open the outside door and hurled Broussard onto the sidewalk, where he crashed to the pavement, breaking both the radius and ulna in his right arm and partially tearing off his right ear.

There were four bombs planted under the pews in the sanctuary. Their combined force turned the seating into a hurricane of sharp projectiles that peppered the walls with shards that in some cases were driven completely through the sheetrock. At the same instant, a million dollars worth of stained glass was turned into at least as many pieces of shrapnel that slashed at the parsonage next door. Phil Gatlin had been the last person out of the sanctuary. When the compression wave blew the big front doors off their hinges, one of them nearly fell on him. But he wasn't hurt. He'd also managed to get Kit and Teddy and all the rest of those in his charge out onto the front sidewalk unharmed.

"What the hell just happened?" Kit said, brushing the blast dust from her hair. She looked frantically over the crowd. "Where's Andy. Did he get out?"

"Not with us," Gatlin said, stutter stepping around a small bewildered group so he could see if Broussard was somewhere beyond them.

Teddy had separated himself from Kit and Gatlin and was now standing about fifteen feet away, looking at the side of the church opposite the parsonage. "There's an exit door over here," he shouted, pointing.

Teddy waited for Kit and Gatlin to join him, then they all headed for the door he'd found.

A moment later, facing away from them, they saw a big body that could only be Broussard, lying motionless on the sidewalk. Gatlin ran up to him, knelt, and felt for a pulse. "He's still with us."

"Ambulance on the way," Teddy said, putting his phone

back in his pocket.

Forehead so heavily furrowed with worry that his bushy eyebrows met over his nose, Gatlin leaned down and said into Broussard's intact left ear, "Don't you even think about dying. I'm not spending the rest of my life remembering you like this."

Chapter 43

"So, how's the food?" Gatlin asked.

"I'm puttin' it on my list of top spots in the city," Broussard said from his hospital bed, where he was wearing a big gauze pad taped to his injured ear and had a cast on his right forearm.

"We were going to bring you flowers, but thought you might like these better," Kit said, producing a glass canister of unwrapped lemon drops. She took the top off and held the canister out to his left side.

"Where'd you get 'em?" he asked, fishing a yellow candy out of the container and putting it in his mouth.

"From the bowl on your desk."

"Hope you didn't scoop 'em out with your bare hands."

"Look who's talking," Kit said, setting the canister on the rolling table suspended over Broussard's lap. "Before I came to work in your office, you used to carry them loose in your pockets."

"But I have very clean pockets."

"By the way," Gatlin said to Broussard from the other side of the bed. "You look like crap."

"You mean in general or just after what happened?"

"What *did* happen?" Kit said.

"I got hurt in a bomb blast," Broussard replied, expertly talking around the lemon ball.

"You know what she means," Gatlin said. "Give it up."

"Short version or the long one?"

"Lemme help you," Gatlin said. "I wasn't sure at the time who that was you took out of the funeral service with you, but we found what was left of Remy LeBlanc's body in the hall by that exit door you used. When I checked out his truck, I saw an article about an Afghan funeral bombing on the seat. Is that what tipped you off to his plans?"

"Yeah."

"But you obviously knew he was the one who killed all those people before you saw the article."

Broussard tucked the lemon ball in his cheek. "I was suspicious of him for a couple reasons. For one, although he did sign Uncle Joe's Birthday card, I noticed that his signature looked different than everybody else's. Lookin' carefully at the reverse side of the card under a dissectin' scope with some alternate light sources, I saw that all the other signatures had a distinct hollow center to the lines the pen made on the paper, an effect produced by the hard clipboard Amelia used for a backin' when she had everyone sign the card at the picnic. On Remy's signature, the lines were all solid, which by experiment, I saw was what happens when the card is signed on a soft surface. That made me think he didn't sign the card at the picnic, but did it earlier, when he was in Amelia's kitchen talkin' to her about a job she had for him. She does all her paperwork on a counter in there. I'm guessin' he saw the card when he came to her house. Knowin' he wouldn't be at the picnic, he signed it right then, on a magazine, maybe. Amelia just didn't notice what he'd done."

Broussard paused, reached for the glass of water on his lap table, and took a sip from the bent straw.

"Later, when I was talkin' to him about the shootin', he said somethin' about how excited the rangers were when they came runnin' out of their office. But they weren't *in* their office when it happened. They were eatin' outside at their own picnic table. If he'd been with the rest of us he'd have seen that. The shooter didn't know it because the ranger station wasn't visible from where he anchored his boat."

"You must have realized early on that you hadn't actually seen Remy at the picnic," Gatlin said.

"I thought of that, but I got there late and didn't talk to hardly anyone else but Joe before he was killed. Then I had more important things on my mind than checkin' attendance."

"I thought we decided that whoever killed Betty would have scratch marks on him," Kit said.

"They must have been under Remy's hair on the back of his head," Broussard replied.

Gatlin looked at Kit and Teddy. "You two notice how much better his color is now that he's getting to show off for us?"

"I'm just followin' your instructions to 'give it up' as you put it," Broussard said.

"Yeah, yeah. Keep going."

"Remember how we were thinkin' that Betty Bergeron and Joe might have discussed my sister, Belle, but we didn't know why . . . Well, last night Grandma O and I drove back to my home town and talked to the guy who was sheriff when my sister was killed."

"Jesus, what's it like being in the same vehicle with *her* for a couple hours," Gatlin said, quickly making the sign of the cross on his chest for saying, 'Jesus.'

"If you want to hear this, you're gonna have to focus," Broussard said.

"Yeah, okay, I'm with you. What did you find out?"

"Belle was born deaf and was progressively goin' blind. So she had the Acadian version of Usher's Syndrome. It's caused by a gene mutation that makes an abnormal version of a protein important for function in the inner ear and the visual cells of the retina. The mutation apparently happened to one man back in the days before what became the Cajuns migrated from Nova Scotia to Louisiana. They were such an isolated group for so long, there was a lot of intermarriage, which means the gene got passed around. I'm convinced that Betty Bergeron and Remy both had it."

"So they were secretly seeing each other," Kit said.

"Secretly, because I think Betty was uncomfortable with the fact Remy was her third cousin. But I believe they were plannin' on gettin' married. Kit, you told me Betty was studyin' molecular biology and wanted to be a genetic counselor. I'm sure she knew about Usher's syndrome. That's why she went to see Uncle Joe, to find out if he knew about any history of the mutation in the family."

"And he told her about Belle," Gatlin said.

Caught up in Broussard's story, Teddy chimed in, "I'll bet Betty insisted that she and Remy be tested to see if either of them carried the mutation."

"I'm sure of it," Broussard said. "And the test came back positive for both of 'em. Now they had a problem, because it's a recessive mutation. You can only get a child with the syndrome if the kiddo gets a copy of the defective gene from both parents."

"Betty didn't want to risk it, so she called off the marriage," Kit said.

"Has to be what happened," Broussard said.

Now Gatlin jumped in. "She tells Remy she doesn't want to see him anymore, he goes nuts and strangles her. Dumps her body down by the river, drives around awhile still nuts, goes back and stabs her dead body 15 times."

"Then he gets the idea to punish everyone up the genetic pedigree for passing the defective gene down to Betty," Kit said, "starting with uncle Joe."

"That's why when he killed Betty's parents, he focused his anger on her mother," Broussard said, his teeth clacking against the lemon ball, which he'd shifted out of his cheek. "Her father wasn't a Broussard and therefore not responsible. Remy gave us a big clue as to what his motive was when he left that condom in Julien's mouth."

"You don't think . . ." Teddy began.

"Think what?" Kit said.

"I was about to suggest that Remy then decided to also punish his side of the family for giving *him* the gene, starting with his daddy, Zach. But what kind of man could do that to his own father?"

"The same kind that was planning on killing the whole clan in the church," Gatlin said.

"He must have had more than one defective gene," Teddy said. Then, to Broussard, "Sorry, I didn't mean . . ."

"No apology necessary," Broussard said. "Your thought has occurred to me too."

"Not that we really need it now, but in Remy's house we found the gun that killed Julien," Gatlin said to Broussard. "And the suppressor was with it. They weren't even well hidden."

"He was planning' on killin' himself at the church so what did he care," Broussard said. "Did you find the car Remy drove when he met Betty at the dollar store?"

Gatlin nodded. "Gray Mazda, right in his garage. The raincoat and Guy Fawks mask he wore when he killed Zach were in the trunk. It was like Christmas. His boat was there too, with clothes in it that belonged to the fisherman he planted in the water at the picnic."

"What about the men who were harassing Kit?"

"All taken care of. You know you've been a pretty talkative

old geezer while we been here. You're not even out of breath. Why not get dressed and go home?"

"They want to observe me until tomorrow."

"Guess they never saw anybody as odd as you before. Let me know if you need anything before they get tired of you."

"I will."

"We're leaving too," Kit said. "Great job at the church. See you when you get out."

"I'm glad you're okay," Teddy said.

A few minutes later, while waiting for the hospital elevator, Gatlin said to Kit. "If you're interested, I got another assignment for you."

"I'm interested. What is it?"

They were still talking about it when the elevator door opened and they got on.

Back in his room, Broussard was wondering how long it would take Gatlin and Kit to realize that in order for his parents to have produced Belle, they must have been related to each other . . . no way to know how close or how distant. Could even have been cousins.

The hospital ventilation system blew a familiar odor into his room, gardenias. Looking toward the door, he saw a familiar taffeta-clothed figure.

"Still in bed," Grandma O declared. "And it's nearly ten o'clock."

"She ain't really bein' judgmental," Bubba said, popping into view from behind her. "Dat's jus' how she is."

"Good to see both of you. What's in the sack?"

"I saw your eyes get big when I gave da sheriff dat bread puddin', so I brought some for you. Want it now?"

"You're not gonna feed me are you?"

"You ain't hurt bad enough for dat."

She got him set up with the open container of pudding and a napkin on the lap table and put a plastic spoon in his good hand. Wasting no time, he dug in. After savoring the first bite with obvious pleasure, he gestured at the container with his spoon and said, *"Fantastique."*

"Thought you didn' know any French," Grandma O said sternly, hands on her massive hips.

"Learned that one from the sheriff. Bubba . . . you keepin' out of trouble?"

"Seems like trouble only comes my way when I'm with you or Doc Franklyn. So for now . . . I'm good, unless you get outta dat bed and drag me into somethin'."

"On da way in we saw Philip, Kit, and Teddy," Grandma O said. "Anybody else been to see you?"

"Just Amelia, one of Uncle Joe's daughters. She apologized for no other member of the family comin' by but they all got reasons . . . lots of 'em traumatized by the relatives they lost, some so confused they blame *me* for what happened." He shook his head. "At Uncle Joe's birthday picnic, after seein' all those people I was related to but didn't know, I felt like I'd been missin' somethin' . . . that in the future I should be more . . . interested in them. At least reconnect with all Joe's kids, considerin' how close we'd all been when we were young. But now everything's a mess."

"Lemme tell you somethin'," Grandma O said. "Bein' related by blood ain't da only way to have family. Philip an' Kit, an' Teddy are your family now. Me an' Bubba are too. So stop feelin' sorry for yourself." She came closer to the bed, leaned over, and kissed him on the cheek. And in that moment, Broussard saw that Grandma O had never said anything that made more sense.

Down in the hospital parking lot, Kit and Teddy were sitting in Teddy's red truck, about to get underway, except Teddy was just sitting behind the wheel staring at the windshield.

"What are you doing?" Kit asked.

"I've been thinking . . . about our problem of me living in Bayou Coteau and you living here . . . how that's going to work after we're married."

"What did you decide?"

"I have a guy who can run the gator farm without me there. And I've got enough property to manage in New Orleans that I'll have plenty to do here. So, it makes sense all around for me to live in New Orleans full time. What do you think?"

"Does this have anything to do with me being attacked while I was jogging?"

"That's part of it. If I'd been here, we'd have been running together."

"Then they would have found a different time, when you weren't with me."

"What are you saying?"

"I love that you want to protect me, but even if you're here, you can't follow me everywhere I go. And, despite what happened in Pirates Alley, I'm not helpless. I want to be sure you realize that."

"Hey, remember, I was there still hiding behind the gator carcass the time you jumped over it and took down that guy with the shotgun. Helpless? Furthest thought from my mind."

"Well, you *were* unarmed when it happened. It wouldn't have been smart of you to do anything else."

"As for Pirates Alley, I heard a guy left there with at least one less functioning testicle than he had when he arrived. It's just that when I can help you, I want to be only minutes or seconds away, not hours. And that includes giving you a foot message."

Kit nodded and pretended to think hard about what he'd said. "Okay then. I believe it's time to set a date for the wedding."

Sometimes an active mind can be a curse, especially if the one it belongs to has a Ph.D. in psychology. Even as she answered Teddy's question and they reaffirmed their engagement with a kiss, Kit wondered if there would be a time in the future when Teddy would come to resent her for making him leave the love he'd had long before they even met.

As Teddy started the truck and backed out of their parking space, Kit wistfully recalled something one of her favorite Tulane profs once said: "The trouble with life is that you have to live it to find out what happens."

The Broussard & Franklyn Series

Cajun Nights

(ISBN: 9781941286371)

Young and vibrant New Orleans criminal psychologist Kit Franklyn has just been assigned her most challenging case yet—a collection of victims with similarities that include driving old cars, humming nursery rhymes, committing murder, and then killing themselves! Welcoming the help of her jovial boss, chief medical examiner Andy Broussard, the two set out to solve the case, thinking only along strictly scientific lines. Not once do they consider the involvement of Black Magic, a New Orleans cultural staple, until an ancient Cajun sorcerer's curse surfaces with an ominous warning: "Beware the songs you loved in youth."

NEW YORK TIMES BOOK REVIEW — *His writing displays flashes of brilliance… Dr. Donaldson's talent and potential as a novelist are considerable.*

WASHINGTON POST BOOK WORLD — *SUSPENSFUL… likeable protagonists…Broussard and Franklyn are an engaging team…a welcome debut.*

HOUSTON POST — *A deadly portrait of this steamiest of Southern cities…mighty fine.*

MEMPHIS COMMERCIAL APPEAL — *A novel of creepy suspense…. It won't be easily put down, through your heart races to dangerous levels… a fast-paced thriller that deserves a wide audience.*

THE PHOENIX REPUBLIC — *Donaldson has relieved the tedium of the murder mystery grind with this engaging tale.*

BOOKLIST — *We close this remarkable, intoxicating book like a first-time visitor leaves New Orleans: giddy, a bit disoriented and much less confident in our own assumptions about life.*

THE BROUSSARD & FRANKLYN SERIES

Blood On The Bayou

(ISBN: 9781941286982)

New Orleans's hugely overweight chief medical examiner, Andy Broussard, and his gorgeous assistant, criminal psychologist Kit Franklyn, set off to investigate a series of violent murders. Examination of the victims leads to the discovery that each had their throat ripped out, as though they'd been attacked by something that wasn't human. 'Blood on the Bayou' is written in Donaldson's unique style: A hard-hitting, punchy, action-packed prose that's dripping with a folksy, decidedly southern, sense of irony. Add in Donaldson's brilliant first-hand knowledge of forensics along with the sultry flavor of New Orleans, and the result is a first class forensic procedural within an irresistibly delectable mystery.

LOS ANGELES TIMES BOOK REVIEW — The bayou atmosphere is redolently captured…

BOOKLIST — Donaldson combines an insider's knowledge with a real flair for making the reader's skin crawl.

MEMPHIS COMMERCIAL APPEAL — It's hard to beat his combination of cool science and explosive passion in the heart of humid Louisiana.

No Mardi Gras for The Dead

(ISBN: 9781681209364)

Kit Franklyn, lately drowning in personal doubts about her life and career, has to put those concerns aside after finding a corpse buried in the garden of her new home. Together with her boss,

The Broussard & Franklyn Series

the loveable and unconventional chief medical examiner Andy Broussard, she sets out to solve this case that's growing colder by the minute. Though they identify the body as a missing hooker, now dead for twenty-seven years, all hope of finding the killer seems lost—until the unorthodox duo link the body and two recent murders to a group of local, wealthy physicians.

PUBLISHERS WEEKLY — *Likable protagonists, abundant forensic lore and vivid depictions of colorful New Orleans and its denizens...*

WASHINGTON TIMES — *Kit...and Andy make a formidable team.*

BOOKLIST — *Donaldson's genre gumbo keeps you coming back for more.*

MEMPHIS COMMERCIAL APPEAL — *No mystery has ever started in a more clinically riveting and elegantly horrifying style.... If you haven't met Broussard and Franklyn, you should make your introductions.*

New Orleans Requiem

(ISBN: 9781938231384)

It's a bizarre case for Andy Broussard and Kit Franklyn. A man is found in Jackson Square, stabbed, one eyelid removed and four Scrabble tiles with the letters KOJE on his chest. Soon, there's a second victim, also stabbed and devoid of one eyelid, but this time with only three letters on his chest, KOJ. Does the missing letter mean there will be two more victims and then the killer will cease, or is he leading up to something bigger and deadlier? Broussard and Kit use their respective disciplines to profile the killer, but it quickly becomes clear that the clues and objects they've found are part of a sick game that the killer is playing

The Broussard & Franklyn Series

with Broussard; a game most likely engineered by one of the hundreds of attendees at the annual forensics meeting being held in New Orleans. Has Broussard finally met his match?

PUBLISHERS WEEKLY — Lots of Louisiana color, pinpoint plotting and two highly likable characters... smart, convincing solution.

NEW ORLEANS TIMES-PICAYUNE — An accomplished forensic mystery. His New Orleans is worth the trip.

JACKSON MISSISSIPPI CLARION-LEDGER — Andy and Kit are a match made in mystery heaven.

MEMPHIS COMMERCIAL APPEAL — Nicely drawn characters... plenty of action and an engaging descriptive storytelling style... An investigation you'll be thrilled to make.

BOOKLIST — Donaldson is a master of the gothic mystery.

KIRKUS — Ingenious... This is one for those who like their lab talk down and dirty. -

Louisiana Fever

(ISBN: 9781938231353)

Andy Broussard, the portly New Orleans medical examiner, obviously loves food. Less apparent to the casual observer is his hatred of murderers. Together with his gorgeous sidekick, psychologist Kit Franklyn, the two make a powerful, although improbable, mystery solving duo. When the beautiful Kit goes to meet an anonymous stranger—who's been sending her roses—the man drops dead at her feet before she can even get his name. Game on. Broussard learns that the man carried a lethal pathogen similar to the deadly Ebola virus. Soon, another body

The Broussard & Franklyn Series

turns up with the same bug. Panic is imminent as the threat of a pandemic is more real than ever before. The danger is especially acute, because the carrier is mobile, his identity is an absolute shocker, he knows he's a walking weapon and he's on a quest to find Broussard. Kit isn't safe either. When she investigates her mystery suitor further, she runs afoul of a cold blooded killer every bit as deadly as the one searching for Broussard.

PUBLISHERS WEEKLY — Delivers... genuinely heart-stopping suspense.

KIRKUS — Sleek, fast moving.

NEW ORLEANS TIMES-PICAYUNE — Broussard tracks the virus with a winning combination of common sense and epidemiologic legerdemain.

BOOKLIST —This series has carved a solid place for itself. Broussard makes a terrific counterpoint to the Dave Robicheaux ragin' Cajun school of mystery heroes.

JACKSON MISSISSIPPI CLARION-LEDGER —A dazzling tour de force... sheer pulse-pounding reading excitement.

MEMPHIS COMMERCIAL APPEAL — (A novel of) "terrifying force.... utterly fascinating... His best work yet.

LOS ANGELES TIMES — The autopsies are detailed enough to make Patricia Cornwell fans move farther south for their forensic fixes. ...splendidly eccentric local denizens, authentic New Orleans and bayou backgrounds... a very suspenseful tale.

DEADLY PLEASURES — A fast moving, ... suspenseful tale. Andy and Kit are quite likeable leads ...The other attraction is the solid medical background against which their story plays out.

The Broussard & Franklyn Series

KNOXVILLE NEWS-SENTINEL — Vivid crisp writing... If your skin doesn't crawl with the step by step description of the work of the (medical) examiner and his assistants, it certainly will when Donaldson reveals the carrier of the fever.

MERITORIOUS MYSTERIES — Donaldson paints the Crescent City with the vivid hues of summer while evoking the autopsy rooms of Gray's Anatomy. His protagonists meanwhile, are those you'd like to invite to dinner.

Sleeping With The Crawfish

(ISBN: 9781938231414)

Strange lesions found in the brain of a dead man have forensic pathologist Andy Broussard stumped. Even more baffling are the corpse's fingerprints. They belong to Ronald Cicero, a lifer at Angola State Prison... an inmate the warden insists is still there. Broussard sends psychologist Kit Franklyn to find out who is locked up in Cicero's cell. But an astonishing discovery at the jail and an attempt on her life almost has Kit sleeping with the crawfish in a bayou swamp. And Broussard, making a brilliant deduction about another murder, may soon be digging his own grave.

KIRKUS — Streamlined thrills and gripping forensic detail.

MEMPHIS COMMERCIAL APPEAL — With each book, Donaldson peels away a few more layers of these characters and we find ourselves loving the involvement.

BOOKLIST — Cleverly plotted top-notch thriller. Another fine entry in a consistently outstanding series.

The Broussard & Franklyn Series

SAN ANTONIO EXPRESS-NEWS — *The pace is pell-mell.*

BENTON (AR) COURIER — *Exciting and realistic. Donaldson... starts his action early and sustains it until the final pages.*

MERITORIOUS MYSTERIES — *The latest entry in a fine series which never disappoints.* —

Bad Karma In The Big Easy

(ISBN: 9781938231322)

Among the dead collected in 'The Big Easy' floodwaters after hurricane Katrina are three nude female bodies, all caught in the same brush tangle, none with water in their lungs. No water. Medical Examiner, Andy Broussard, knows this was not an act of God; not the work of Katrina. There's a killer on the loose and by God, Broussard means to find him. But Broussard has perhaps the biggest challenge of his colorful career. The city and all its records are destroyed, practically the entire population is scattered, the police force has no offices and many of the rank and file (who haven't defected) are homeless. And if that's not bad enough, Broussard discovers that the bodies were all once frozen solid, completely obliterating key forensic clues. Soon, Broussard and his alluring assistant, Kit Franklyn, are on a dangerous and labyrinthine journey through the obscenely damaged, ever mysterious, irresistibly seductive, city of New Orleans; leading them to a kind of evil that neither of them could imagine.

TESS GERRITSEN — D.J. Donaldson is superb at spinning medical fact into gripping suspense. With his in-depth knowledge of science and medicine, he is one of very few authors who can write with convincing authority. .... Donaldson has established himself as a master of the gothic mystery.

THE COMMERCIAL APPEAL (MEMPHIS) — With each book,

The Broussard & Franklyn Series

Donaldson peels away a few more layers of these characters and we find ourselves loving the involvement.

BOOKLIST — Andy and Kit are a match made in mystery heaven.